LABOR OF FOOLS

MARCUS A. BUCKLEY

Hope Again Books

"LABOR OF FOOLS"

BY MARCUS A. BUCKLEY

Published by Area613 an imprint of 613media, LLC in partnership with LifeFilters, LLC.

❀ Created with Vellum

BOOKS IN THE THOMAS HAWKINS SERIES

All Have Sinned

Labor of Fools

For Lea Ann: You're always the hero of my story.

ACKNOWLEDGMENTS

Projects like a novel are never done in a vacuum; there are so many people whose insights and encouragement make it possible. To thank them all would take many pages, and more than a few wouldn't want to be recognized anyhow, so I'll just say "thank you"—you know who you are.

I also want to thank you for buying this book and taking the time to read it. I hope it gives you a fun escape from the real world for a while, and that maybe you'll learn a little something in the process.

The labor of fools wearieth every one of them; for he knoweth not how to go to the city.
--Ecclesiastes 10:15, ASV

PROLOGUE

The new French president, Louis Paquet, sat in the weekly meeting of the Council of Ministers. He was still getting acclimated to his position, having taken office only a few short months prior. His predecessor had been removed from office after the debacle with BEAR Pharmaceuticals. Evidence had arisen that suggested the former president knew more about William Matheson's plan to produce and use biological weapons than he admitted, and rather than endure a potentially disastrous investigation took the offer to step aside and avoid any further trouble. The fact he was allowed to get off scot-free had caused even more issues for his political party, so when the new election took place his opposition easily swept into power. Paquet had named a new Prime Minister, but a number of the other Ministers had not yet been replaced. Changing too much at once could indeed upset the apple cart, and France was dealing with enoughAt the moment. The last thing it needed was a perceived power vacuum. This meant Paquet was forced to navigate the treacherous political waters with Ministers and Secretaries who were not necessarily of the same mind or political intentions.

"The only language the United States understands is

violence," the Minister of Armies said forcefully. "They continually press their strength. Perhaps it is time someone pressed back."

"Absolutely not," President Paquet said, pointing his finger directly at the director of the French military. Paquet knew that the Minister had ordered the French fighters to fire on the American jets sent to destroy the facility producing and preparing to ship the bioweapon at the heart of Matheson's misguided war on religion. The only thing accomplished was the loss of an expensive French aircraft, a French pilot who was now an inch shorter from the ride in his ejection seat courtesy of a USAF F-22, and the image of French fighters defending a bioweapons plant on French soil. "I will not allow bruised egos to lead us into armed conflict, particularly against the United States." The Minister started to speak but Paquet continued. "France is seen as being in the wrong for the events involving BEAR Pharmaceuticals, to the point of being accused of collaboration. The last thing we need is to do anything that furthers that impression, and starting a fight with the United States is the height of foolishness."

"But we cannot allow France to appear weak," the Minister of Social Affairs and Employment said. "Something must be done."

"And something *will* be done," the Prime Minister injected. "We have been making great strides in conveying to the world that France was not involved in the bioweapons issue in any way, and that we are willing to do our part to make reparations for any damages our oversight might have allowed."

"Do you have any idea what that could cost?" the Minister of Labour exclaimed.

"Indeed, I do," the Minister of the Economy and Finance declared. "And it is much lower than our costs if we are perceived to be in collusion with the terrorists who perpetrated those attacks."

The Minister of Europe and Foreign Affairs leaned in. "We

cannot afford to have another year like the one we have had. My predecessor did almost irreparable damage with most of our allies, and we cannot afford to stand alone on the world's stage. There are too many threats to our national sovereignty to allow shortsighted thinking to rule the day. We must consider what is best for France in the long term and follow that course."

"We must press forward on a path of peace," the Prime Minister said.

"And what if peace doesn't get us what we want?" the Minister of Armies said, almost shouting at this point. "We are still a sovereign nation..."

"That is perceived as being at least partially responsible for the death of hundreds upon hundreds of innocent people as a result of biological weapons being created under our collective nose," President Paquet interjected calmly. "I realize that some of you were serving on this Council when these events transpired. I know you are frustrated, angry, and disappointed. But we must assume responsibility for the failings of those who were in authority before, and show the people this new government can be trusted to do what is best not only for France but for the entire world." He paused for a moment, letting his words sink in with the Council members. "We must do our part so France— indeed the whole world—can become all it was meant to be." The Council members were quiet for a moment, then nods of approval rolled around the table like a wave.

The French President stood, signaling the end of the meeting. "I am grateful for your service to your country, ladies and gentlemen. Vive la France." The Ministers stood nearly in unison and began filing out of the meeting room. One by one they filed past the President, each nodding in affirmation or speaking briefly to voice their agreement. They were not all happy, to be certain, but they all knew Paquet was correct. They could not afford any more bad blood with their allies and neighbors. The world was too dangerous to find yourself standing alone. They would go along with him, and the nation would be better for it.

As the last Minister left the room, the President closed the doors and sat down once more. He picked up the secure landline, tapped in a series of numbers verifying secure and anonymous communication, then dialed a number. The receiver clicked on the other end, but no one spoke.

"An altogether excellent meeting," Paquet said smoothly. "Even the continuing Ministers are in agreement with my guidance. I believe most everyone is settled down now and we should finally be able to put the Matheson incident behind us." The other end remained silent.

"There may yet be one or two Ministers who are not in full agreement, but they're coming around. If not, then they'll be removed from the playing field. We will be able to move forward accordingly." Still silence. "There may yet be some other issues that need to be dealt with, but they will also be handled appropriately." The silence was broken only by the slight digital crackle of the secured line.

"Bien," a voice finally said. Then the line clicked off. Paquet replaced the telephone receiver, leaned back in his chair, and lit a cigarette. Things were moving slowly, but that suited him well enough. They were at least moving in the direction he desired, and he was patient. *When one takes the long view, one can afford to be patient*, he mused.

CHAPTER ONE

"No, the cars are not part of the deal," FBI Special Agent Thomas Hawkins said into his phone, perhaps a bit more sternly than intended. "I don't care how much they're willing to pay; the cars are not an option. In fact, I've got transporters coming to get them in a few days."

"I understand you're very attached to the vehicles, Mr. Hawkins," the real estate broker on the line started.

"I don't think you do. The cars are a no-go. Tell them thank you, but no thank you."

"Mr. Hawkins, the buyer's wife loves the home very much, but the buyer himself indicated that if he couldn't work a deal with you on the vehicles then he wasn't interested. He's very wealthy and used to getting his way."

"Then I'm happy to be a departure from the norm for him," Hawkins deadpanned. "No cars. If they don't want the house, then someone else can buy it." Hawkins had finally gotten around to putting his home in Jacksonville, Florida on the market. After stopping William Matheson and his bio-weapon plot, Hawkins had found himself to be very popular within the law enforcement and Intelligence communities. He had been reassigned to Washington, where he was in process of becoming an operational liaison with CIA. He had transferred a few months after the case had closed—over a year ago now—and had spent some of that time going through specialized training at various locations like The Harvey Point Defense Testing Activity facility, known colloquially as "The Point." Now that all of that was behind him, he was trying to get the Jacksonville house sold and get all of his stuff out of the house. He didn't want to bring it to DC; the townhouse he had inside the Beltway had room for only one car in its small garage, so his Bureau car sat outside. There was certainly no need to have all of his vehicles stored in a warehouse in the Beltway area, so he had a massive garage built at his place in Cosby, Tennessee that had more than enough space for his beloved collection. Technically, most of them had been his parents' cars, but since their tragic death years before he had kept them all in perfect condition.

"I understand completely, Mr. Hawkins," she said, although her voice expressed disappointment in greater measure than understanding. She undoubtedly had visions of a big commission getting away from her. Hawkins sympathized, but those cars meant too much to let go of them lightly. He had too many memories of traveling to auctions around the country with his mother and father, gathering them up over the years, to ever willingly let go of them. Since his parents were gone, those vehicles were the last—and strongest—connection he had to them.

Hawkins considered for a moment, then spoke again. "I'll tell you what. I'll make him a deal on the Shelby, but that's it." He referred to a 1968 Shelby GT500 they had bought years before. The car had been plagued with one problem after another, and they had never gotten it to run quite right. Now that he thought about it, maybe getting rid of one wouldn't be so bad, especially if it was a car none of them had particularly been fond of. Hanging onto something problematic out of blind sentimentality was rarely a good idea, he supposed.

"I believe that was the buyer's favorite," the realtor replied, clearly pleased at Hawkins' change of heart. "I'll let them know and get back to you with a number as soon as possible."

"Sounds good," Hawkins replied. As he placed the phone back into his pocket, he stepped into the coffee shop he had frequented while stationed in Jacksonville. It was located in one of the ubiquitous strip shopping centers that seemed to pop up overnight, but the ordinary location was no indicator of the quality of their coffee. It was a little *too* good, Hawkins thought, because it was almost always packed with customers. The little shop was one of the few places outside of New Orleans Hawkins had been able to have true café au lait made with chicory, the ingredient that made the Big Easy's Café du Monde's coffee his personal favorite. He had yet to find anywhere in the DC area that had comparable coffee. Everything up there was overpriced, bitter soup that everyone raved about only because it was the chic thing to do. He had to get to the airport to catch his mid-day flight back to DC, but he had more than enough time for a good cup of joe.

The store was even more packed than usual. It was in the high 60's that morning, so everyone needed a cup of hot coffee as Florida's version of fall crept in a little ahead of schedule. It seemed to Hawkins the shop may have been a little shorthanded behind the counter, as there was a lot of activity and a good deal of shouting back and forth from the register to the other baristas on deck. The small shop was packed, tables filled, and the line behind Hawkins quickly stretched outside the entrance. There were five people between the FBI agent and the register, with three young men directly in front of him. Now that he was no longer distracted by the telephone conversation with his real estate broker, they garnered his full attention.

One stood slightly in front of the others, and while they were clearly together none spoke or interacted with each other. They weren't messing around with their phones, weren't joking with one another. They were just *standing there*, which made them stand out to Hawkins as clearly as if they had glowing auras around them. The two who stood slightly behind the lead were in their early twenties, tall and thin, dressed in faded t-shirts, skinny jeans, and Vans. Hawkins caught the slight but distinctive smell of marijuana, suggesting that they smoked with sufficient frequency to firmly ensconce the scent into the fibers of their clothing. They looked like they spent most of their time smoking and playing video games while tossing back energy drinks and listening to bad music.

The one in front drew Hawkins' attention in particular. He wore a gray hoodie and a scarf—not terribly unusual for late November in Jacksonville, but that too seemed to be the trend. He was shorter than the others but stockier. Even under his hoodie it was obvious that he lifted weights, although Hawkins noted that he looked as though he skipped leg day. His long hair was pulled up into a bun on top of his head. While others in line were looking at the menu board, scanning their social media accounts, or being otherwise distracted, the young men faced straight ahead like predators locked onto prey. Hawkins' senses were highly alert now, and he tried to visualize what the men were staring at. He looked past the young men, and the woman in front of them in line, and saw the cashier: a pretty red-haired girl whose nametag said "Jersey." Hawkins and other special agents from the nearby Field Office stopped in regularly so they had gotten to know most of the baristas. Jersey had worked in the store for at least a couple of years. She was a student at one of the local universities and worked there when her class schedule allowed. She was there at least two days a week when Hawkins and some of the others would stop in. As busy as Jersey was, she hadn't noticed she was being stared at.

The woman in front of the young man stepped up to the counter and placed her order. When Jersey looked at the customer Hawkins caught her glancing over the woman's shoulder. The young man shifted slightly, making sure he was behind the woman in front of him. The door to the coffee shop opened once more, and as the inside air rushed to escape into the atmosphere a whiff of alcohol rushed past him—the man had apparently been drinking early, or maybe continuously since last night. Hawkins saw a shadow of concern cross Jersey's face. Did she recognize him? Maybe a jealous ex? Jersey continued taking the other woman's order but was clearly distracted now. She made eye contact briefly with Hawkins. He knew the look—she was scared. He didn't know the relationship between the man and the cashier, but Hawkins knew the young man was clearly the cause of her concern.

The female customer stepped aside. As soon as Jersey saw him, she froze. "Tim?" she whispered, struggling to hide her obvious fear. "You aren't supposed to be here."

"Hey, Jersey," Tim said as he pulled the scarf away from his mouth and made a "pfft" sound. "I can go wherever I want."

"Restraining order says otherwise," she said, mustering her courage.

"Just a piece of paper," he replied coolly, spreading his arms sarcastically. "Here I am. And I've got something to say to you."

"You have to leave," Jersey said a little louder. "Right now."

Tim's two friends stepped around beside him. "Or what?"

Hawkins spoke up. "Hey, 'Tim.' If you're not going to order anything, how about moving along so the rest us can get our caffeine fix."

Tim spun around, followed more slowly by his two friends. "Who do you think you're talking to, tough guy?" he said angrily, balling his fists. He was a good 6 inches shorter than Hawkins, and bounced up onto his tiptoes at the realization. The smell of alcohol and weed rolled off of Tim and hit Hawkins like a hot, wet mop. "I'm having a conversation with my girlfriend!"

"Sounds like a judge thought that was a bad idea," Hawkins replied.

"The judge ain't here," Tim replied, his countenance going suddenly calm and he flattened his feet. "And he can't stop me from saying what I want to say to Jersey." He reached into the pocket of his hoodie and spun back towards the young cashier.

Before Tim's hand cleared the pouch Hawkins grabbed his wrist, spun him back around, and drove his right knee into his groin. Tim grunted as his breath was taken away, his legs went out from under him and he dropped in a heap on the floor. A small pistol clattered away as it fell from his limp hand. The two friends were slower to react, but their hands also went to their pockets. Hawkins drove his fist into the nose of the one on the left with a satisfying crunch, pivoted slightly, pressed his left hand against his right fist and jabbed his elbow into the jaw of the other. Both men tumbled to the floor, the one on the left trying to stop the substantial flow of blood from his now broken nose. Several of the other customers screamed, while two others rushed from the door towards the counter.

"You good, Hawk?" Special Agent Renee Cortez asked, her service pistol in the low ready position at her side.

"Yeah," Hawkins replied. He glanced at the men crumpled on the floor moaning. "They came between me and my coffee. You got cuffs?"

"I do," Special Agent Susan Nash replied. "I thought you just wanted to meet for coffee. I didn't know we'd be rousting some mama's boys that don't know how to fight."

"Just wanted to show you ladies a good time," Hawkins said. "Phone JSO and give them a heads up." It was almost certain that someone would have called the Jacksonville Sheriff's Office by now and they would be here any minute. Better for them to know that three FBI agents already had the bad guys in custody so they wouldn't come in overly hot. He handed his cuffs to Cortez then turned to the counter. Jersey was still standing, frozen in place. She hadn't moved an inch.

"Jersey," Hawkins said softly. "Are you okay?"

She stood silently for several seconds, as if slowly taking in all that had just happened. "Yes," she said finally. "He, uh...he had said he wouldn't let me go. He wouldn't let *anyone* have me if he couldn't."

"You don't have to worry about him anymore," Hawkins said. "You're safe now."

Jersey looked up from Tim's moaning form, and her tear-filled eyes locked with Hawkins'. "Am I?" she asked. "Am I safe?"

He looked at her and found himself unable to say anything. Cortez stepped around the counter. She wrapped her arms around Jersey, who immediately began sobbing and leaned into the female agent. Cortez held her and looked at Hawkins worriedly. *Safe*. Such a small word, fraught with such meaning. But after all he had seen, Hawkins no longer felt qualified to tell anyone they were truly safe anymore.

"Paquet is definitely saying all the right things," David Hathaway, The President of the United States, said as he leaned back in his chair behind the Resolute desk in the Oval Office. He held a file in his hands with the paper copy of the President's Daily Brief. The PDB was among the most highly guarded documents in Washington, containing up-to-the-minute intelligence gathered by the United States and its allies. It had been delivered on a daily basis to POTUS since 1946, and was currently prepared and delivered by the Office of the Director of National Intelligence without fail. The section on France had been substantial since the BEAR incident the previous year, and the replacement of the French president had not diminished the watchful eye of the Unites States Intelligence Community. Paquet was earning the cautious favor of those concerned with France's open hostility towards the U.S. and its allies only a year previous. "Granted that doesn't mean a lot in the world of politics, but he seems to be backing it up with the right actions so far."

"*So far*," Director of National Intelligence Jack Price repeated, his eyebrows raised over his rimless glasses indicating his suspicion. "Just because someone offers an olive branch doesn't mean the arrows aren't still in the other hand," he said, tapping the front panel on the desk. The seal of the President of the United States was there, but it was one of only a handful in the White House that featured the eagle looking toward the talons holding arrows rather than the normative pose of gazing at the ones holding the botanical symbol of peace.

"True enough," POTUS replied as he leaned forward and placed the file on the desktop. "Talbert's pretty good at reading people," referring to Kirk Talbert, the Vice President. Talbert had been a prosecutor before running a successful campaign to become the governor of Iowa. Hathaway had wisely chosen the influential and well-liked governor as his running mate, which had made the outcome of his presidential campaign nearly a foregone conclusion. Talbert was a people-person who could connect with almost anyone immediately, knowing just what to say and how to say it. He was also sharp and insightful, capable of seeing through the veneers of a person to determine who they really were, extremely useful during both his time as a prosecutor and as a politician. He was a real asset to Hathaway, and his current assignment would be no exception. "He'll have a pretty good sense of Paquet before the first cup of coffee is gone. As one of my predecessors said, 'trust but verify.'"

"We need to be cautious, regardless of how this visit goes," Price said. "You'll see in the PDB that we have concerns about some way-back connections Paquet has. He and his people went to a lot of trouble to cover them up."

"Almost everyone has things in their path they'd rather not have brought to the light of day, Jack."

"Which is why I don't trust anyone, Mr. President."

"Well," POTUS said with a smile, "that *is* your job. And one you're extremely good at."

Price returned his own grin. "Only because my job is to make sure you have the absolute best information to make the decisions that only you can." His smile faded somewhat, and he raised his eyebrows again. Hathaway had learned that was one of the few tells Price allowed himself. He only gave away what went on in his head to a handful of people, POTUS being one of those few, but even then he knew Price held his own counsel. "There's just too much that we don't know yet."

"But you're still digging."

"Oh yes," Price replied. "We've got all of our antennas directed that way." He sighed, then continued. "I just feel that this whole thing isn't over yet."

POTUS leaned back in his chair again, rubbed his hand over his chin and thought for a moment. He locked eyes with Price. "We need to know who we're dealing with." Price nodded back but remained silent. Hathaway exhaled, then continued. "Do what you've got to do. Follow those trails. Let's just try not to tick them off if we can help it."

Price smiled broadly. "You can count on us, Mr. President."

CHAPTER TWO

Thomas Hawkins was not a runner. He had enjoyed lifting weights and even bike riding throughout his life, but running was an acquired taste that had eluded him with the same certainty as broccoli. Running with a certain level of performance had been a requirement for his entrance to the FBI several years prior, so he had done it, and even gotten to where he was pretty good at it. But he never achieved the nirvana so many claimed running had brought them. He did it because he had to, and he dreaded ever having to start at ground zero again, so he ran five miles most mornings. Some days he was slower than others, and this seemed to be one of those days. It was November, which generally meant cold air in Washington, DC. Maybe being in Florida for a few days had thinned his blood again, and now the normally welcome colder temperatures were dragging down on him. He wore a thermal watch cap on his head, with a fleece pullover and joggers, and he was *still* cold. Whatever it was, he was struggling to find a good pace this morning.

"On your left," Samantha Land said as she sprinted past. Thomas Hawkins marveled at the effortless way Sam ran. She never seemed to tire, barely even appeared out of breath, and had stamina that was endless in its supply. Her feet seemed as though they barely touched the pavement, her muscular legs propelling her effortlessly past him. He huffed in slight frustration, then increased his pace to catch up. It was, honestly, easier to run when he could see her. Her short blonde ponytail bounced and swayed happily in rhythm with her stride, underlined by a dark gray fleece band that partially covered her ears and encircled her head. She wore a gray Under Armour windbreaker with coordinated leggings, almost a perfect match for the early morning sky above.

"That never gets old," Hawkins said trying to speak through his own dripping sarcasm with the same ease as his running partner.

"But it works every time," Land replied easily, glancing to her right as Hawkins caught up. "And here you are closing the gap." They were running a circuit that brought them past the Washington Monument, past the World War II Memorial, and down the trail running alongside the Reflecting Pool in front of the Lincoln Memorial. This morning they were meeting on Hawkins' side of the Potomac. Tomorrow he would meet up with Land closer to her workplace.

"Hard to argue with results." The two had been seeing each other for over a year, and although they would often go weeks without seeing one another in person they made the most of times they were in Washington together. They had even met up in Paris when their follow-up investigation on GODKILLER necessitated the trip. It had been much more relaxed than his previous trip to France with the CIA operative, which had resulted in a shootout and car chase which ended with their vehicle being hit by a grenade. They had grown accustomed to the madness of such a relationship and were both happy with how it was going.

"In that case, I'll race you to the top of the steps," and Land sprinted forward toward the Lincoln Memorial.

"Oh, you've got to be kidding me," Hawkins grunted as he put everything he had into propelling himself at top speed.

DEA Agent Logan Nash sat in the passenger seat of a Dodge Ram 1500 in full tactical gear at 0555 hours. Even in the massive front seat, he felt like he was crammed into a locker. It was cold in Greenville, South Carolina, reading 36 degrees on the truck's thermometer. Even so, he felt hot and claustrophobic. He had been an agent for nearly two decades, but he still hadn't gotten used to the gear they made all agents wear when serving warrants. He remembered the days when all they needed was a light vest with "DEA" and "FEDERAL AGENT" emblazoned on it. Now they were required to wear level-IIIA armor, tac helmets, headsets, knee and elbow pads—the list seemed to get longer ever quarter as some new flunky at the Justice Department came up with new rules based on what the legal team said. Avoiding liability was as important as arresting bad guys nowadays, it seemed, and Nash frustration grew accordingly. Still, he loved the work, especially the undercover part. They didn't let him do as much undercover as he used to, saying he was more important in a supervisory role. He frequently told them what he thought of that, but they would laugh it off and send him on his way. One of these days, he would hit his limit and walk out the door for good.

"Hey," a voice said, the fist belonging to it jostling the cup of coffee in Nash' hand. "Are you awake? We need to go kick a door in if you're done with your beauty sleep." It was Mike Rhodes, Nash' friend and partner for the last ten years. Rhodes sat in the driver's seat, geared similarly to Nash, but he had yet to put his helmet and headset on. Rhodes had long black hair beginning to streak with gray, that touched just below the neckline of his vest. As cold as it was outside, Rhodes wore a short sleeve shirt under the vest. Tattoos covered every square inch of his exposed arms, the muscles beneath the skin twitching in anticipation of the coming action.

"I'm awake, you idiot," Nash grunted, "just burning up in all of this crap."

"I told you not to wear that jacket under the vest," Rhodes said with the enthusiasm of a sibling proved correct.

"It's freakin' freezing outside! I'm not going outside just wearing a t-shirt like you,"

"And here you are passing out from the heat." Rhodes smiled broadly, his beard pushing his cheeks upward and forcing his eyes into a pleased squint.

"Well, genius, you're about to be freezing, so I guess it balances out."

"We'll see," Rhodes replied. The radio beeped and a voice came over the comm. "Target is confirmed inside. No movement for an hour." The subject of the federal warrant was one Darius Cheever, a low-level hoodlum who had worked his way up to the big time. Starting out as a neighborhood drug and firearm dealer, he had stumbled into a major supplier of stolen weapons out of Texas. Cheever had gone from being the darling of city cop watch boards to getting the attention of the feds almost overnight after he successfully brought in a shipment of drugs and weapons with a street value of over $20 million dollars. He had used a school activity bus for that one, taken from a storage yard during the summer when no one noticed it was missing. They had caught him, but the drugs and weapons were long gone. The evidence was circumstantial, and the district attorney didn't want to touch it, so Greenville had its newest millionaire. His legend grew, and so did his business. No one was able to figure out how a bumpkin like Cheever was able to go high-stakes so quickly—and so well, quite frankly—but the fact remained that he was there. He continued to move drugs and guns with seeming impunity. It's been said that police don't catch the smart ones.

Fortunately, Cheever messed up. He spent some time with a

stripper one night, who happened to be a confidential informer of Nash, by the name of Luna Roberts. She had grown up in the area and had been a star gymnast. She was accepted to a prestigious college in the area and received a scholarship for her gymnastics. Her parents were killed in a car wreck and she didn't have enough money to pay for school. She had heard how much money strippers made at the big nightclubs, so she went it for an interview. The manager was a female, a former dancer herself, who looked out for her dancers. She hired Luna on the spot, gave her the stage name "Carrera," and put her on the schedule. Luna was uncomfortable at first, but security always made sure none of the customers got too close. The money was better than she could have imagined, so much so that she kept working there even after she had graduated three years earlier. She planned to work there for another couple of years, padding her bank account even further, then do whatever she wanted with the rest of her life.

Guys like Cheever made her career choice possible, loved the feeling of power their money gave them. High rollers who came in from out of town were the most extravagant. The car she drove, a late model Corvette, was a gift from a fan. The condo in which she lived was a gift from a foreign visitor who gave it to her to avoid losing it in a divorce. Most were like Cheever, though—losers who had gotten their hands on some money and loved to show off. He kept throwing dollar bills as the girl danced, and he kept throwing back the alcohol as well. Over the course of an hour he bragged to her about how he had outsmarted all the cops with his methods of trafficking drugs and weapons from out of state. Luna knew she was on to something, and when Cheever started to get sleepy from the booze she slipped away and gave Nash a heads up. He told her to keep him on the hook. That, she told him, she could do.

The next night Cheever was back, and once again was drawn to Luna. On the first drink he bragged about how effective his methods were at bringing in merchandise. He then made the mistake of telling her what those methods were. After his first few drinks, he told her he had been approached by a foreign high-roller about expanding into the Carolinas. This foreigner was looking for an unknown, but someone who was willing to risk it all for a shot at the big time. Cheever knew he had nothing to lose, so he agreed. A few drinks more, and he began talking about his methods: stolen school buses, fake medical transports, even a bus for a nursing home with mannequins in the seats, all invisible to the eyes of the cops looking for contraband. Shortly before he passed out in the club, he was telling her that he was keeping a load of merchandise at his home in Greenville just because he could. He would be shipping it out the first of December but was keeping it at his own home in the meantime, so confident he was of his own cleverness. No sooner than he had passed out in his chair the informant went to her locker and called Nash. He brought the info to his supervisor, they took it to the prosecutor's office, and they in turn took it before a judge. The surveillance warrant was issued, and Nash and his team were ready to go. Cheever continued to frequent the strip club over the next three nights, and continued to prefer Nash' informant, so they were able to monitor his activity pattern. If Luna was working, he would stay and drink until closing, about 0430. He told her about how many millions of dollars he had in the house, but not in cash—it was all merchandise. He had cocaine, heroin, fully automatic weapons. This load was enough that he was going to need two buses to haul it all, but this was the big payoff for him. He was going to sell it and then move overseas. His biggest days were yet to come, he repeated every night that week. Because he had spent so much money at the club, he was given a driver who would chauffeur him home and make sure he got inside. Nash made sure Luna was on the schedule, verified that Cheever was partying the night away, then readied his team. Cheever had arrived home at 0445, an hour and twelve minutes ago now, so he would be happily passed out and in deep sleep. Exactly when Nash and his team liked to make entry on a subject. They had been watching the house for five days, so they knew no one ever came and went from the house except for Cheever.

"Roger that," Nash said into his headset mic. "Let's cue up." He looked over at Rhodes. "That means you, mister mosty-toasty. Let's go." Rhodes snapped the chin strap of his helmet and checked his headset.

"Right on, brother," Rhodes said as he readied his SIG .556 rifle.

The two men climbed out of their truck as six other agents followed suit from their vehicles down the street. Cheever's house was in an upscale neighborhood, his way of thumbing his nose at everyone. It actually had made it easier to put surveillance on his house. There was no comings-and-goings in the neighborhood other than the residents and service vehicles. A little subtle electronic surveillance and Cheever's every movement around the house was mapped. He was currently in the master bedroom, face down fully dressed on his king size bed. He hadn't even made it under the covers before he passed out.

The breacher readied the battering ram, and the agent responsible for the shield stood ready to lead the way. Rhodes took up position directly behind the shield man, with Nash at his left shoulder. The rest of the agents stacked up behind, ready to fan out and clear the house. Nash gave the sign, and the breacher slammed the battering ram into the door casing, shattering it on the first hit. The agent with the shield went in first, shouting "FEDERAL AGENTS! WE HAVE A WARRANT!" repeatedly. He quickly moved his way down the hall to the master bedroom. When they rounded the corner, Cheever was still lying facedown on the bed.

"Darius Cheever, you are under arrest," Nash shouted. "Do not move!" Rhodes moved in quickly, snatched Cheever's arms behind his back, and secured him with plastic zip cuffs. Shouts of "clear" began ringing out as the remaining agents determined there were no other occupants in the house.

"He ain't movin', Mike," Nash said.

"He's hammered," Rhodes said. "Of course he ain't movin'." As he continued to frisk him, he noticed something indeed seemed off. He removed a glove then put his fingers to Cheever's neck. He swung around to Nash. "No pulse."

Nash cursed as he holstered his pistol. The agent holding the shield dropped it and reached for his backpack. Rhodes flipped Cheever onto his back, then noticed the black sheets where he had been lying were soaked. Nash saw the holes in Cheever's shirt first, then Rhodes ripped it open. Two shots had been fired at close range directly into Cheever's heart, killing him instantly. The agent moved over to them with a trauma pack in his hands but stopped short when he saw it wouldn't do any good.

"What gives, man?" Rhodes said as he stood up next to the bed.

Nash swore again under his breath. "The chauffeur," he said. He looked to the agent in the room with them. "You guys stay here and secure the house."

"Where are you going" the agent asked as Nash and Rhodes rushed past him.

"My CI is about to wind up dead, too," Nash shouted. "Do *not* let anyone else in here until our forensics people arrive!" he shouted as he ran out the door, Rhodes right behind him. Nash was barely in the truck before his partner had it in gear and roaring away.

"Where we goin', hoss?" Rhodes asked.

"She lives in the River Mill lofts," Nash answered while dialing his phone.

"River Mill lofts," Rhodes repeated, then whistled. The lofts were in an old industrial building that had been converted into high-end luxury townhouses. There were a number of such redevelopments around Greenville, but this one commanded top dollar with its interior appointments and views of the Reedy River waterfall. There wasn't a unit in the building available for less than $600,000. "Strippin' is paying big money nowadays."

Nash flipped on the lights and sirens on the truck and pointed forward. He was focused intently on the phone pressed against his ear, willing his informant to answer her phone. He knew there were two units from the Greenville PD that were watching the building because of some of the other well-to-do occupants, and the condo itself had a guardhouse manned 24 hours by retired cops, but he wouldn't feel any better until he could get there himself. There was a click, and Nash thought it was going to her voicemail.

"Really, Nash?" a female voice said wearily. "I just got to sleep. Did you get him?"

Nash relief was palpable, but he couldn't relax yet. "Luna, listen to me. Do not open your door for anyone. Cheever is dead, and I think you may be in danger. Rhodes and I are on the way to you right now."

"What?" she said, suddenly awake. "What should I do?"

"Lock yourself in your bedroom. You've got a gun, right?"

"Yeah, I've got it right here."

"Then be ready to use it. Stay on the phone with me until I get there." He could hear Rhodes on the phone with the units posted outside her building telling them to warn security and post up on her hallway. He caught her up with what had happened.

"How far away are you?" she asked, her voice quivering slightly.

"Two minutes," he replied as the truck caught a little air as it hurtled through an intersection. "You're gonna be okay. The Greenville officers are posting up on your hallway, and security has the front gate locked down. No one else is getting in there but us. Did you see who the chauffeur was tonight? Was it the usual guy?"

"I didn't notice, to be honest," Luna said. "The drivers don't usually work regular shifts. They kinda come and go."

"Okay, we can talk more about that after we get you secured.

Get some clothes on and grab what you need. We're going to leave in a hurry."

"Getting dressed now. I'll put some clothes in a..." The line went silent.

"Luna?" Nash looked at his screen. It said, "Call Ended."

CHAPTER THREE

"This coffee is too hot to drink." Samantha Land said, taking the lid off her cup and blowing on the steaming liquid inside.

"Isn't that the point?" Hawkins asked. They had this same dialogue nearly every time they got coffee. She always complained that the coffee was too hot and waited until it was room temperature before drinking it. As they were currently resting on the steps of the Lincoln Memorial, that meant she would have an iced beverage if she waited too long in the pre-sunrise hour.

She took another sip, then shook her head. "I suppose." She smiled as she turned to look at him. "You know, I'm really glad we get to do stuff like this."

"Run too fast and drink coffee that's too hot?"

"Exactly." She leaned into him. "I was pretty sure that the life I'd chosen wasn't going to lend itself well to finding someone I wanted to spend my down time with."

"And yet, here we are. Funny how that works, isn't it?" He paused. "Wait. Is this where you tell me you're breaking up with me?"

"No such luck for you. Who else would make sure you ran at least 4 days a week?"

"I'm *so* glad to know you have my best interests at heart." Hawkins stole a glance at his watch as he took another sip of his coffee, which he felt was not at all too hot. "I'd better get going. I don't like driving through downtown after sunrise."

"I complain about coffee, you complain about traffic," Land said as they stood. "You coming over to Langley this week?"

"Yeah, I'll actually be there tomorrow for a meeting. Lunch in the food court?"

"It's a date," she said. "Call me later."

"You can be certain of that," he said. Land leaned in and kissed him, handed him her cup with a smile, and jogged away. He stood for a moment and watched her as she ran. Her presence had warmed him more than any coffee could. He tossed his empty cup in the trash and began sipping hers as he headed to his nearby condo. If he hurried, he could get ready and be in his car by 6:45. He didn't have far to drive, but the thought of being stuck in the grid of early morning DC traffic made him pick up his pace.

The Dodge Ram had barely stopped when DEA Agent Logan Nash jumped out and sprinted toward the entrance, his partner sprinting up behind him. Security had been waiting to let them in, and remotely triggered the maglock entry door that led to the emergency stars. He sprinted to the third floor, which was the equivalent of six due to the fact that each condo was two stories high. When he reached the level with Luna's residence, he burst through the doorway and almost bowled over the two Greenville Police officers waiting.

"I was on the phone with her but lost contact. We're going to have to make entry."

"Sir, we don't have anything that will breach that door," one of the officers said. "We'll have to get SWAT up here."

"I got it covered," Rhodes said as he reached into his vest and pulled out a small device that looked like several phones strapped together. Nash knew it was a shaped charge that would destroy the handle mechanism and gain them entry through anything short of an armored door.

As they approached the door and Rhodes readied the charge, Nash phone rang. He looked at the screen and saw it was Luna calling. He quickly answered. There was silence on the line.

"Luna?" he asked. "Luna, are you there?"

"I think there's someone in the main hallway," she whispered.

"We're here, Luna," Nash answered. "Can you buzz us in?" The sound of magnetic locks in her door mechanism confirmed that she could, and they hurried inside. The condo was dark with the exception of a couple of nightlights on the appliances in the kitchen. In the dim light Nash could see that the appliances cost more than some people's houses. "Luna, we're in. Open the door and come out."

A door lock clicked, and Luna walked out into the hallway. Nash recognized her, even without the bright pink wig she normally wore in the club. She had jet black hair that was cropped short on the sides and back. She was wearing a hooded sweatshirt, jeans, and running shoes. A small duffle bag hung from her left hand, and a large black pistol was clenched in her right. She was clearly frightened but was still in control. "Can we get out of here?"

"Right now," Nash replied. They whisked her down the stairs, got into the truck, killed the LED strobes, and eased out of the parking lot.

"What happened, Nash? Why did they kill Cheever?" Luna asked from the back seat as soon as they turned away from downtown.

"I have no idea who killed him, much less why," Nash said as he continued to look in the rearview mirrors. "I'm pretty sure his suppliers are the ones who ordered it, presumably to keep him from talking. But how did they know we were coming?" He turned and looked intently at her. "Have you been talking to anyone else, Luna?"

"No!" she shouted. "I know how this works. I wouldn't tell anybody anything. I don't want them coming after me." She paused for moment, then shrugged. "Although I guess that didn't help much."

"So how else would they know to kill him on the very night we're coming to hook him up?"

"I don't know! Maybe it was someone in your office!"

Nash bit back an angry reply. He knew she could be right. It wouldn't be the first time someone in the chain had been compromised. It didn't have to be a cop on the take, either; there were enough hands and eyes with access to the forms that it could have come from the good guys. Nash preferred to think it was someone with a criminal background who would do such a thing, but experience had told him that money could get to almost anyone.

"We're going to have to keep her somewhere secure until we figure out who blabbed," Rhodes said, giving voice to Nash' next thought.

"We can use the old house in Asheville," Nash replied. Each Field Office had various safe houses that were made available for other Divisions' use. It didn't always make sense to hide someone in the same town where a threat was coming from, so they were often temporarily quartered in a neighboring Division's area of operation. The "old house" was actually a cabin perched on the side of a mountain just to the east of downtown Asheville, North Carolina. A little more than an hour from Greenville, it was remote enough that the only people who knew its location were those who needed to know.

"Sounds like a plan," Rhodes replied. "We'll take your truck, in case this one was made."

"Land Cruiser's a good idea," Nash said, and Rhodes nodded in agreement. The Land Cruiser was a dark green 2004 model, a luxurious brute appreciated for its off-road capability and reliability. Nash had obtained it as a bug-out vehicle several years prior, and had it registered under one of the identities he had used while undercover. It comfortably rested at his house in a secured garage most of the time, only being driven enough to ensure everything remained ready for use. His home was in a gated community a few miles north of Greenville—they could make the swap without fear of any watchful eyes. It almost sounded paranoid to him, but he had stayed alive through years of dangerous undercover work by being smart and careful.

"Right," Rhodes said. I've got a go-bag at the office. We can head to your place from there. Guess we should let the boss know we'll be out of the office for a couple of days."

"But nobody else," Nash added quickly. "We don't need..."

"I know, dear," Rhodes intoned sarcastically. "Don't forget, Ive been at this longer than you."

"14 months," Nash said as he rolled his eyes. "And you were on probation for 11 of those."

"You're just jealous that I have more fun than you," Rhodes said with a chuckle.

"You and I have very different ideas of fun."

"I don't know about that."

"Oh, for crying out loud," Luna said from the back seat. "Are you guys going to get married or what? Can you focus on keeping me alive?"

CHAPTER FOUR

How do people ever get used to this, Hawkins though to himself. It was a quarter to 7 in the morning and traffic was virtually impassable in Washington, D.C. He was within sight of the Brutalist monstrosity that was the J. Edgar Hoover Building, the headquarters for the Federal Bureau of Investigation. The storied building was well past its prime. Concrete had demonstrated a propensity for falling off onto the sidewalk, leaving exposed rebar to begin the slow decay of rust for all to see. A study had been done well over a decade prior to examine the possibility of renovating the structure, but the cost was deemed too high. Worse, engineers determined that the original construction was so compromised even exorbitant amounts of money would only make the building slightly better than its current condition. A push to relocate headquarters followed, but even that had stalled in recent years as funding was allocated to sexier projects. Even so, Hawkins was a little awestruck every time he saw the Hoover Building. Something about it embodied everything about the FBI, good and bad, and he never failed to be moved by the sight of it.

Hawkins' actual destination was the Washington Field Office several blocks away, and as the light turned green the Hoover

building vanished quickly from his sight. HQ was where all of
the administrative personnel had their office, and in this case
field agents actually had a better setup at the newer FO. He
turned onto 6th Street NW, then turned right toward his new
duty station. He pulled his black Dodge Charger into the drive
that led to a security post and rolled his window down, the cold
November wind stabbing its way into his warm vehicle. The
checkpoint was only slightly less than a bunker with bigger
windows, topped with multiple antennae and a climate control
unit. Concrete stanchions eight inches thick blocked further
entry. The checkpoint's windows were slightly steamy at the
edges, but the guard inside was bundled up as though he was
sitting outside on the cold sidewalk. He stepped forward and the
door opened, giving Hawkins a better look at the man. He was
young, a few years Hawkins' junior. He had the bearing of former
military, a swagger that carried a sense of confident invincibility.
Even so, it was evident the officer was chilled to the bone. It was
possible that the young man had spent time overseas stationed
in a tropical climate, took a job with the FBI upon his discharge,
and immediately found himself tossed into the concrete refriger-
ator of the nation's capital during the late fall. Steely eyes peered
out at Hawkins from under a hat that bore a shield and "FBI
POLICE" in prominent letters. His winter jacket likewise bore
the regalia of the FBI's uniformed division, and his hand rested
comfortably close to the sidearm slung low on his thigh.

"Good morning, Agent Hawkins," the young officer said,
even before the agent could present his credentials.

"Morning, Justin," Hawkins said as he handed his credentials
to the officer. Although the younger man's jacket had a gold plate
that read "Jeffries," he had already come to know him by his first
name. The young man returned with his credentials momentarily, and Hawkins handed him a styrofoam cup. "Here's something
to warm you up."

"Coffee?" Jeffries said excitedly. "Thank you, sir. I need that
in a bad way," he chuckled. "I spent the last couple of years

burning up in the desert. Now I'm freezing my..." He paused, catching his language choice at the last second. "Well, I'm just plain freezing, sir. I really appreciate it."

"Least I can do, Justin. Have a good one." The concrete stanchions retracted smoothly into the ground, and Hawkins eased his car down the ramp into the subterranean garage. Hawkins aimed toward his assigned spot, gathered his gear, and walked across the deck already rapidly filling with vehicles. Anyone driving to work inside the Beltway knew that if you weren't in place by 7:00 a.m. you would be stuck in gridlocked traffic until well past 9:00. He entered his code at the elevator and stepped inside. He had only been in D.C. for a couple of months, and while he was still getting used to certain aspects, he felt like he was catching the rhythm of the place. Unlike many of the agents he had spoken with, he liked being assigned to a big metropolitan Field Office. D.C. ran at a hectic pace, the traffic was a nightmare, and being in the center of all things political certainly had its drawbacks. But all of these things also contributed to why Hawkins enjoyed it as much as he did. He felt much the same way about the Headquarters building itself. For all of its maintenance shortcomings, there was just something about being in the Hoover building. And even though living and working in a major metro area had its drawbacks, Hawkins found the trade offs to be worth it. It also made his time in the mountains of Tennessee at his getaway home more enjoyable.

The elevator chimed its arrival at the appointed floor, and Hawkins stepped out. He walked down a short hallway then stepped into a large open area filled with kiosks, not unlike office buildings in any large city. Neutral-colored partitions gave each person their own work area, with soft backlighting at each desk. Massive monitors were the focal point of the desktops, with just enough room for the agents and support employees to personalize their individual spaces. This area housed a counterterrorism squad, one of several scattered throughout this

building and several others in the metro area. Each team had
their own focus, based on where the funding for the terrorist
activity came from. Hawkins' unit dealt with groups funded by
foreign governments, either directly or through intermediaries.
Many times the leads came from other squads, but once a
foreign power was determined to be involved, it was Hawkins'
group that took point.

His promotion to this squad had been a little circuitous.
Shortly after he and his team had stopped the biological attack a
little over a year prior, he had been promoted to a supervisory
position in Jacksonville. The FBI was certainly proud of the
work Hawkins and the others had done. They had stopped
several murderous conspirators and saved countless lives. The
fact that the Bureau had gotten a lot of good publicity out of it
didn't hurt, either; such things were very helpful when budget
appropriation time rolled around. It wasn't enough to get the
ball rolling on relocating headquarters yet, but perhaps that
would come soon.

The Bureau wasn't the only institution that had taken note,
however. His work with CIA Case Officer Samantha Land had
garnered the attention of the people at Langley, and they had
been fairly insistent in their attempts to woo Hawkins to come
work at the Agency. While flattered, Hawkins loved the Bureau
and didn't want to leave. Jack Price, The Director of National
Intelligence and Land's boss, had proposed an alternative:
Hawkins could become a liaison for the FBI and CIA. Intrigued,
Hawkins talked it over with his friend Mark Woodley, former
Navy SEAL who had become an FBI agent and Hawkins'
partner for a time. Woodley himself had been promoted to
ASAC in Jacksonville, while the former ASAC had taken the
SAC position when Tom Shear took the job of Assistant
Director of the Counterterrorism Division in Washington.
While Woodley hated to see his friend leave Jacksonville, he
knew it was a great opportunity. Shear was in favor of it because
it would get Hawkins to D.C.

Then there was Samantha Land. Hawkins had fallen hard for the strong, beautiful Case Officer. Sam had, quite fortuitously, felt the same way. She was operating out of CIA Headquarters, so the idea of moving to D.C. meant it would also be easier for them to see each other more frequently. That had been the final push Hawkins needed, so he accepted the transfer. Over the next few months Hawkins found himself in training facilities operated by several of the government's agencies, teaching him technologies and techniques he would need to be familiar with in his new role as CIA liaison. Sam had been in and out of the country, but they still made time for each other whenever possible. The three months since he had officially transferred to D.C. had been amazing, in no small part to the fact that he and Sam were able to spend almost every free moment together.

"Well, don't you have a warm glow this blustery Monday morning," a voice called out. Hawkins turned his head slightly to see Barry Morris smiling widely as he peered over the top of his cubicle. Morris was a decade older than Hawkins, a seasoned agent with a lot of experience. An easygoing man with a ready laugh, Morris' favorite hobby seemed to be giving Hawkins a hard time. His real hobby was body building, and his black skin stretched taut across massive muscles that bunched and relaxed constantly beneath his Under Armour polo shirt. "What's got the spring in your step today?"

"I got a good run in this morning," Hawkins said without breaking stride as he walked towards his desk. "I like cold weather."

"Especially if you've got someone to keep you warm, huh?" This was Jenn Moreland, Morris' partner. Moreland's father had been a Marine and met her mother while he was stationed in Japan. They were married in Okinawa, and Jenn was born on her parents' first anniversary. An only child Jenn was as proud of her Japanese heritage as she was of her service in the Marine Corps. She had made a name for herself as a JAG before the Bureau made her an offer she couldn't refuse. About the same age as

Hawkins', her military and legal experiences gave her an air of someone much older. "I'm pretty sure you weren't running alone, were you?"

"So, they call that 'running' now, huh?" Morris said, and the other agents around made various jeering noises.

"Be careful if Hawk asks you to go for a run," Dave Culver said sarcastically. Culver was an accounting genius, someone who Hawkins believed could actually smell an electronic trail of illicit funds being shuffled around over the internet. His accounting skills were matched by his lack of athletic prowess. Almost painfully thin, Culver was often teased for his lack of physicality in the world of federal law enforcement, but he more than made up for it when it came to the financial and technical side of things.

"Yes, Sam and I ran together this morning, but that's it," Hawkins said dismissively. "You bunch of dirty-minded middle schoolers," he added with a smirk. The group of agents laughed and continued ribbing him as he walked over to his desk. Hawkins and Sam would run together most mornings they were in town together, and the whole squad knew it. Hawkins and Sam would take turns meeting close to one another's work—one day running along the George Washington Parkway, another running through the National Mall. Land was much more naturally athletic than he. She had been a star athlete in high school and had earned her reputation as being exceptionally capable physically, both in the Army and her current position as a CIA Case Officer. Running seemed to come so naturally to her, while it was always a struggle for him. He didn't mind at all, however, as long as he was running with her. "What do we have going this morning other than morbid curiosity about my personal relationships?"

"I was just sending some stuff over to the boards in the war room." Culver was referring to the conference room, a glassed-in soundproof area large enough to hold 20 people with a long table that filled the center. The glass outer wall could turn opaque, and every wall could become a giant interactive touchscreen. Anything "written" on the walls was saved to a file so it could be recalled in future meetings or sent to those with a need to know. "Supposed to be a big meeting here in a few."

Hawkins curiosity was piqued. "Really? Who's coming in for that?"

"Not sure," Culver replied. "You're the SSA, so I figured you'd know." At that moment Hawkins phone chimed. He glanced at the screen and saw a message from Tom Shear, the new Assistant Director of Counterterrorism. Shear had been promoted from the Special Agent in Charge position in Jacksonville shortly before Hawkins had been bumped up. Shear had agreed to the promotion as long as he could pick his replacement. He had chosen his former ASAC, Walter Simmons, to take the SAC position. Mark Woodley, Hawkins' former partner, had been moved up the the ASAC position. Shear had also insisted on Hawkins being put in as Supervisory Special Agent over one of the CT squads, and HQ had been happy enough to allow for all of those. Shear's message was brief: "Meeting in your conference room in 5. Eyes only."

"And there's my heads up," Hawkins said.

Culver shrugged. "Don't feel bad. I just got the data files sent to me that they want for the meeting. They're encrypted, so I don't know what's on them. Sounds like 7th Floor to me." He referred to the administrative level at FBI HQ. Hawkins noted to himself that it was also the top executive level at CIA Headquarters across the Potomac.

"Alright, I'm going to head in and try to look reasonably prepared. You guys try and make yourselves look busy for the brass."

Moreland said something entirely off-color about upper management, which elicited chuckles from her squadmates. Field agents generally felt that everyone at HQ was out of touch with what happened in the day-to-day work of the Bureau. Many considered it an unwritten rule that in order to be promoted you had to screw up enough that they moved you up the chain of command just to get you out of the way. While that was clearly an exaggerated view, the fact was many people in the upper ranks of federal positions seemed to get there due to their failures more than their successes.

Such was not the case of the leadership that walked through the door of the squad office shortly after Hawkins had entered the conference room. Assistant Director Shear had been around long enough that his reputation for excellence preceded him. He had high expectations for everyone that worked for him, but he didn't ask anything of anyone he hadn't done or wasn't willing to do himself. He was an agent's agent, and was well respected by those who knew him. At his side was James Van Horn, the Director of the FBI, and Jillian Stott, the new Attorney General. She had taken the place of the previous AG who retired shortly after the GODKILLER Case was resolved.

"Hawk, you know Director Van Horn."

"Indeed," Hawk replied and shook the Director's hand. "Good to see you again, sir."

"Hope you're getting settled into the area," Van Horn said with a smile. "DC is a different world."

"That, sir, is an understatement."

"I don't believe you've had the pleasure of meeting the Attorney General yet," Shear said.

"No, sir," Hawkins replied as he extended a hand towards the AG. Stott had been an FBI agent herself for a time before she was appointed as a U.S Attorney. She served in that capacity for nearly a decade before she was tapped by President Hathaway to serve as Attorney General shortly after the previous AG's retirement. "Thomas Hawkins, ma'am. A pleasure to meet you."

"It's nice to finally meet you, Agent Hawkins," Stott said. "Director Van Horn and AD Shear have really been talking you up. You did a good job on GODKILLER."

"Thank you, ma'am, but that was definitely a team effort."

"Every team has its captain, Agent Hawkins," she said, raising her eyebrows over the tortoise shell rim of her glasses.

"I suppose you're right, ma'am." Hawkins wanted to get the focus off of himself as quickly as possible. He knew that the route to success in the federal realm was often shameless self-promotion, but he was certain he would never be comfortable with it. Praise wasn't why he did what he did. He had to admit, however, it felt awfully good. "The conference room is right this way." Hawkins felt the eyes of his squad following him as he went into the conference room and shut the door behind him. He flipped a switch and the walls went opaque. The room was completely soundproofed, and the soft hum of the climate control was almost distracting in the silence.

Director Van Horn spoke first. "Agent Hawkins, what we're about to share with you is eyes only. We will give you a redacted version of this briefing to share with your squad, but for now this is close hold."

"Understood, sir."

Shear touched a glass pad on the table and entered a code. When he had finished, the walls of the room displayed files, photographs, video clips—an almost overwhelming display of information—in high resolution. "There is a degree of concern that the French government is not being straightforward with us in the aftermath of GODKILLER. The new president, Louis Paquet, talks a good talk, but the Intelligence Community suspects that there's more than meets the eye there." Shear touched the picture of Paquet, and a cascade of photos and other files opened on the wall. "So, they want to take a look. They want us digging around on the financial side. Looking through his books, seeing if there's anything out of place. He has a few known business associates and such, but he seems to have kept his nose clean over the years. He has no known associations with any groups that would raise even a yellow flag. He's supportive of restoring normative relations with the U.S. after that mess, going so far as to own up to France's improper inflammatory actions."

"Sounds like exactly who we would want in office there," Hawkins said.

"That's what has the IC wound up," Stott responded. "They have a sense that all of this went a little too smoothly, which makes everyone at Langley nervous."

"It makes us nervous, too," Van Horn said. "The DNI called me and briefed me on a conversation he had with the President. He made very clear that we are to look into this thoroughly yet circumspectly. We don't want anything to happen that would upset the tenuous apple cart of cordiality that's going on now. The White House doesn't want the bad press, and we don't want the blame for heightened tensions."

"Unless there's a reason for tensions to escalate," Shear interjected. "If it turns out there's something wonky going on inside Elysée Palace, then we need to know. If it's actionable, then we need to be able to pass that information up the chain. If there's nothing there, then we can all breathe a sigh of relief."

Van Horn leaned in. "We want your squad to begin digging into President Paquet's numbers and see what turns up. See where the trails lead. But discretion is key. Your squad can't know just yet that we suspect Paquet may be dirty. They should think this is just an informal evaluation of a new ally, looking for weaknesses where someone might want to take advantage of him."

Hawkins raised his hand, then felt like a child in the principal's office asking permission to speak. "I understand the need for secrecy, but why keep my squad in the dark? They have high-level clearances and work on compartmentalized intel all the time."

"Because we're not sure who we can trust," AG Stott said. "We can't risk anyone in your unit knowing something too early and have it getting out."

Hawkins felt himself flush slightly. "With all due respect,

ma'am, my squad mates are Federal Agents on a counterter-rorism unit charged with investigating foreign powers' financial involvement in support of terrorism. Just what part of that makes them unworthy of trust?" Shear cocked an eyebrow at him. It wasn't usually a good idea to get feisty with the Attorney General.

If the AG was upset with Hawkins' tone, she didn't show it. "This doesn't have anything specifically to do with your unit, Agent Hawkins." She sighed, then continued. "We have reason to believe that our information system has been compromised at some point."

"What?" Hawkins asked incredulously. "What would lead you to believe that?"

"Our French counterparts have known things they could only know if they had been *made* aware," Van Horn said with no small amount of frustration evident. "CIA thinks it's someone in the White House, the White House thinks it's CIA, and we think it might be both. Secret Service has got their technical guys putting eyes and ears 24/7 on everybody who sets foot within a quarter mile of the Oval Office. We don't want to spook off the leak, if there is one, before we can nab them." Hawkins felt honored to be trusted by his three superiors, but then it occurred to him: *what if they're doing this to see if* I'm *the leak?*

Shear tapped the wall, and another image popped up: Samantha Land. "DNI Price has launched his own investigation that will be a bit more—hands on. Samatha Land is going to be working this on behalf of the IC. As liaison, you will have access to the case at Langley, but you will not be able to share what you hear on that side of the river with your squad just yet."

Hawkins knew that would be the case when he agreed to be an FBI liaison with CIA. He would be privy to things at Langley that would be so compartmentalized it was possible even the FBI Director wouldn't have clearance to know them. Secrecy was a part of the life of every Federal Agent, but for those involved in the Intelligence Community it *was* their life. "I understand," he said.

The AG nodded. "Good. You have a meeting at 10:00 am today with DNI Price and D/CIA Sullivan. Assistant Director Shear mentioned you'll be going back to Jacksonville soon?"

"Yes, ma'am, just for a couple of days. Getting the last of the stuff out of my house there so it's clear to close next week. If I need to postpone..."

"No, that'll be fine," she replied. "We have a conference call with SAC Simmons about this in 25 minutes since that office was the one that took point on the GODKILLER case. You can get with him while you're there and compare notes." Shear typed another code in. A message appeared on the walls that said, "SAVING SESSION," then there was only opaque glass. "If anything changes suddenly, we can send one of our aircraft to get you."

"Yes, ma'am," he replied. "Thank you all for the opportunity."

"Of course," she said, then turned to the other men. "Gentlemen, if I could have a word privately with Agent Hawkins before we go."

"You've already done us proud, Agent Hawkins," Director Van Horn said as he shook Hawkins' hand and clapped him on the shoulder. "Keep it up," and he walked out. Shear patted Hawkins on the back as he walked past, whistled almost inaudibly then chuckled softly. He could almost hear what Shear was thinking: "Way to tick off the AG, Hawk. What could possibly go wrong there?" Hawkins was bracing himself for a good chewing out when he noticed the AG didn't look angry at all. In fact, she looked at him proudly.

"Not many squad supervisors would get mouthy with the AG on behalf of their squad," she said with a smirk.

"My apologies, ma'am," Hawkins offered. "I meant no disrespect at all. But I know the work this squad was doing long before I got here. These are seasoned agents with immaculate track records, and they have proven themselves worthy of trust with their previous casework. I wouldn't be much of a supervisor if I didn't stand up for them."

"You're exactly right, Agent Hawkins," the AG said, taking a step forward. "You've proven yourself an effective leader, particularly in a crisis. I'm afraid we've got more of that coming our way, and it's going to be important that you continue to be who you are. You're a supervisor *because* you're a natural leader. There are plenty of people with more experience than you, including the people on your squad, but you have something they don't—you're a leader. You do what's right, no matter who it ticks off." She looked over the top of her glasses again. "You just make sure you continue to do that. Am I clear?"

"Perfectly, ma'am."

"Good," she said as she shook hands with Hawkins once more. "Be sure and give my best to DNI Price" she said with a smile, and stepped out of the conference room. Hawkins flipped a switch on the wall and the walls were no longer opaque. He saw the other members of his squad, and the other agents in the office, looking at him expectantly. Morris finally threw up his hands, and mouthed "Well?"

Hawkins stepped out into the office toward his squad. "Okay, everybody," he said. "Here's what we've just had served up to us."

CHAPTER FIVE

Hawkins turned onto Highway 123 heading toward MacLean, Virginia off of the George Washington Parkway. He hadn't traveled far when he saw a green highway sign that read "George H. W. Bush Center for Intelligence, Next Right". Immediately afterward he saw a white sign with large red letters advising people who had no business entering the land occupied by the Central Intelligence Agency headquarters complex to just keep going straight, and not to even think about taking the next right. Hawkins *did* have business there, and so entered the turn lane. The road arced right and looked more as if it were the entrance to a college campus than the headquarters of the world's premier intelligence agency. He didn't go far before the true nature of the place revealed itself.

The road was a four-lane, divided by a well-manicured curbed grass median lined with trees and other foliage. The outgoing lanes were relatively unobstructed, but the two lanes going in were randomly blocked by retractable steel barriers, necessitating some slow and cautious maneuvering to weave in between them. Another 50 feet or so and he arrived at the large checkpoint station, manned by the CIA Police. There were two lines, one for employees and another for visitors on official business.

He veered his car to the right and approached the lowered bar at the first checkpoint, where there was only a small box with a black button. He held his credentials up to it and waited. He had a set of CIA credentials that allowed him access, but he still felt like an underage kid with a fake ID at a liquor store. The bar raised and Hawkins pulled forward. He approached the hard-looking structure that housed the employee section of the guard post. A woman in a dark blue police uniform stepped out of the building and approached his car.

"Good morning," she said pleasantly. The small brass name badge on her uniform said "Keller". The patches on her sleeve bore the seal of the CIA and its heraldry, with the words "POLICE" emblazoned beneath. She was young, in her mid-twenties, and Hawkins knew beyond any shadow of a doubt that she was one of the toughest people to wear a badge anywhere. Far from rent-a-cops, the CIA Police were a force to be reckoned with, each highly trained CIA personnel in their own right. They had federal law enforcement jurisdiction not only on CIA grounds, but anywhere their duties might require them to go. Any one of them could immediately join the ranks of the most elite SWAT teams in the country and not miss a beat. "Can I see your ID, please?"

Hawkins complied, and waited while she compared what he gave her to the images she no doubt was looking at on her tablet. When she was satisfied that Hawkins was indeed who he was supposed to be, she handed his creds back.

"Here to see the Director?"

"Yes, ma'am,' Hawkins replied.

"I know you're fairly new to Langley, Agent Hawkins. You know where you're going?" CIA kept a short leash on everyone who came onsite. Hawkins was a liaison with the Agency now, but he was still viewed by some as an outsider. Perhaps he always would be. There had traditionally not been a great deal of love between the Bureau and the Agency, and it would take more than a title to fully ingratiate him into the culture of Langley.

"I've been here a couple of times. VIP lot?"

She smiled. "Yep. Just go straight, follow the road on around, and you'll eventually see the old entrance. Turn left there, show your ID to the officer at the guard post, and he'll give you a pass to park in the lot."

"Got it. Thanks a lot."

"You have a nice day," the officer replied, then turned and walked back inside. The bar lifted, and Hawkins was able to proceed once more. He marveled at the beauty of the settings, lush woods surrounding him on both sides. Cars were parked everywhere one could fit—along the road, in large lots, once again bringing to mind the image of a well-manicured college campus. He went a little farther, then saw the large water tower on his left, and the two connected buildings that comprised the CIA Headquarters--at least, the part that could be seen from above ground. He continued going straight and approached the Old Entrance, the original building with the entryway everyone sees in the movies. He turned to the left past a Dodge Durango and a Chevrolet Suburban with satellite receivers on the roofs and stopped at the guard shack. He once again showed his ID, as well as the colored card the officer had given him, and the guard gave him a VIP parking pass in exchange. He pulled into the lot, found a corner spot, and parked.

When he walked into the main lobby, he once again felt a rush of adrenaline. Here he was, an FBI agent with several years of experience, having done some pretty exciting things in his life, and yet he felt like a little kid every time he had been here. He stepped forward and saw the massive CIA seal on the marble floor and felt a chill run up and down his spine. He looked to the left and saw the statue of Colonel William J. Donovan, the founder of the World War II Office of Strategic Services, or OSS, that would become the CIA a few years later. Nearby there was a memorial to those members of the OSS who gave their lives in service to their country. Etched into the wall nearby was a passage from the Biblical Gospel of John, chapter 8, verse 32:

"And you shall know the truth, and the truth shall set you free." On the other side of the columned lobby, was another memorial, this one to those who had given their lives in the service of the CIA. There was a book with years written on the pages. Some years had a name or two next to and under the date, some did not, but they all had black stars. Hawkins knew that the black stars represented those Agency employees whose jobs were so secret that their identities could not be revealed even after their deaths.

Hawkins' gaze lingered on the CIA memorial book. He looked at those black stars and thought again about the individuals they represented. He hoped that Case Officer Samantha Land would not be one of those remembered by a black star in the book. He thought about the names of the OSS operatives who gave their lives during World War II. He thought about the Bible verse etched into the opposite wall, about the truth setting one free. The converse of that, he knew, was that lies bound and tripped people up. He was hoping for truth in his visit this day.

Four CIA Police officers stood at the guard desk offset to the right. To the left of the desk were massive turnstiles with black square pads with keypads just below. He held his card to the scanner and punched in his code. One of the officers took note of him and nodded as the turnstile chimed its approval. The light blinked green and the gate unlocked.

As Hawkins passed through the turnstile a well-dressed man that looked to be about his age walked up. Several inches shorter and much thinner than Hawkins, he wore rimless glasses, a blue suit with a white shirt and red-and-blue diagonal-striped tie. He looked like he belonged in D.C., lobbying for some special interest group or another.

"Good afternoon, Agent Hawkins. I'm Carlisle Welch, the Director's personal assistant. She's currently on an international call right now, so she asked me to come down and escort you up." Welch looked down at Hawkins' credentials clipped to his breast pocket, subconsciously verifying he had the clearance needed to get to the 7th floor.

Hawkins thought back to his first time at Langley. Although he was already an FBI agent at the time, he had been given a limited access visitor's badge to clip onto his jacket on that trip. Regardless of one's security clearances, if you weren't an employee of the Central Intelligence Agency, you were going to wear one of several colors of visitor's badges. Red and white meant that the guest had no clearance and must be escorted by authorized personnel at all times. Yellow with red markings indicated a visitor with limited access. Green with yellow lettering signified a civilian with security clearances sufficient for travel within most areas of the building. A green badge with black lettering signified the highest level of clearance for non-Agency personnel, and someone with that kind of clearance wasn't usually seen strolling the hallways.

The two men walked up the few stairs that led to the main hallway. They took a left and entered one of the elevators that went to the seventh floor. Welch didn't seem to have much to say, didn't offer any comments on the weather, absolutely nothing in the way of polite small talk. In fact, it seemed he made an effort *not* to say anything. It was as if Welch was afraid that if he opened his mouth he couldn't be sure what would come out. Hawkins noticed that Welch seemed a bit uncomfortable, almost nervous. He wondered perhaps if the man were sick. Hawkins hoped that the guy wasn't about to puke here in the elevator. That would not be fun at all. Hawkins could stand just about anything apart from vomit. If someone else did in his presence, he joined in.

It was at that moment Hawkins noticed a few beads of sweat at the edge of the other man's hairline, and noticed that the skin on his neck just above his collar was a splotchy red. Something had this guy agitated. Hawkins filed his observations away for future reference and followed the man off the elevator.

They walked down a hallway much like any other—white

walls, gray carpet, windows looking onto the outside world, and doors leading into other offices. More accurately these windows actually looked out through the windows of another building constructed around the one he was walking in. This precaution had been necessary to prevent any signals from within being picked up by anyone on the outside. The Soviets had tried aiming laser mics at the Agency's windows from their satellites decades ago, but the building-within-a-building helped squash their attempts. The ordinary-looking office doors on this hallway were armored and electronically-secured doors leading to offices built like bank vaults. They rounded a corner, walked past a couple of offices, and Welch opened a door on the right that bore a bronze crest, a circle nearly filled with the image of an eagle. On the eagle's chest was a shield containing a globe with a large star in the center and 13 smaller stars all around the globe's edge. On the outer edge of the circle was written, "DIRECTOR OF CENTRAL INTELLIGENCE AGENCY, INTELLI-GENCE COMMUNITY". Welch looked at the Director's closed door, behind his own desk.

"Let me see if she's off the phone," he said. Hawkins tried in vain to remember if Samantha had ever mentioned the name of the D/CIA's assistant. He was fairly certain that "Welch" didn't ring any bells. The other man tapped on the Director's door and stuck his head inside. Hawkins couldn't put his finger on why, but he didn't like Welch at all.

"The Director will see you now, Agent Hawkins." Welch opened the door and Hawkins walked in. Seated behind a mahogany desk was the Director of the Central Intelligence Agency, Dorothy Sullivan. She was far younger than previous D/CIA—and current DNI—Jack Price, some twenty years his junior. A four-star Marine General, Sullivan had distinguished herself over the years as a brilliant mind encased in a warrior's body. A combat veteran, Sullivan had eventually completed a law degree and joined the JAG corps. She worked her way up through the ranks and found herself increasingly involved in operational oversight and international diplomacy. No-nonsense on the battlefield, she was perhaps more nuanced but equally fierce in the courtroom and halls of Washington. She was nominated by the President based on the recommendation of Price and several of the Joint Chiefs. Although the POTUS was of a different political affiliation than Sullivan, his advisors were in unanimous agreement. The gesture was not lost on a Congress trying to make some bi-partisan progress, and Sullivan was easily approved.

"Come in, Agent Hawkins," Sullivan said as she rose from her chair. The CIA Director extended her hand and Hawkins shook it. "I've heard so much about you I feel like I already know you. That was some excellent work you and Land did together last year."

"Thank you, General." Hawkins turned and saw they were not alone in the room. To his right was the legend himself, Director of National Intelligence Jack Price. Further to the right was Samantha Land. "Director Price," Hawkins said.

"Hello, Agent Hawkins," Price said as he extended his hand. It was hard to believe Price was as old as he was, Hawkins thought. The man's bald head and white goatee gave the impression of age, and his cream-colored turtleneck sweater beneath a navy blazer exuded a calm demeanor, but he gave off a sense of restrained energy. Hawkins had no doubt whatsoever that, regardless of his age, Jack Price was a man who cold still take care of business. "I believe you know Case Officer Land," he said with a smile.

"Indeed I do," Hawkins said. Land wore a black business suit with high-heeled ankle boots. He never ceased to be amazed at how she looked good in every style of clothing. She smiled at him. "Always a pleasure."

The Director motioned to the chair directly in front of her desk and Hawkins took a seat.

"I understand you were briefed by the DOJ this morning, and they told you the nature of what we would be discussing."

The compartmentalized nature of what they were about to discuss was clear in Sullivan's tone.

"Yes, Madame Director, they did."

"This is never the kind of conversation we look forward to having, Agent Hawkins," Price said, his slight Southern drawl at odds with his serious tone. "But we fear that all is not as it seems in France and, even more troubling, may also be problematic here at home. We believe that French President Louis Paquet may, in fact, be connected with a group that would like nothing more than for the United States to find itself in a conflict with her Western allies."

"Conflict," Hawkins repeated. "Exactly what is the nature of this potential conflict?"

"That we can't answer," D/CIA Sullivan responded. "That's why Justice is running an investigation through your squad, and we're running an investigation through ours. Case Officer Land has been assigned to a unit comprised of British Intelligence agents to investigate President Paquet's connections on the ground in France. They will be operating under non-official cover."

Hawkins bristled slightly at the phrase. He knew that NOCs operated with near total impunity, but they had no recourse if they were caught. CIA operatives often worked under the auspices of the closest U.S. Embassy as State Department employees. If they were caught, they could invoke diplomat status, at which point they would be treated poorly for 72 hours then released. NOCs had no such benefit. Total deniability on the part of the U.S. Government was the price NOCs paid for the operational freedom they had. He glanced over at Land, who nodded ever so slightly at him.

Sullivan continued. "Case Officer Land and her team will conduct their operation and report their findings. Those findings will be shared with you. We expect the same courtesy on any of the FBI's findings."

"Absolutely. We're all on the same team on this."

"We'd like to think so, but that's not always necessarily the case," Sullivan said.

Price broke in. "Even more so than usual," he said with a mirthless chuckle. "In all seriousness, we have concerns that our high-level classified communications on this matter may be compromised. I know you were briefed on this issue to some degree. Our Science and Technology Directorate is working in conjunction with the Technical Security Division over at Secret Service to try and shore things up at the White House, but we aren't taking any chances. The eyes-only nature of this operation across all involved agencies will ensure that we'll be able to track any leaks very easily from this point forward."

"What do we know about Land's team?" Hawkins asked. He wasn't sure, but he thought Land tilted her head in a slight sign of disapproval. "Are we sure they aren't compromised?"

"Director Price has history with one of the British operatives in particular," Land said. "I've worked with him a number of times myself. They are Tier 1 operators, and completely trustworthy."

"Land is right, Agent Hawkins," Price agreed. "Their team lead and I go back more years than I care to admit. He's verified and vouches for the rest of the team. MI-6 is running this the same way we are, eyes-only with fewer than a dozen people including the British Prime Minister and their operators. We can't ask for more secure personnel than what we've put together there."

"Obviously, it is of the utmost importance for Land's team to be completely off the radar," Sullivan said. "No one outside of this room can know about them."

"Does Director Van Horn know? Or AD Shear?"

"They know we're running an op, but that's it," Price replied. "Operational details are limited to those of us in this room and POTUS." Price's expression grew more serious. "This is not just for the safety of our team. If the French President is up to some-thing, and he finds out we're snooping around, it wouldn't take much for this to turn into an international incident. It could very easily be made to look as though we're trying to control who's running things in France. The last thing we want to happen is to be perceived as empire building in Europe."

"The stakes are high on this, Agent Hawkins," Sullivan interjected. "We've already been through this with Land. If there are agents in power who were connected in any way with the battle virus last year, they may have another play. We can't afford to let them get by us."

Hawkins looked at Land, who gave him a determined nod. "We'll get it done."

CHAPTER SIX

Donald Molson took a sip from his double café au lait. He was sitting at a table for two, the outdoor café he frequented now enclosed slightly by an extended awning. Portable propane heaters radiated heat as fire danced in glass enclosures at the top. It was almost 4:00 p.m., dangerously close to being too late for such a dose of caffeine. It seemed like only yesterday that he could drink espresso at bedtime and fall asleep immediately. The older he got, however, the more he found evening caffeination to be problematic for his sleep patterns. As the FBI's Legal Attaché in Paris, many would consider his position to be relaxed, if not outright cushy. Only those who didn't understand what the job actually entailed thought that, however. His investigative days were mostly over. Now, Molson's schedule consisted of bureaucrats looking to see how much help the French could get out of the United States for whatever project they were peddling. He didn't begrudge them—after all, he did much the same thing. While he had vastly underestimated the workload when he accepted the position, he came to enjoy it more than he had ever thought possible. He worked with some genuinely exceptional people, both in his own offices and those of the French Government. But it was nonetheless exhausting, and often exasperating, work. Molson was generally in bed by 10:00 and up at 5:00 every morning, and in order to maintain that schedule he drew the line on coffee intake at 4:30. He couldn't bring himself to drink decaf, so it was an accommodation he was willing to endure. And he wasn't about to let the man walking up to his table sense any kind of weakness.

Molson rose to his feet as Philippe Dupain approached the table. His counterpart in the French government smiled as they shook hands. "Good afternoon, Donald," he said smoothly in perfect, unaccented English. "I trust that's decaf? You're not as young as you used to be. You'll never get to sleep drinking a double this time of day."

"It's not usually a problem," Molson smiled as he responded in flawless French. "If I find myself restless at bedtime, I generally just smoke a nice Rocky Patel, unlike the candy sticks you call cigarettes."

They both grinned at the exchange. As much as both men might be loathe to admit it, they had become good friends over the last few years. The nature of their work brought them into frequent contact, and it had spilled over into personal relationships between the men and their wives. The ladies generally shook their heads as their husbands tried to one-up the other at every opportunity. A waiter walked up and Dupain ordered a cappuccino.

"I trust things are going well for you?" Molson asked.

Dupain removed a pack of cigarettes from his coat pocket. He offered one to Molson, who declined, them flicked open a stainless steel lighter. The flame caught the end of the cigarette, and he took a deep drag.

Molson chuckled as he took a sip. "That answers that," he said.

"You Americans have a saying: 'Never ask what else can go wrong,' no?"

"Something like that."

"Well, someone in France has clearly said it. And I would like to have a word with them about it." He took another long drag from the cigarette as the waiter brought his drink. "Things are absolutely chaotic."

"What do you mean it's all still there?" DEA Agent Logan Nash asked.

"This house is filled with drugs, Logan," the agent on the line back in Greenville repeated. "There's coke, heroin, pills, you name it. The blow alone is worth $30 mil."

"That's nuts. Why would they kill him and leave that stuff there if they knew we were coming? What about cash? Any weapons?"

"No to both. No money, other than a couple grand in Cheever's pocket. He had a gun in the nightstand, but that's it."

"So why did he say he had cash and guns if he didn't?" Agent Mike Rhodes was sitting next to the speaker phone. "Just trying to look more 'Scarface' for Luna?"

"I don't know, man, but he was big time with that much narcotics sitting around in here."

Nash shook his head. "Alright, thanks, man. Let me know what else you guys find." He tapped the screen and ended the call. He threw his hands up in exasperation.

"That's some weird stuff, Logan." Rhodes said. "If it was the supplier who killed Cheever, why would he leave millions of dollars' worth of narcotics just sitting there? Was he sending a message?"

"What message? 'We've got so much money that $30 million isn't worth us picking it up?'" Nash shook his head. "I've got no idea, but I need some coffee."

"Maybe you should crash for a bit," Rhodes suggested. "I know you never sleep before we serve warrants. Why don't you catch some shuteye while Luna's out? You can interview her when she wakes, and I'll catch some Z's then." Luna had said she was too wired to sleep after the excitement, but she fell asleep in the cabin's upstairs bedroom almost instantly.

"I guess it couldn't hurt," Nash admitted. There wasn't anything to do until she was awake, or the forensics crew found something—*anything*—to work with. As it was, they didn't have much at the moment. Sure, there were a lot of drugs that would never hit the street. Allegedly, and most alarmingly, there were also quite a few fully automatic weapons floating around now that had once been in Cheever's possession. That wouldn't be good for anybody. And they had no idea who was behind any of it. It seemed their case had dried up with the blood on Darius Cheever's sheets.

Kirk Talbert sat comfortably in the back of the armored vehicle known as Cadillac Two. The Vice-President of the United States required transportation that not only adequately projected the image of American power but was also safe, so the previous version of the Presidential Limousine passed to him. Cadillac One, the President's conveyance, was referred to by insiders as "The Beast," an appropriate nickname if ever there was one. The modern Presidential vehicle was a Cadillac in name only. Custom built using bleeding-edge technology, it was more armored tank than car. While the capabilities of The Beast were one of the nation's most closely guarded secrets, it was public knowledge that the vehicle was a massively heavy, massively powerful brute capable of protecting its occupants under most any circumstance and bringing them home safely. The Vice-President likewise needed protection, but that position merited the previous-generation model. The older model of "The Beast" was nothing to look down on. There weren't many obvious differences to the untrained eye between the version of The Beast Talbert was riding in and the newer version assigned to POTUS, but he knew they were there. It didn't bother him, though. This vehicle, the twin of it that served as a backup in front of him, and the motorcade filled with armored Suburbans gave Talbert the confidence that as long as he was tucked away inside its armored embrace had nothing to fear from anyone who meant him harm.

The motorcade wound its way from the airport to Elysée Palace. He had a meeting with the French President, and everything had to go perfectly. There was a lot riding on this visit. The eyes of the world, not to mention those of his boss, would be watching. Things were still tense globally as a result of the United States and France coming to blows over the chemical weapons plant that had been in the French countryside. France had come across too forcefully in its defense of the facility, and as a result had incurred the wrath of the United States and many of their mutual allies. There was a great deal of instability as a result, and this meeting was necessary to put restless minds at ease. Talbert and Paquet would meet, the press would shoot video and take photos while they chatted and shared a meal together, and everyone would breathe a little easier when it was clear that France and the United States were mending their fractured relationship.

Talbert lived for moments like this. He was taught from an early age that the easiest way to get what you want is to be gracious, agreeable, and grateful. Those lessons had served him well through college, law school, and his entry into politics. As he made his way through the ranks, his polished speeches and winsome personality won him friends everywhere he went. He earned a reputation for being able to broker deals between even the most partisan bureaucrats, a skill that earned him a spot on his party's ticket as Vice-President. He was often asked if he aspired to the highest office in the land, if he would run for President himself. He always said that he would discuss that at an appropriate time in the future. It would be unseemly to talk about such things at this point, and President Hathaway was very good to him. POTUS allowed Talbert a great deal of leeway, and offered opportunities that some VPs never got. No, Talbert was happy with where he was and what he was doing. He had a job to do, and he was going to do it. He was going to make the world a better place if he could, and every day that passed made it seem more likely that he would do exactly that.

The motorcade arrived at the French presidential palace. Agents from his Secret Service detail opened the impenetrable door of Cadillac Two, and Talbert stepped out into the French afternoon. Louis Paquet waved warmly and made his way toward the motorcade. Talbert returned the gesture and turned to wave at the cheering crowd who had gathered. American flags waved throughout the crowd. Everyone in attendance was hopeful, optimistic, that this was a sign of great things to come. Talbert knew they were right—great things were indeed on the horizon.

"Sorry if I went out of bounds in there," Hawkins said sheepishly as he walked the halls of CIA next to Samantha Land. "I know you're more than capable of dealing with any situation that comes your way, but I just…"

"No, I get it," Sam said. "It's actually very sweet of you to worry. But you've got to remember, this is what I do. It's what I've been doing for years."

"And you're very good at it," Hawkins admitted. "I've seen you in action." He paused for a moment. "There's just something about this whole thing that just…"

"Just what?"

"I don't know. It's like an itch I can't quite reach." He shrugged. "Maybe I'm just still getting used to the world of cloak and dagger."

"Remember what they taught you at the Farm about your intuition. If something feels wrong…"

"It probably is. Yeah, I know that one pretty well."

"So, we both agree to stick with that, and everything will be fine." Hawkins wasn't sure, but he decided to leave it alone. They made small talk as they went down to the food court, grabbed lunch, and found a table.

"You know we really need to talk sometime," Hawkins said.

"That's what we're doing now, isn't it?" Land said with an impish grin. Hawkins loved it when she grinned like that. It was almost a dare, like she was encouraging him to do something that would be dangerous but also a lot of fun.

"Can we please be serious for a minute?" Hawkins asked in mock frustration. She shuffled in her seat slightly, then gave him her full attention. "Sam, I love you. I am happier when I am with you than I have ever been in my entire life." Her expression softened, the amused look turning to genuine affection. "I know our lives are crazy and, like now, we are going in different directions half the time. But I just want to know: is this something you want? I mean...us. I know you love your work, and I would never want to take you away from that, but do you think we could..."

Land reached across the table and took both of his hands in hers. "Yes," she said softly. "I think we could. I think we can make anything work that we want." She looked down at their intertwined hands for a moment, then locked eyes with his. "Thomas Hawkins, you have made me feel like I never thought I could. You take me just as I am. You aren't intimidated by me, and you don't try to put me in a box or keep me on a shelf. You let me be who God created me to be. And I love you for that. Yes, what we do is dangerous. And I don't know what a 'normal' life looks like for us. But I can tell you that I adore you, and there is no one I would rather figure out how to make this life work with than you."

Hawkins sat for a moment and looked into Land's green eyes, her blond hair framing her tanned face. "Well," he said after a moment. "That went well." They both laughed and started eating again.

"I was a little afraid you were about to propose to me in the CIA commissary."

"So that's not a good idea then?"

"Not in the CIA commissary anyway," she said with a wink.

"So you're saying there's a chance."

"Hope springs eternal."

"Well, at least you're an optimist," he said

"And generous," Land said as she looked at her watch. "Want to share a ride to the airport?"

Nash was sitting across the table from Luna Roberts, notebook and audio recorder in front of them. He was going over everything from the previous few nights, everything that Darius Cheever might have said before his untimely death that might give Nash some desperately needed information. He needed to know who Cheever was running drugs and guns for, who might have killed him, why they killed him now, how they knew the DEA was coming for him, and, at the top of Luna's list, were they coming for her next.

"I know this is a lot to deal with, Luna, but we're got to go over this stuff now while it's still fresh. We can't get behind the eight ball."

"I know, Logan," she said anxiously. "I don't want to wind up dead over this craziness. I want to do everything I can to help you."

"I don't question that at all," Nash replied calmly. "Is there anything else he said about who his contacts were? Did he say any names, mention any phone numbers, anything like that?"

"No, he never..." Luna paused for moment, then shook her head. "¡Estúpido!" She picked up her phone and unlocked it.

"What?"

Luna tapped at her screen hurriedly, and an excited look came over her face. "He wanted to show me his bank account balance. His phone battery was dead, and I told him he could show me on my phone."

"He logged into his bank account from your phone?" Nash asked. "We can't be that lucky." Luna handed him the phone and he started swiping through. Sure enough, Cheever had used the phone's browser to login to his bank account, and the phone had saved the password. He wrote the login information and account on his notepad, then logged in. He went to the "Account Settings" tab, then looked up the personal and account retrieval information. There was a cell phone number and an email. *What's the chance of that?* he thought to himself. He grabbed his laptop out of his backpack, and entered the web address for Cheever's email service. He typed in the username and entered the same password that had been saved in Luna's phone for the bank login. He prayed a swift, silent prayer before he clicked "Login."

Nash was in. All of Cheever's emails were laid out before him on the screen.

"Rhodes! Get the printer!" The other agent had dozed quietly in a nearby loveseat, but sprang up wide awake at his friend's call. He grabbed a portable printer out of the backpack and quickly set it up.

"Good to go," Rhodes said as the printer's indicator lights all went to green. "What do we have?"

Nash was reading emails and hitting print as fast as he could. "Everything, Mike," he said in a stunned voice. "We've got freakin' everything."

CHAPTER SEVEN

Samantha Land pulled the silver Porsche 911 into the parking spot in the Parisian garage. She looked in the mirror at the woman who had gotten off the Gulfstream G650 in her place: a pink wig cut in a bob, blue contact lenses, and bright pink lipstick changed her features enough that even someone who knew her well would have to look closely in order to recognize her. She stepped out of the sports car and walked to the staircase that led to the safe house she would call home until her mission was complete. It was actually a lovely apartment on the third floor. The staircase leading up to it wound skyward under a glass ceiling and ended on a deck at her front door. No one would accidentally walk up to her residence. If someone came up those stairs, they had a reason to be there or their night would not go so well for them. She was wearing a white faux fur jacket over a white cashmere turtleneck, pink leggings, and white boots that went up to the middle of her thighs. She carried a dark gray duffle bag filled with her necessities. It wasn't quite as fancy as the rest of her attire, but function overrode the fashionable cover her arrival required. Cold weather made it easier to carry hardware, and in this instance she had a Sig Sauer P938 in a band under her sweater and another just inside the top of her left boot. Several spare magazines were tucked into the band and the pockets of her coat. A composite spring-loaded blade was attached to her right forearm. Sam didn't ordinarily carry this much kit, but she considered herself to be in enemy territory. She jogged easily up the stairs, tapped a secure code into the keypad lock, gave the hidden retinal scanner a moment to do its work, and the door popped open.

A text five minutes earlier had told her to expect a visitor in the apartment. As she walked in, the quaint nature of the place instantly appealed to her. It was located in an old building but decorated in a style that had classical elements combined with white and chrome new tech. Old fashioned and cutting edge, all rolled in to one.

"It's a lot like you and I, isn't it?" a male voice with a British accent intoned from a sofa across the main room. "Old world charm and sharp-edged modernity."

Land smiled. "Are you saying there's no charm in modernity?"

"I would never presume to insult the lady in such fashion." The man looked to be in his early fifties, grayish-brown hair swept to one side. He stood smoothly from the low sofa with ease, his hands in front of him extending outward as he rose. "It's good to see you again, Samantha."

"Always a pleasure, Chris," Land said. Chris Chapman was former British Special Air Service, and now served within a part of the most clandestine section within MI-6. She had worked with Chapman a dozen times over the last few years and trusted him as much as anyone. He was a consummate professional, had a genuinely gracious personality, always stayed cool, and was as deadly as they came.

He leaned in a gave her a kiss on each cheek, a platonic gesture not unlike Land would get from a visiting uncle. "The pleasure is most certainly mine. I hope you find these accommodations to be acceptable. Your previous place was unavailable this time."

"Probably for the best." It was highly unlikely that anyone

would make the connection if Land stayed in the same safe house she had used on previous missions in Paris, but the nature of this operation meant they would take no chances. "How are things going so far?"

"The rest of the team is already geared up and ready." He pulled a tablet out of a satchel on the table and unlocked it. "The meeting place is a dozen blocks or so from here, so you'll probably want to get changed and head over there soon. I can brief you while you're getting ready."

"Sounds good," she said, and walked into the bedroom. She opened the closet and found an unusual outfit hanging in front of other clothes that would be in her size. "Um, exactly where are we meeting the rest of the team?"

"Believe me, it wasn't my choice," Chapman said with a laugh. "Glad I'm on overwatch. I'd stick out like a sore thumb in there, no matter what I was wearing."

She pulled the outfit from the rack and looked at it questioningly. "Which is all the more reason why I'm suspicious of the location."

Chapman was clearly amused. "I promise you, I am not to blame."

"I'll take your word for it," she said as she walked into the bathroom and began changing. This was going to take some effort. "I read the file you sent right before I landed. What do we have on this Surmonter Corporation?"

"Diversified financial and logistics company. Based out of Paris, with offices in a dozen port cities around the globe. Founded shortly after World War II. Although low key, they have grown into a substantial mover and shaker in the financial world thanks to their willingness to make low-interest financing available on commercial projects that might not otherwise get funded."

"Risky," Land called out as she removed her wig.

"Indeed, but it's paid off for them. They also do quite a bit of shipping and transport on the Continent. They spread into

Eastern Europe in the mid-90s. Large office in Romania serves as their 'official' headquarters."

"So who owns it?"

"That's the catch," Chapman said. "The companies are privately held, and as such their reporting is slightly cloudy. Since the home offices are in Bucharest, they are able to work the system there and be mysterious." Romania was well-known in federal law enforcement and the IC for being a hotbed of financial crime. If you had enough money, and knew who to give it to, you could get almost anything signed off on.

"Tax evasion?"

"That would be the common reason, but I have a sinking suspicion there's more. I was digging around and found a name I thought seemed familiar. I dug through some old files—the paper kind—and found a connection that, while tenuous, bears further investigation."

"And what would that connection be?"

"I'm not quite ready to talk about it out loud yet. It may be nothing, and I don't want to needlessly chase rabbits. We're going to have our hands full with enough here as it is. We'll go down the line with that we know and see what turns up from there."

"Fair enough," Land said. "You have history with our teammates?"

"A couple of them. Jean Leblanc is a good one. About your age, GIGN for several years before joining up on our French unit." Land nodded to herself in approval. The GIGN, or Groupe d'intervention de la Gendarmerie Nationale, was the tactical side of the French National Police, comparable to the FBI's Hostage Rescue Team.

"How does he feel about spying on his own president?"

"He works for us now," Chapman said. "And he is no fan of how France conducted itself during last year's debacle. He also has his suspicions about the current regime. He's a professional, so we can count on him to do what's needed."

"That's certainly reassuring. Who else do we have?"

"Leblanc brought one of his people from GIGN along, Paul Brodeur. He has a great record. Hasn't been at the game as long, but definitely has the required skill set. Benny Duncan and Wally Morgan are two of my guys, worked with me for years. Rock solid, absolutely will not flinch under pressure. Leblanc and Brodeur will be close contact with you, Duncan and Morgan will be next up."

"And you'll be on overwatch. Got it," Sam said as she walked out of the bedroom in her attire for the meetup. "I can't imagine why you wouldn't want to be in there with us."

Chapman smiled broadly as he looked Land up and down. "Like I said, I wouldn't exactly blend in where you're going."

"That, Chris, is the understatement of the year."

CHAPTER EIGHT

DEA Agent Logan Nash waited for his boss in Greenville to join the virtual meeting. He had gone through dozens of Darius Cheever's emails and found more than enough evidence to prove the dead man's guilt on drug and weapons trafficking charges. They would be able to seize all of his assets now, and he had no beneficiaries to lay claim to any of them, so nearly $10 million in cash and physical property would go into the DEA's coffers. He wondered idly who would get Cheever's Mercedes AMG S65 for undercover use. A chime sounded, bringing him back to the matter at hand. His boss, Supervisory Special Agent Keith Linden, appeared on screen.

"Logan, I just finished looking over the stuff you forwarded to me. How did a nobody like Cheever get mixed up in this?"

"All I know is he was in over his head, and he had no idea until it was too late. And probably didn't know it then because he was so hammered."

Linden made a "pfft" sound. "Now what's this about the supplier. You don't think this is out of Latin America?"

"The drugs, maybe. I'm more concerned about the guns. There are dozens of fully automatic rifles, grenade, explosives—military level hardware—that's in the wind."

"So, we pass that on to ATF," Linden shrugged. "That's their bread and butter."

"Yeah, but there's something about the money that seems hinky," Logan said. "Everything was coming out of an internet bank based out of Romania."

"And? Romania is a hotbed for financial crime"

"The transactions all sourced anonymously, except for one. Somebody slipped up and left a fixed IP address."

"Another lucky break," Linden said. "You need to go buy a lottery ticket. Let's send that over to the Bureau's Financial Crimes division and let them chase it down."

"Why would we want to do that?" Nash said angrily. Although they were part of the Justice Department as well, he had no love for the FBI. He had frequently said that the DEA actually arrested criminals, while the FBI just held press conferences and took credit for it.

"Because they have technical assets we don't, and we're already going to be covered up with this case on the narcotics end of things. Let's spread the love around." In other words, we don't want to mess with the paperwork chasing financial crimes requires. Linden was a good enough guy, but he liked to take the easy route when he could. Nash tried not to let his face wrinkle up in disgust too badly.

"Fine, I'll send the packet to them."

"Good. How's your CI doing?"

"Doing alright," he said, looking over at Luna as she watched tv on the sofa. "Any luck on grabbing that chauffeur?"

"The strip club owner said that the driver that night was a new guy, a last-minute replacement. The registered owner of the car that carried Cheever home doesn't match up with the description we got, unless he grew 9 inches taller and gained about 130 pounds."

"Well, that guy's dead," Nash stated flatly.

"Probably," Linden nodded in agreement. "We found the car earlier at the downtown airport. A guy matching the driver's description apparently got on a private jet and left out about the same time you guys hit Cheever's house."

"Well, of course he did," Nash exhaled.

"What if this really is all just luck?" Mike Rhodes said from the other side of the table.

"What are you talking about, Mike?"

"What if the killer had no idea we were coming? What if he just happened to kill Cheever the same night we were coming to hook him up?" Nash looked dubious. "Think about it, Logan. The killer didn't stick around to tie up loose ends because he didn't know there was any. If he didn't know we were coming, then that means he didn't know Cheever had been running his mouth to Luna."

"Which means he wouldn't know about her at all," Nash nodded. "And they wouldn't know we had access to his emails."

Rhodes shrugged. "It's possible. Why else wouldn't he make sure Luna was out of the picture before he flew away? This guy was a pro. If he thought someone else knew something, he would have taken them out, too."

"Cheever had outlived his usefulness," Nash stated. "He got the military hardware, which was clearly the priority since they just left the narcotics."

"It would have been a lot harder to move all of the drugs than a few cases of weapons," Linden offered.

"But what if the narcotics were a decoy? What if they just wanted us to think it was a drug deal gone bad and nothing more?"

"You've been watching too many movies, Logan," Linden said.

"Maybe, but after last year's mess, nothing would surprise me."

"The suits at the Bureau are going to have a field day with this," Rhodes said.

"Pass all of this to them and let them run with it," Linden

said. "If the killer is gone then we can assume your CI is in the clear. Come home and let's wrap this up."

"Alright, Keith. We'll see you tomorrow," and Nash ended the meeting. He looked angrily at Rhodes. "Just where did that come from?"

"I've been sitting here thinking about it. It just didn't add up. If whoever this was needed some hardware, it made sense to find a nobody in a smaller town to bring in the gear. They clearly have a lot of money to throw around, and they don't give a rip about narcotics, so they get what they want and throw investigators off the trail." Rhodes raised his eyebrows and waited.

It dawned on Nash what his friend was saying. "You think this is terror related?"

Rhodes tilted his head sideways. "I don't know, but it sure seems like it fits."

Nash thought for a minute. "We've gotta call somebody at the Bureau on this."

"Agent Culver," the thin FBI agent said into the handset receiver at his desk.

"This is Agent Logan Nash with the DEA in Greenville, South Carolina. I got bounced over to you about a case we're working." He gave Culver a quick rundown of what had transpired thus far. "If I send you the info, can you trace where those money transfers came from?"

"That's literally my favorite thing to do, Agent Nash." Culver gave him the secured email address.

"Alright, I'm sending the packet to you now. And if you wouldn't mind, I'd like to know how this all winds up, if possible. I've got a CI who would sleep a whole lot better at night if she knew someone wasn't gunning for her."

"Will do, Agent Nash. Thanks for the referral. Stay safe."

"You, too," Nash replied, and ended the call.

Culver began poring over the file immediately. He wasn't

exaggerating when he said his favorite thing was digging through the financials of criminals trying to hide something. He had worked dozens of cases that were considered too murky to ever find anything of prosecutorial value and hit paydirt, time and time again. The static IP address on the one transaction stood out like a sore thumb. *Someone had gotten careless,* he thought. He was almost disappointed. *Now this is going to be* too *easy.* Within an hour he was calling Nash back.

"Hey, Agent Nash, this is Agent Culver with the FBI in Washington. I told you I'd give you a heads up when I got something."

Nash looked at his watch. "Well, that was fast."

"We aim to please. I traced the company dumping money at your perp in Greenville. It's a financial and logistics company in Romania called the Surmonter Corporation."

"Surmonter," Nash repeated. "That sounds French. Why is a French finance company, based in Romania, sending millions of dollars, narcotics, and weapons to a dirtbag dealer in Greenville, South Carolina?"

"I was hoping you could tell me."

"I got nothing on my end. There's no place around here with that name." He wrote "Surmonter" on a piece of paper and held it up where Mike Rhodes could see it. Rhodes shook his head and shrugged.

"Okay," Culver said, "we'll keep going on our end. Thanks again for the tip, Agent Nash. I'll keep you posted," and he hung up.

"So, what does Surmonter want with a bunch of untraceable kit? And why would they be willing to dump millions of dollars to do it?" Agent Barry Morris asked.

"The answer to the second question is that they have staggering amounts of money, from what I've been able to find," Culver said as he tapped the opaque wall in the conference room. Window after window opened showing account ledgers.

"Surmonter is privately-held and owns about 100 smaller companies it runs everything through. They have no debt on record, and have a significant revenue stream just through the main Surmonter business. All of the others have a great deal of money in reserve with no relative expenses."

"How much money are we talking about?"

"I've found $10 billion in liquid assets. That's not counting investments and funds that I haven't been able to track down yet. If I had to guess, I would say the actual figure could be ten times that."

Morris whistled, and Moreland swore out loud. "That would definitely qualify as high-roller status," she said. "Who sits at the top of this? And why have we never heard of them?"

"Can you name any of the companies who provide financing for commercial development projects? How about transoceanic transport ships and fuel tankers? They've been intentionally low-key without having to try really hard. The dozens of small companies are not that uncommon when it comes to sheltering money, especially in countries who gladly look the other way if the right palms are greased."

"Which is why a French company has its headquarters in a place like Romania,"

Morris said.

Culver touched the tip of his nose with his finger. "Bingo. As to who sits at the top, because it's a private company they only release limited information publicly. Romania allows for such because they claim to protect the privacy of wealthy individuals for their safety and protection." He smiled. "But I can still find out who they are."

Without warning the images on the screen froze, "SESSION TERMINATED" flashed in red for a few seconds, and the walls were opaque glass once more.

Morris looked at the confused financial expert. "What just happened, Culver?"

"I don't know," he said. "I've never seen it do that before." He tapped the glass pad on the table. "I'm locked out."

The conference room door burst open, and AD Robert Shear stormed into the room. He had a cell phone to his ear, saying, "I'll get right back with you, sir." He closed the door behind him and looked at the three agents. "What have you done?"

"I'm sorry, sir," Culver stammered, completely confused by the turn of events. "I don't understand."

"That was the Attorney General. You all are in a world of trouble."

CHAPTER NINE

I feel like I'm on the set of a bad vampire movie, Samantha Land thought to herself. In fact, she felt like she *was* in a vampire movie. She was in the 11th *arrondissement* at a place called *La Grotte du Vampire,* a Goth nightclub not far from the Opera Bastille. While not a big fan of opera, she did think blaring sopranos and blustering tenors might be preferable to hearing the wailing coming from the band on the stage. The place was filled with pasty-skinned men and women of all ages, covered from head to toe in black trenchcoats, leather, and velvet. The guys were all skin and bones and looked as though they had indeed been dead for a couple hundred years and come here to suck the blood of someone, some with unkempt black hair swept back and others with blood-colored dreadlocks. The girls were a bit more variable, but they all had the same dark colors contrasting against pale white skin, and, cold weather or not, they showed a lot of it. Apparently vampires, at least female ones, were immune to the cold.

There were no mirrors in the place—vampires hated those, after all—but Sam remembered what she had looked like when she left the safe house a couple of hours before. A wig composed of kinky, jet black hair tumbled past her shoulders, a major change from her genuine straight blond cut; her eyes were wrapped in heavy black eyeliner and mascara, with a substantial dose of grey eyeshadow. Black lipstick covered her lips, and the foundation she applied made her tanned skin a few shades more pale than usual. She wore a black cropped leather jacket with the appropriate number of metal studs over a dark grey tank top, black form-fitting jeans, and black tactical boots. Thick metal-studded black leather bands covered both her wrists, and a satin choker with a small cross on it wrapped around her neck. She definitely fit the part, and that made her somewhat uncomfortable.

At the bar, about twenty feet away, was Jean Leblanc. The former French Intelligence officer, now working for MI-6, looked a little out of place because he was one of the three biggest guys in the nightclub, aside from the bouncer and the DJ. Leblanc was leathered out, looking something akin to a Harley-Davidson version of Dracula with close-cut dyed black hair. He was talking to the bartender, looking for all the world like he was asking him about nothing at all, but Land knew they were speaking to one another in code: the bartender was also a covert operative, and he was the link to get them information on their target. The Clandestine Service was compartmentalized, so that no one person knew everything. If one operative was captured, they couldn't tell anything other than the small stuff they knew personally. It was the most basic of intelligence community principles, but Sam was reassured somewhat by their vigilance.

As Sam watched him, Leblanc's newly blackened hair made him, just for a moment, look a little like Hawkins. The Case Officer looked away as her heart shifted within her chest. Sam couldn't allow herself to think of Hawkins, not right now. She knew better than to dwell on what-ifs any more than necessary, but he had made her think more about her life away from the job than—well, more than she ever had. Everything she did was dangerous, but NOC work was always another level, and she hadn't done any since they had met. The thought of never seeing him again, never telling him all the things she wanted to, was more than Sam could deal with right now, so she put it back in the mental box where she kept such thoughts. There was no doubt Leblanc was competent, extremely so, but she would still have preferred to be with Hawkins. He turned to her, and the moment was gone. He *definitely* wasn't Hawkins.

Sam stood and walked toward the bar. A Goth girl bumped her slightly, smiled and said something in French that made Sam even more uncomfortable than she already was. She swore that she could hear Chapman laughing from wherever he perched outside. She wasn't sure exactly where he had setup on over-watch, but she had no doubt he was taking in every word they said. Chapman had come to be referred to as The Ghost, gifted with the almost supernatural ability to appear and disappear any time, any place. She was quite certain that wherever he was he would be in disguise—if the other team members had seen him an hour earlier, she knew they would not recognize him now. She ordered a rum and diet cola. A young man with piercings across both eyebrows started to slide closer, clearly intending to make a move. Sam cut a look sideways at him. The ice blue contact lenses almost glowed in the nightclub's eerie lighting, and he took the hint. She tossed her hair over her shoulder and walked to a booth where Leblanc and three other men were sitting.

"Mind if I join you?" Sam asked in perfect French.

"Of course," Leblanc responded and extended a hand as he slid over in the booth. Brodeur and Morgan were on the opposite of the crescent shaped booth. It was covered in a crimson leather with black velvet tracing the contours of the cushions. Red LEDs backlit every seating area, giving privacy while providing some illumination. At least the owners of the nightclub understood that the red lights wouldn't affect their clients' ability to see in a dark area. Everyone at the table had a drink and a cigarette. Sam hated smoking, but it would be easier to cover her conversation if she used it as a prop. She raised her eyes and pointed at the pack lying on the table. He picked it up and gave her a cigarette, pressing on the side of the pack as he set it down. The seemingly ordinary pack of cigarettes was also a white noise generator. Anyone trying to listen in on their conversation would get nothing but static.

"So," Sam asked as she took a puff from the cigarette, "what are we looking at?"

"We've confirmed our location is green," Brodeur said. Even with all of their precautions, there was no need to be obvious about their target. The report Chapman had sent to Sam while she was flying over the Atlantic contained the basics: they were planning a surreptitious entry at the Surmonter building in Paris after hours.

"I still don't understand why we're here and not the primary," Morgan huffed. Although the company's main offices were in Romania, the Paris office is what had garnered Chapman's attention.

"The internal servers allow access company wide, so this will be an easier point of access than the primary. This does not mean we can afford to be complacent. Although it is not the primary, there will still be some level of security to deal with." Leblanc took a puff, then continued. "The building itself has been under watchful eyes, and it had been determined that there are only minimal security personnel on site, no more than three at this time of night, and audio/video security is rudimentary at best."

Sam reached into the inside pocket of her jacket and pulled out her phone. She swiped it open and took a peek at a social media app on the screen. She nodded, then wiggled in her seat as she tucked the phone back into place. No one at the table noticed anything amiss. Even if someone had been watching intently, they would not have been able to see a tiny fly detach itself from the phone case. They certainly would not have been able to trace its flight pattern out of the nightclub and into the dark Parisian night. Even if someone had noticed, they would never believe the tiny fly to be a robotic drone piloted by a CIA operative sitting at a console in a submarine parked in the English Channel. The drone was headed to Surmonter to map the place out in case Sam needed the information herself. Since Leblanc already had verified building schematics, she made no mention of her own personal reconnaissance. In this business, it was sometimes best to keep some things to oneself.

"Morgan and I will go inside," Leblanc continued, "while you three separate and watch the exterior from a distance to alert the team in case of a problem."

"And why should you two get to have all the fun?" Brodeur asked.

"Because I said so, now settle down," Leblanc said, and Brodeur indeed seemed satisfied by the reply.

"So, what is it we're looking for in there?" Sam asked. "There's got to be more than money-laundering for all of this trouble."

"Okay, our boy at the bar Remy said Surmonter has been hopping. He hears they're connected with someplace else in Paris, an old warehouse or something. He hasn't been able to find out where it is, but he says there's a lot of back-and-forth on the down-low. The rumor is that it's a little boy."

Sam worked hard to hide her shock. "A tactical nuke?"

Leblanc nodded grimly. "Apparently, it is a Russian suitcase bomb. Low yield, but big enough."

"How low?"

"Not sure," Leblanc said. Land knew the Russians had developed low-yield nuclear devices, just like the United States had. The main difference was that the U.S. had experienced some degree of success in developing a nuclear warhead with limited-duration radioactivity following the detonation. The Russians had not been so successful in their early attempts, but the former Soviet Union was not known for giving up on weapons programs easily. There were two examples of a new version supposedly superior to anything the U.S. had been able to come up with. They had a yield of only .25 kiloton, but they weighed less than 75 pounds and could be carried in a backpack. No one in the West had ever seen them, and there was only minimal confirmation from within the former Soviet government that they even existed, because no one knew where they were. The bombs had vanished shortly after the collapse of the Soviet Union, but just the rumor of their existence was enough to spark a global search that had continued to this day. It was entirely possible that these two devices were the legendary backpack bombs that had gone missing at the end of the Cold War.

Thoughts of these devices being detonated in a major metropolitan area roiled through Sam's brain. "We have to assume the worst. Do we have any idea where the device might be? Is it under guard? Is someone walking around with it on their back?"

Leblanc shrugged. "That's why we need to find out what's inside Surmonter."

Duncan whistled. "I would say that definitely upped the stakes." Sam agreed. News of this needed to get back to Langley ASAP. This was going way beyond the capacity of a small NOC team. If nukes were in play, they were going to have to up their game. Who inside Surmonter wanted tactical nuclear weapons, and for what purpose?

"That's why we're going in now," Leblanc stated flatly.

"Now?" Duncan replied. "I don't think we're ready for that."

"We don't have time to wait for a better opportunity," Leblanc argued. "We need to get in and find out what's going on now while we have the chance. The longer we wait, the higher the risk of that chance slipping away." Everyone seemed a little uncomfortable with the idea of the intrusion taking place imme-diately, but the intel regarding nukes had changed the situation quickly. They all nodded in agreement.

"It's settled then," he continued. "Here's your earpieces. Take up positions nearby and call out anything you see. Stay out of sight and we'll be fine. No one knows we're coming." He handed the small in-ear communicators to each person at the table. As he handed the last one to Sam it slipped from his hands and into a glass of water. He cursed and retrieved it quickly, dabbed at it on his pant leg, then handed it to Sam. "Sorry, mademoiselle," he said curtly, angry at himself for his carelessness. "It's waterproof, so it should be fine. Just give it a few minutes before you turn it on."

Sam nodded, put the device in her pocket, then got up from the table. As she walked to the door several club goers looked her over enticingly, but she ignored them as if they weren't even there. She walked outside and around the corner to where her Dark Stealth Ducati Diavel 1260 was parked. Sam reached for her helmet which was locked onto a loop on the back. She pulled it over her head and dropped the visor in place. As she did, it registered her biometrics and revealed its full capabilities. A HUD appeared in front of her, giving her a full array of telemetrics regarding her position, the motorcycle's diagnostic information, and communications options. As she started the bike and roared away into the night, she activated the secure mode and dialed DNI Jack Price. He answered on the first ring.

"Hello, Sam. Chris already contacted me about the discussion your team had." She never ceased to be impressed with the Ghost's ability to get information and move it quickly. "That's quite an issue."

"Yes, it is, sir," Sam said. "I deployed the drone to get inside Surmonter and do a little extra recon. Should be helpful given our advanced timetable."

"Absolutely," Price replied. "That's why I'm ordering you to go in yourself."

"Sir?" Sam asked, surprised at the instruction. "What about the rest of the team?"

"They have different parameters than you. I need you to get in and plant some tech in case they come up short. There's a dead drop waiting for you three blocks ahead of your position. It will be under the left arm of the third bench from the corner. We're sending the operational details to your display now."

"Sir, what about the team's entry? I'm supposed to be on overwatch for them."

"Using an earpiece that one of them dropped in a glass of water?" Price chuckled. "They planned on doing this without you anyway, my dear. That's why Chris is working directly with you and not them. That's also why that drone is going to show you the way in. Our analysts have already gotten the telemetry back from its scan. We'll be sending that over to your HUD momentarily as well."

"Can we patch into their comms anyway? It would be nice to know what they're doing."

"Got you covered," Price replied. "Once they're up and talking we'll put it in your helmet feed. They won't know you're listening."

"Even better," she said. *Jerks*, she thought to herself. She had caught Morgan ogling her from the moment she approached the table. She had worked really hard for a lot of years to get where she was. She had dedicated countless hours studying and training to be the best she could at what she did, and her record spoke for itself. She didn't think of herself as all that attractive, but Sam knew she was in top shape physically, and understood she certainly had physical traits that could garner attention. But none of that diminished her capabilities in any way, and she resented how men—and even some women—treated her as disposable eye candy. It just served to motivate her even more. "I'm heading to the dead drop now."

"Good. Just so you know, I'll be out of contact for the duration of your mission," Price said almost apologetically. "I wouldn't have reached out directly now if the parameters of your mission hadn't changed so drastically. Watch yourself," Price said, and ended the call. She piloted the Ducati to the location Price had given her and walked over to the bench. She sat down to adjust the laces on one of her boots, and in one fluid motion removed a canister from the armrest exactly where Price had said it would be. She smoothly put it in the inside pocket of her leather jacket, zipped it up to her neck, then got back on the bike and rode towards the Surmonter offices. There was traffic on the streets even at this late hour—or early hour, depending on one's perspective— but the Ducati powered easily through.

Within minutes Sam arrived at the Surmonter building. It was a nondescript concrete structure six stories tall. The main entrance featured a glass lobby that evoked every other generic office complex in the known world, but each successive floor featured windows that were increasingly smaller than the last. The top floor had no windows at all to speak of except for one small section, with only a vent-like slit running around the perimeter just below the roofline. Sam parked the bike a block away in a small alley tucked between two older buildings. She kept her helmet on, the blacked-out visor revealing nothing of the high-resolution night vision view afforded her, and moved through the darkness toward the Surmonter building.

The headset in her helmet came to life. "The others are arriv-ing," Chris Chapman said on their private comm channel. "I'll patch you in." Within moments she heard the slight click as her "teammates" activated their radios as they arrived on site.

"I still feel bad about Land," Duncan said in his thick Cockney accent. "That was no way to treat a teammate."

"We don't need her," Brodeur said. "She's an unknown quan-tity. We've all worked together."

"And we're all professionals," Morgan added. "I don't need a skirt trying to prove she can run with the big boys on a job like this. We can't afford any mistakes." Sam seethed quietly but said nothing.

"She seems more than capable based on what I know of her," Duncan said sternly. "Sounds to me like you're afraid she might show you up."

"Enough," Leblanc interjected. "We can talk equality later. Right now, we've got work to do. The guard at the rear takes his smoke break in two minutes. Morgan and I are going around to make entry when it's clear. You all keep watch. Chapman will have his eyes open also. If she shows, just leave her alone and let her take up position. Radio silence unless absolutely necessary."

Sam liked to think she had gotten used to the "boys club" but it still irked her. The men were going in the entrance their plans had allowed for, but the scan provided by her drone revealed a route perfectly suited for her mission. As she looked at the building, an overlay appeared with a highlighted route. The analysts at CIA had already run several simulations showing the best path to her target. It was almost like playing a video game with waypoints highlighted for the player to more easily figure out where to go. It never ceased to amaze her how quickly the technology of her work was changing. The arrow in her HUD went yellow so she slowed her pace and crouched slightly. The analyst must have seen something they didn't like, but it cleared quickly, and the path indicator returned to green once more. She smiled to herself. Too bad the boys didn't want to let her play. They would have benefited from the "eyes" she had available. Granted, the analyst plotting the course was only focusing on her direct pathway, but it never hurt to have more assets at your disposal.

Sam moved closer to the building's perimeter and spotted the chain link fence that encircled the service area of the building. As she approached the fence it was apparent the bottom had been lifted from the ground just enough to allow her to gain entry. She looked around and nodded slightly, quite sure The Ghost had paved the way. Sam wiggled under the fence and made her way to one of the building's exhaust ports when her path turned yellow. Air was ducted from the elevator shaft through the port, and it also allowed excess heat from Surmonter's server rooms to be vented if necessary. Those vents were her point of access. As if on cue the fan shut down and slowly stopped spinning, and the path on her display turned green. She pulled open the access latch, stepped in between the still blades, and closed the latch behind her. Within moments the fan resumed. She eyed the shaft that ran from the server rooms. Of course, it was on the sixth floor.

No time to moan about it, Sam thought to herself. *Get to climbing.*

CHAPTER TEN

"There is clearly some mistake here," Agent Morris said.

"It's a mistake alright," AG Stott said to AD Shear, completely ignoring the agents in the conference room. "One that's going to wind up with people in the unemployment line. Or worse."

"Until we know what's really going on, we don't need to jump to any conclusions," Shear said.

"It's not jumping to conclusions, Bob," the AG said, almost shouting. "These three have compromised an investigation that no one was even supposed to know about."

"We were following up on a lead that came from a DEA agent in South Carolina earlier, ma'am," Culver interjected. "I just started digging into this Surmonter company a couple of hours ago, and then our workstation in here locked us out. Hawkins doesn't know anything about this."

"Wait a minute," Stott said. "What DEA agent?" The three agents filled their superiors in on what Nash and Rhodes had discovered.

Shear shook his head. "Boy, did you guys walk into it. It's good work, but you really walked into the deep end quick." He instinctively made sure the door was secured. "From this point on, everything is close hold. Nothing leaves this room."

Stott took a deep breath. "I got a call from the CIA Director saying someone here in one of our CT units had initiated a search that matched keywords involving a highly sensitive operation they were working on. You three set off every alarm at Langley when you started looking into Surmonter. They have a task force with Secret Service that is starting to look into the same financials you were. If anyone gets careless, it could tip off Surmonter that they're under suspicion."

"I apologize, ma'am," Culver said, "but we had no idea. This seemed like something with potential terror characteristics so we felt we should look into it."

Shear spoke up. "You were doing the right thing. It just so happened that you stumbled onto something that Langley was already working on. You had no way of knowing that."

"But the mutual connection with Hawkins made it look questionable," Stott added.

"Questionable?" Morris repeated angrily. "Thomas Hawkins is freakin' Mr. Clean. There's no way he would spill compartmentalized intel and potentially endanger an operation." His volume climbed with each sentence. "And besides that, we're the counterterror squad tasked with investigating international financial supporters of terrorism. With all due respect, ma'am, if you think we're not capable of keeping matters of national security confidential, then maybe you need to find some other agents to do this job."

Shear intervened. "Morris, that's enough."

"I don't know what kind of ship you're running here, Tom," Stott said angrily, "but you'd better get your people under control."

"Actually, Agent Morris is right," Shear said. "This is one of our elite CT squads. Agent Hawkins got cleared to be a CIA liaison. Accusing him—*anyone* on this team—of having loose lips is a bit of a stretch."

"Well somebody is talking that shouldn't, and you'd better figure out who," the Attorney General said. "I'm not going to sit idly by and let another agency head talk to me like I'm running a clown show."

As if on cue, Director James Van Horn walked into the conference room. No one said anything. "Well," he said, "I've clearly come at a good time."

"Director Van Horn," Stott said. "We were just discussing the particulars of the case the CT squad is working. As well as some decorum issues."

"Such as trusting the people who work for you," Morris said. He headed for the door.

"This meeting isn't over," Stott said.

"Then court-martial me," Morris replied, and slammed the door behind him.

Van Horn looked at the other agents and tilted his head toward the door. Without another word, they left the conference room and closed the door behind them.

"So, what in the Sam Hill just happened in here?" Van Horn asked. "Those are three of the best CT agents we have, and they all look like they're about to turn in their resignations."

Stott raised her hands slightly and nodded. "I may have come in a little hot on them." Shear said nothing, only raising his eyebrows and looking away slightly.

"General Stott, if I could make a suggestion?" It wasn't a question. Van Horn was one of the few people in Washington with enough experience that when he spoke everyone listened. "If you want the people who work at Justice to have confidence in you, then you need to show more confidence in them. This isn't the military."

"*I'm* the one who's getting reamed by the CIA Director and DNI."

"And that's part of your job," Van Horn said. "You've got to take the heat so the agents can do their job. If you don't run blocker for them, then they will just sit back and let the world go by. These agents need to know that as long as they're doing their job, they will have your support. Whatever they find. That's the mandate, isn't it? 'Investigation?'"

Stott sighed. "It really *was* easier in the military. You have my apologies."

"We aren't the ones you need to apologize to," Van Horn said and nodded toward the outer office. "Here's your chance to show them how a leader owns their actions." Shear sat unmoving, waiting for the AG to explode and fire every one of them on the spot. Instead, she nodded once and walked out of the conference room.

"Everyone, listen up, "Stott said as she walked into the squad's work zone. "I came in sideways and made the very worst mistake anyone in our line of work can do—I made assumptions without evidence. I owe you all an apology. Hawkins, too."

The three agents looked at each other, nodded, then looked at the Attorney General. "Not a problem, ma'am," Morris said. "We were all running a little hot in there. I shouldn't have said what I did, either."

Stott raised her hand. "I deserved it. Let's just not make a habit of it, shall we?"

"Understood, ma'am."

"I'll reach out to Director Sullivan and tell her the situation and what you've discovered. I'll have the workstation unlocked and the session reloaded. Can you be ready to compare notes with CIA and Secret Service on what you've got in the next few hours?"

Morris nodded, then looked at Culver, who smiled widely. "Ma'am, by this time tomorrow I'll be able to tell you who the head of Surmonter is and what they bought their kids for Christmas."

Samantha Land had successfully made her way into the maintenance area at Surmonter's office building in Paris. Having located the main ventilation ducts into the building, a CIA operative had remotely shut down the main fan on one of the ducts. Now inside, she looked up into the metal duct running parallel to the main elevator shaft. The HUD in her helmet confirmed the composition of the metal used in the construction of the maze of ducts that ran in and out of the shaft, ultimately connecting with her target destination on the sixth floor. She touched the metal studs on her motorcycle gloves and the top rim of her boots, activating magnetic plates in each. They would not be strong enough to hold her fully in place, but they would give her enough of a handhold to the metal ductwork to make the multi-story vertical climb easier. She had made many such climbs before without them, but once again the march of technology kept improving things. She made her way up to the third floor without incident, then had to shift over to the main elevator shaft in order to access the next set of ducts, which led higher.

She looked out into the shaft and saw two elevators, one at ground level below and the other parked at the top. She had just enough room in the shaft to turn herself around so she could go out feet first. Sam slid her feet out of the duct and into open space for a moment before she located the service ladder. It was just to the side of the duct opening, recessed so as to allow needed travel for service technicians without getting in the way of elevator operation. It would be too tight for someone to be on the ladder while the elevator was running. She was glad to be in the building at night when that shouldn't be a problem. The ladder led to the next duct opening above, at the fourth floor. There were several other ducts on her current level, but they were across the shaft and didn't lead to where she needed to be, so she started making her way up the ladder.

The comlink squawked to life in her helmet, startling her momentarily. It was Leblanc. "We're in," he said. "Getting in the elevator now." Sam's heart jumped. She looked down and saw the elevator below shift slightly, moved by the entrance of two passengers. She looked up and started climbing as fast as she could, the slight magnetic effect both helping her to hang on to the rungs but also slowing her slightly. She reached down as she climbed and switched off the magnets in her boots but didn't risk switching off the gloves. The HUD in her helmet started flashing red, warning her of the climbing elevator car. She realized she wasn't going to make it inside the duct before the car would crush her. She took a deep breath and pushed herself out into space as far as her legs would propel her. She cleared the rising car by less than an inch, grabbed the cables for the car that ran parallel, and swung around like a performer in one of those French acrobatic shows. Her momentum carried her around in a circle twice before she slowed enough to grasp the cable firmly. The car stopped on the floor above. *Why are they going to the fourth floor?* She swung over the cables hanging down from the car, then veered over to the duct and scampered inside. She needed to get to the sixth floor, and quickly. She suddenly had a very bad feeling about this operation.

"You met the AG?" Woodley asked. "And didn't turn to stone?"

Hawkins tilted his head and turned his palms upward. "What can I say? I fear no man."

"Well, you ought to fear that woman," Jacksonville SAC Walter Simmons said as he pointed a piece of ribeye impaled on the end of his fork at Hawkins. He couldn't help but notice that even at the end of the day Simmons' dress shirt was as impeccably ironed as it had been that morning. There was likely a starch shortage in Duval County to keep the SAC's shirts looking as smooth as they did. Now that Woodley was an ASAC he was wearing a shirt and tie as well, but his was loosened at the neck and the button of his collar was open. Hawkins didn't mind that he was in a suit and tie again most days in the Washington FO, but Woodley chafed against it. The three men were eating in one of their favorite haunts, the Stonewood Grill and Tavern. Nice without being overdone, Stonewood had become the steakhouse of choice for several of the agents in the Jacksonville Field Office. It wasn't particularly close to the office, which they viewed as a plus, and the steaks were always consistently excellent. "She was already a JAG when I left the Corps for the Bureau. She had a well-earned reputation as someone who would tune you up if you got sideways."

"Maybe age has mellowed her," Woodley offered. "That does happen sometimes."

"Or maybe she was just softened by my winning personality."

"Oh, that's definitely it," Woodley responded with a grunt.

"Whatever the reason, it's a big deal," Simmons said. "They've put a lot of confidence in you."

"No pressure or anything," Woodley interjected. "You've only got all of the honchos at the Bureau and Justice watching your every move. What could possibly go wrong?"

"Because you said that, when everything goes south, I'm taking you with me."

Woodley laughed and raised his hands in mock surrender. Simmons continued. "There's a lot of eyes on you, for sure, but you're up to the task. Shear's a good judge about who's ready for what. He wouldn't have put you in the position you're in just because you made a big bust. If he didn't think you could lead well and bear up under the pressure, you wouldn't be where you are."

"I appreciate the vote of confidence," Hawkins said. The waiter saw the break in conversation and hurried over to check on drink refills and to clear away unneeded dinnerware. He refilled their glasses and carried away the refuse on a tray.

"And the Agency put you through some of their training, too," Woodley reminded him. "Even a few weeks at the Farm and their other facilities is worth a lot in terms of prep for the real world."

"No doubt," Hawkins said. It was true that the training he went through since his entry into the liaison program had been rigorous, but it had also given him an edge he didn't have before.

The Bureau had an outstanding training program at Quantico, but to say that the CIA had a different way of doing things was something of an understatement. "It's just still a little strange to me that I find myself in this world, you know?"

"This is your life now, Hawk," Simmons said. "Better get used to it."

That sentence stuck in Hawkins' head on the drive back to his soon-to-be-former home on the river. His life as a pastor was far enough away now that it almost seemed like someone else's entirely. Hawkins was confident that he was doing exactly what he was meant to do, and he enjoyed the work immensely. There were still times he felt as though he were role-playing though, pretending to be someone he was not. Here he was, a successful FBI Agent and CIA liaison, preparing to start an investigation on a world leader that stemmed from his own prior case. He found himself in the middle of history in the making and was humbled by his place in all of it. The stakes were certainly high enough. He prayed the rest of the drive home that God would give him what he needed to do his job well.

As he pulled into the driveway and opened the center garage door he was struck by a tinge of sorrow. His collection of his parents' cars was visible in the LED-lit garage though the now open portal, and he thought again of all the years spent with them before they were taken in a terrorist attack in Spain. The cars were the most substantial link he still had to his parents. Hawkins knew he didn't particularly need all of vehicles, but he found it hard to part with them. Even selling the Shelby with the house made him feel as though he was discarding their memory. He knew that was foolish, but he felt it, nonetheless. It was amplified by the fact that his new life, and his relationship with Sam, had made looking backward less important than it had been. He had said many times that God designed us to move forward, not backwards. There was also something in the Old Testament about looking backward and turning into a pillar of salt, but he was pretty sure the context didn't fit. He got out of his car and noticed that the lights along the driveway and those that shone upwards onto the house were out. The home inspector probably turned them off and forgot to switch them back on when he had been there earlier. Still, Hawkins had a strange feeling about it. He quickly brushed the sensation aside.

He walked in the house and looked around at the furnishings, most of which had been sold with the house. Only a handful of items were already taken to either his condo in DC or his mountain retreat in Tennessee. It already felt like someone else's house. Well, technically it *would* be someone else's house the day after tomorrow. The buyers had cash, so they didn't need to wait for a lengthy loan approval process. Hawkins had the title deed to the home, so they were able to move the closing along very quickly. A car hauler was supposed to arrive in the morning to pick up the remaining vehicles he was relocating to Tennessee, so he would oversee their loading. He would finish up a few things at the Field Office, go to the closing in two days, then leave Jacksonville behind for good. He was sorry that his neighbors were out of town and he couldn't say goodbye to them in person. The Allens were sweet people and had been good neighbors. He would have to send them a gift of some kind as a way of saying thanks.

Hawkins made his way up the steps to his bedroom when he noticed movement outside in the driveway. It was still dark inside the house, and only the light from the open garage door shone outward, but he caught...what? Was it something really moving or just his imagination? That strange feeling that something was off ramped up significantly. He squatted low and moved to the window. In the slight wash of light from the open garage Hawkins saw four figures, crouched and moving fast along the dark side of the driveway. He couldn't make out much detail, but he could tell they were wearing tactical gear, headsets, and what looked like suppressed MP-5 submachine guns.

It took a fraction of a second to register—there was a hit squad coming for him at his own home.

CHAPTER ELEVEN

Sam pressed her arms and legs against the sides of the ventilation duct. Every so often she would get a flow of warm air with the particular scent of electronics at work. This section was made trickier than the first due to the laser beam motion sensors in the ducts. This section was meant to be serviceable, but the building owners wanted to be made aware when anyone was in this shaft. It was the only one that connected directly to the main server room, the only other access being though heavily secured doors on the sixth floor. Her clothing had technology woven into it that would trick the beam into thinking it was unbroken, allowing her to pass undetected. The only problem was that she had to move very slowly to ensure it worked correctly, so she was having to remain in the vertical shaft longer than she would have otherwise.

The tightly bunched muscles in her arms and legs burned slightly as she supported her full weight by pressing against the sides of the shaft. She had switched the magnetic assists off in her gloves and boots to ensure they didn't interfere with the laser eye countermeasure. Sam was remarkably strong, her muscular frame capable of more than most would suspect, but even she was beginning to feel the effect of the last three stories of slow climbing. She eased past the last laser eyes and pulled herself up into the horizontal portion of the shaft. She lay there for a moment to give herself a chance to catch her breath. It wasn't a bad spot to rest for a moment. The motorcycle helmet she wore sealed itself around her neck and had its own temperature-regulated air supply. The air in the shaft alternated between the cold backflow from the outside and the 85 degree-plus temperatures of the air being drawn out from the server room. She was sweating from the exertion, but the combination of airflow had kept her from being uncomfortable due to either extreme. As she lay there, the fan started pulling cold air back through the shaft. She heard the comms go active again.

"1, this is 3. Got an update?" Brodeur asked.

"Working on it, 3" Leblanc said, the tone in his voice giving away his frustration. "Stand by." Sam wasn't sure where Leblanc and Morgan were now, but they started out two floors lower than they should have. It was entirely possible they were looking for something else before going to the server room. She would have that discussion with them later. Sam moved forward a dozen feet before reaching the air return overlooking the server room. She looked down and found that one of the massive cabinets holding the servers was just below the grate. That would definitely make ingress and egress much easier and quicker.

Sam opened the grate and lowered herself onto the cabinet, which was topped by a meshed grate in order to allow heat to rise toward the exhaust duct. She then dropped silently to the floor. The room measured twelve feet square, with a ten-foot ceiling. As warm as it was at ceiling level, it was almost freezing in the room itself in an attempt to keep the computers cool. Three rows of cabinets seven feet high ran the length of the room, with barely enough space for a person to slide between the wall and the cabinets at each end.

The HUD overlaid one of the cabinets with a green glow—the wizards at Langley had determined that server was the primary unit, and therefore her target. Two others in different cabinets suddenly lit up in her visor as well, with "2" and "3" superimposed over each. Clearly, they wanted access to those computers as well. She carefully removed the casing from the first server, reading the instructions for the next part of her task in nothing short of amazement. She was simultaneously impressed and terrified at the capabilities of modern technology, and was not surprised she had never seen anything remotely like the tech she was about to deploy.

Sam reached into her inner jacket pocket for the package she had picked up at the dead drop. The small, matte black cylinder housed what looked like several stainless steel straws with a small bulb on one end and a cap on the other. She aimed the "straw" into the server case and squeezed the bulb. With a barely audible "pop" the cap burst open and covered the inside of the computer with a faint, almost invisible film. What would have looked like ordinary dust to even a trained technician was much more, one of the most astounding things Sam had seen yet in her fieldwork with the Agency. The "dust" in fact consisted of thousands of near microscopic transceivers that could tap wirelessly into the computers' systems. Anyone looking in the case would see nothing more than a slight amount of common dust. The instructions did not give her any indications of how it worked, of course, and she wasn't sure she really wanted to know. Technology was advancing so fast it almost seemed like magic at times, and she was pretty sure she wouldn't understand if someone tried to explain it anyway. She just needed to deploy the asset—it was up to someone else to make sure it worked.

Sam repeated the procedure for the other servers, then looked around the room and waited to verify the controllers at Langley didn't need any of the other computers tampered with. The grate she had entered turned green in her display, and she had her confirmation. She replaced the empty straws into the cylinder, resealed it, and zipped it back into her inner pocket. Then she pulled herself on top of the cabinet in one smooth motion, opened the gate, and climbed back into the ductwork.

As she made her way back past the first of the lasers towards the vertical shaft, another message popped up on her HUD. She removed the cylinder from her pocket and opened the other end. There were six bulbs like the ones that topped the straws, with only a cap at the end. A green "X" appeared on the ceiling of the duct. She aimed the bulb at it and squeezed. A tiny fly, not unlike the drone that had been used only hours before to map Surmonter, flew out and mounted itself to the duct. It beeped green in her HUD, telling her it was receiving and transmitting solid signals. These robotic gnats would ferry bursts of information from the transceiver dust in the servers back through the ductwork to satellites waiting to receive the encoded, almost undetectable burst transmissions from the "bugs".

Sam worked her way down the vertical portion of the shaft, releasing two more of the tiny drones while moving slowly enough to defeat the lasers. As she moved through the shaft, she heard the unmistakable sounds of a helicopter coming up through the duct. As the sound quickly faded, she pushed it from her mind. When she arrived at the horizontal section on the third floor, so had to resist two wildly different impulses: to collapse into exhausted sleep, or break out into a full-speed exfiltration from the building. She knew either was a terrible idea given her current predicament, so she trusted the display in her helmet which guided her ever downward. Before she could climb onto the ladder and move towards the lower vertical shaft, her radio came alive in her helmet. At the same moment, her entire display went red. "HOLD POSITION" appeared in each corner of her display.

The bad feeling returned. *This isn't good*, she thought to herself.

"I am absolutely sure there are no monsters in the closet."

"What about under the bed?"

Special Agent Mark Woodley put on his best scowl, looked

under the bed and said, "FBI! All monsters under the bed are unauthorized in this room! Leave at once!" He raised up beside his 5-year old son's bed and looked Mark, Jr. in the eye. "The room is clear, sir." The boy laughed, and Woodley pulled the covers up to his son's chin. "Now you go to sleep, or we're both going to be in trouble."

"Okay, Daddy," Junior said as Woodley kissed him on the forehead. "I love you!" the boy shouted with all of the exuberance a little boy can muster at bedtime.

"Shh!" Woodley held his finger over his lips and looked back over his shoulder as if to see whether or not Mommy would come in wondering why Junior was still awake. "I love you, too," he whispered, then pulled the door closed behind him.

Woodley walked into the hall in time to see his wife, Sarah, stepping into the hallway from their daughter's room. She smiled at him, and he knew what that meant. With two little ones running around the house, it wasn't always easy to find time for one another. But Mark and Sarah Woodley had been together for nearly fifteen years now. Years of separation while Woodley was in the Navy, and then his frequently rotten hours with the Bureau, had taught them to make the most of every minute they had together.

"Got mine down," she said.

"Me, too," he replied. She motioned to him with her finger, *come hither*. He noticed she was wearing one of her big, fluffy terrycloth robes. "Can I help you?"

"I think you can," she said and dropped the robe from her shoulders. He was infinitely more pleased by what he was seeing now.

Then, his cell phone rang.

"I don't believe this." He looked at the screen, then tapped the glass surface. "I'm a little busy here, buddy."

"So am I," Thomas Hawkins said, and Woodley immediately noticed from his voice that something was up. "I've got at least four heavily kitted-up intruders in the river house, and I need you over here now."

It took a second for Woodley to realize his friend was serious, and then he went into battle mode. "I'll call it in. You stay alive, alright? I'm on my way." He ended the call and dialed Dispatch.

"I guess this means later," Sarah said, shrugging her robe back on.

"Four guys are after Hawk in his house," Woodley said, grabbing his bulletproof vest out of the hall closet. Into the phone he said, "This is ASAC Woodley. We've got an incident involving at least four gunmen at Agent Hawkins' former residence on the river. I need units there now."

In that moment, he had the strangest sensation. It wasn't a voice, more like an impression, an urging. "Send units to my house, too." He tapped the screen and looked at Sarah. He walked down the hallway to the front door. He made sure that the dead bolt and secondary locks were in place, then realized he had set his keys down on the kitchen counter when he had come in. He turned to walk down the other hall to the kitchen when a spray of bullets drilled through the door behind him.

Thomas Hawkins tucked the phone into his back pocket. He made his way to a waterproof Pelican case in the corner of his bedroom and opened it. Inside was his backup stash of gear, most of which was decidedly non-standard issue.

He quickly grabbed a suppressed Fabrique Nationale Five-seveN pistol and three magazines, a set of hi-res thermal night vision goggles, and a small remote which he clipped to his belt. If the bad guys were wearing vests, which they almost certainly were, the rounds in the Five-seveN would have no trouble punching through. He quietly closed the case, then moved back through the door into the hallway. He moved down the hall to the bedroom furthest from the stairs, turned on a lamp on the nightstand, then moved through the bathroom that connected to another bedroom and took up position in the corner where he could just barely see the top of the stairs. His night vision headset in place, he gazed out of the darkened room into the dimly lit hallway, illuminated an eerie green by the optics. He saw two figures crouch-walk into view up the stairs, dark shadows made plain in the green haze. The one in the lead pointed with his left hand towards the bedroom with the light on. They had taken Hawkins' bait.

They were dressed in dark gear, carrying what looked like MP-5s. They each wore night vision headgear, although it was an inferior monocular setup. They flipped the lens upward as they approached the lit bedroom at the end of the hall, weapons at the ready. Hawkins considered ways to take them alive, then acknowledged it to be neither feasible nor likely. He watched until they had made entry into the bedroom with the light on. He touched the small device at his belt and every light in the house went off. He watched the gunmen freeze, still crouching, and lower their night vision goggles into place. He raised his own lenses, then pressed the button again, causing every light in the house to illuminate to its brightest setting. The two men recoiled, the sudden bright lights blinding through the light-amplification gear over their eyes. Hawkins leaned into the hallway and squeezed off four shots, two bullets for each man's head. A headshot at that range wasn't as easy as it looked in the movies, but it wasn't that hard if you practiced a lot, and Hawkins did. The two men dropped to the floor. Hawkins hesitated for a moment, waiting for a flood of gunfire to erupt in response to the two men's deaths. When none came, he pressed the remote again, killing the house lights, and quietly moved out into the hallway.

Sarah Woodley had heard what sounded like someone knocking on the door and had stepped out into the hallway to see if Mark would get it. What she saw was her husband running down the hallway towards her at full speed in a crouch-run.

"Grab Gracie, and get into the safe room," Mark Woodley whispered as loudly as possible. He went back into Junior's room and scooped him up. Already asleep, he thought. Just as well. He brought him into the master bedroom and into the bathroom. Sarah already had Gracie, also asleep, in the closet wrapped in her blanket. Woodley handed Junior to Sarah, then placed his hand on a small metal plate on the wall. A panel opened revealing a mini armory inside. He slung a small satchel over his shoulder, grabbed a suppressed MP-5, and chambered a round into battery. He pulled a Remington shotgun from its resting place. racked a shell into the chamber, and handed the weapon to his wife.

"You know the drill."

Sarah nodded. "If anyone other than you opens the door...."

"Right," he said. "If they're with me, you'll know."

"I love you," Sarah said. Woodley smirked.

"Me too, baby," he said, then closed the hardened door behind him.

Hawkins waited a full minute before moving to the two dead men on his floor. He grabbed a radio and earpiece from one of the bodies, then silently moved down the hall. A panicked voice called out in his ear through the captured radio. *It worked in the movies*, he thought to himself.

"Three, are you there? Three, do you copy?" The voice whispered urgently.

A second voice responded. "They must be down. Move up to the house." The lack of radio discipline demonstrated that he likely wasn't dealing with seasoned military operators. When two of your team members aren't responding, it would be a safe bet that your radios could be compromised and, therefore, would be a bad idea to broadcast your intent to whoever might be listening. Just because they were sloppy didn't mean they weren't dangerous, Hawkins noted. Or maybe they weren't being sloppy at all.

Hawkins brought his pistol in close to his chest in a ready position. Most movies and TV shows got it all wrong, having the cop walking around with his arms straight out in front. That's a great way to get your weapon taken away from you. He barely heard the whisper of a footfall coming from the room behind him. Without hesitation Hawkins dropped to the floor as a dozen 9mm bullets ripped through the wall next to him. He rolled over and fired the pistol four times. Two hundred pounds of man and equipment fell to the ground with a dull thud. He hit the remote again, bringing the lights downstairs to their full brilliance, and lobbed a flashbang into the living room below. He squeezed his eyes shut and pressed his hands as tight against his ears as he could, and it was still deafening in the confines of the house. He looked over the railing, and saw a man stumbling out the front door, night vision monocular on the floor,

Hawkins sprinted down the stairs and cautiously looked around the corner of the front door. The man was moving blindly towards the garage, pointing his weapon wildly. Hawkins went down the hallway and through the door leading directly into the garage itself, flanking him. The man was now literally backing right towards him. The man backed into the garage, right next to the Shelby GT500.

"Drop it, now!" the FBI agent shouted. "I won't tell you again!" The man nodded and tossed the weapon in his hand aside. "Now your sidearm. Slowly!"

"Looks like you'll get to hell a little before her," the man said. Hawkins couldn't place it, but he detected a slight accent. The man carefully withdrew his pistol and something else from his belt and dropped them at his feet. Hawkins recognized the pistol as a common 9mm, but it was the other object that dropped at the man's feet that made Hawkins' heart miss a beat.

An explosive pack with a blinking LED.

"Got ya," the man said.

Woodley ran through the various scenarios of what was happening in his head within seconds. He knew it was highly likely there would be more than one shooter. He immediately assumed this was someone who had targeted him. If they had sent four shooters after Hawk, then it was likely they though it would be enough for Woodley. Taking an FBI agent was one thing, but when that agent was a battle-hardened Navy SEAL... well, it was something very different.

He estimated there was likely a team of four. They would draw his attention to the front door and then make entry at another point. The garage was completely locked down, so the only other viable doorway was the one at the back of the house. Woodley had a screened-in pool, surrounded by a 6-foot vinyl privacy fence. It would not be a direct access entry for anyone coming in. He was confident that they would not have ordered the shots on the front door until they were already at the back of the house.

He reached into his satchel and pulled out what looked like an oversized hockey puck. He pressed a button on the side, then slid the device just in front of the damaged front door. Moving as quickly as he could, Woodley stayed low and quiet.

It was pitch black in the house. Woodley flipped his goggles down and his world went green. He worked his way down a short hallway that led towards the rear of the home. The kitchen ran along a large section of the back of the house, with large sliding glass doors looking out toward the pool. He stopped just short of being able to actually see the glass, and he noticed it was completely dark out his back windows. The low voltage LED lights were all off. If they were professionals they would almost certainly have taken out the motion detector lights. That meant they would be coming through the door soon. He assumed they, too, would have night vision. At least he hoped they did. He also hoped he was right about all of this, because the damage he was about to do would be hard to explain to his wife otherwise. He touched another metal panel, which slid out of place and revealed a large red toggle switch. He took a deep breath, squeezed his eyes shut, and flipped the switch.

Even with his eyes closed and looking away, it was like the sun had suddenly burst through. Magnesium flares meant to illuminate a nighttime battlefield burst forth from over a dozen hidden recesses in the wall facing the pool. Shouts and cursing confirmed Woodley's suspicions. He crouch-ran through the kitchen and saw three men fumbling with their night vision goggles and shouting in pain. They still held submachine guns in their hands, so Woodley took no chances. A three round burst went into each shooter, and they went down. A quick visual sweep confirmed no one else was in the back yard. At that moment Woodley heard a concussive thump from inside the house. Realizing someone had tripped the flashbang mine he had set up at the front door, he sprinted back inside. Just inside the front door was a fourth shooter, and he immediately began spraying full-auto fire down the hallway. Woodley ducked behind the wall and squeezed off two three-round bursts. The shooter dropped his weapon, then fell forward in a heap. The former SEAL sat quietly for a moment, listening for any indications of movement. When he was satisfied there were no sounds other than sirens in the distance, he pivoted back towards the back of the house to make sure. When he shifted, he felt a burning pain in his left shoulder and knew immediately what that meant. First things first, he thought. He moved through the kitchen and past the shattered sliding glass doors onto the pool deck. The three shooters were all down. Woodley rolled them over and put zip cuffs on their hands and feet, just to be sure. He made his way back down the hallway to the front door entryway to take care of the other shooter.

He heard the sound of movement almost too late. He rolled to the side, and an 8-inch knife sliced through the air where his neck was an instant before. Woodley spun around in time to catch a boot to his chest. He stumbled back a couple of steps out the front door, hoping to draw his attacker in close. The feint worked, and Woodley caught his assailant's arm as he stabbed at him. With a twist Woodley broke the offending arm and the knife clattered away. Faster than he expected, the assassin drew a pistol with his left hand and jabbed it into the agent's chest. Woodley spun as the gun fired, the bullet grazing across the front of his protective vest. As the man prepared to fire again, Woodley spun back around the way he had just turned. The shooter was thrown off enough to give Woodley time to grab the gun hand and twist it back and upward, forcing the barrel up under the shooter's own chin. Woodley drove his foot hard into the shooter's left knee cap. It gave way with a sickening crunch, and the man cried out in pain.

Woodley dropped to a knee to stay at the other man's level, the gun still pointed up into the attacker's own jaw. "Give it up, man. It's over."

"Yes, it is," the attacker said, and pulled the trigger. The flash and bang of the weapon discharging so close to Woodley, and so unexpectedly, dazed him for a moment. Woodley felt the man's body go limp in his grip, and he dropped him to the ground on the front porch.

A half dozen vehicles with blue lights flashing and sirens screaming roared into the yard. Woodley had his vest with "FBI" emblazoned on the front and "Federal Agent" on the back, so he hoped that would slow them down when they saw him. The last thing he wanted was to get shot by an overeager responder.

"I'm Special Agent Woodley," he shouted as law enforcement personnel began pouring forth from their vehicles. "Welcome to my home."

"Agent Woodley, you okay?" he recognized the voice as belonging to a sergeant that worked his neighborhood. Woodley chastised himself that he couldn't remember her name.

"I've got one here, and three more on my pool deck. They're

all secured, but keep your head on a swivel in case I missed one."
Woodley stood, then the flashing blue and red lights in his yard
turned into a kaleidoscope of colors swirling together. He heard
the sergeant—*Barnes*, that was her name—saying something, but
he couldn't quite make out what. He waved with his hand. "Wife
and kids are in bedroom closet. Safe room. Say 'Hook 'em,
Horns' or you'll get a face full of buckshot." He wasn't sure the
words were coming out right, but Barnes understood and
motioned other officers inside.

"A lot of blood here, Agent Woodley," Barnes said, and
Woodley snapped back.

"Crap," he said as he took mental inventory of his injury.
"Arterial bleed, left shoulder. Lucky shot." He tilted his head
toward the satchel hanging under his right arm. "Clotting pack
in my man purse."

Barnes chuckled in spite of herself. "Are you kidding me?" she
mumbled. She found the pack and injected it into the bullet
wound. Woodley winced as the clotting agent found its mark

"Good as new," he said, then the world went black.

CHAPTER TWELVE

Hawkins wondered for a split second if somehow he had died and wound up in hell. Smoke filled his lungs and fire crackled through the haze. He immediately knew he was alive because he still gripped the gun, and his head and left shoulder were killing him. When he'd seen the explosive drop at the last shooter's feet, he had dived back into the house right before it detonated. The wall separating the house from the garage had absorbed most of the blast but had still tossed him several feet. He became aware of approaching sirens as he crawled to stay below the smoke, and made his way out the front door, coughing uncontrollably as he struggled to replace the smoke in his lungs with cool, clean air. From a prone position Hawkins swept his field of view even though his vision still hadn't completely cleared, scanning for a target. He looked to one side and saw what was left of his attacker. The explosion had taken care of him.

But it had also taken care of Hawkins' garage. The entire structure was ablaze and spreading to the main part of the house. Police units with blue lights flashing and sirens screaming roared down his driveway. He scrambled to his feet to get some distance and get a better look at the conflagration. The gas tanks of the remaining vehicles were igniting now, feeding the flames as it burned hotter. The roof of the main house had caught—it wouldn't be long until the entire thing had burnt to the ground.

"Agent Hawkins!" a voice shouted. "Are you alright?"

"Sir, get back from there, that whole thing could come down!" another said.

Hawkins barely acknowledged them until he heard a familiar voice.

"Hawk, are you okay?" Special Agent Renee Cortez asked as she ran up to him.

"I think so," he replied shakily. "Three tangos down inside the house, and what's left of the fourth is scattered over there." He turned and looked at the house, and the garage filled with his parent's vehicles, bursting into an even greater blaze. "Is Woodley here yet?"

Cortez hesitated for a moment. "Hawk, there's been an incident at Woodley's place."

Hawkins remained still for a moment, then turned toward his car. It was blocked in by all of the emergency vehicles pouring in. "Renee..."

"We'll take mine," she said, and they ran for her car. "I'll fill you in on the way."

"Zulu, this is Victor," Duncan called from his covert location to Leblanc over the secured channel. "We've got a slow mover coming back through the AO." He watched the helicopter pass by not quite directly overhead. It had passed over from the other direction a few minutes before. Probably a coincidence, some might say, but Duncan didn't really believe in chance. He believed everything happened for a reason, he just didn't always understand what that reason was. A perfect example was Leblanc's dismissive treatment of the CIA officer earlier in the evening. Chapman had spoken highly of her abilities in the field, but Leblanc, Morgan and Brodeur had insisted on acting like pre-pubescent schoolboys pulling a pretty girl's ponytails. When this was over, he was going to recommend to Chapman that they not use those three anymore.

"Copy," Leblanc responded. His radio crackled as he spoke. The transmission was coming through, but it was slightly garbled. "We've rerouted to primary target and are preparing to make entry. It that slow mover stationary or mobile?"

"Mobile, opposite heading," Duncan replied, then paused. "Wait. It's coming 'round."

"Zulu, this is X-ray," Brodeur chimed in. "Whatever you're doing, you'd better do it fast. Something doesn't feel right."

"Roger that, X-ray."

Duncan went on high alert as beams of light cut across his line of sight. They were coming from down the side street two blocks from Surmonter. They approached the corner coming from the right and stopped. Duncan was finally able to identify the source of the headlights from its profile, a dark colored BMW 5-series. The hair raised lightly on the back of Duncan's neck as the sedan then turned towards where Brodeur sat in his car

"X-ray, this is Victor. I've got a black BMW rolling towards your 20," Duncan called out to Brodeur. He was lying prone in the back of a Honda Civic Type R hatchback, specially modified for surveillance work The top surfaces of the car were insulated and coated with a material that would mask the heat from the engine and any occupants inside the vehicle from prying eyes-in-the-skies. He lay prone in the hatch area under an anti-IR blanket to both keep warm in the cold night and add another layer of invisibility. The car's backup camera had been replaced with a high-resolution IR unit capable of long-range magnifica-tion and recording. Everything the camera saw was displayed onto a binocular headset. The helicopter passing over had concerned him, but the new arrival to the party put him on high alert.

"I see it," Brodeur replied, "it's just..." The radio was filled will the sounds of shattering glass, grunting, then silence. Duncan watched suppressed bullets light up his infrared display as they sprayed from the window of the BMW into the driver's window of Brodeur's Citroen. He could make out the twitching of his teammate's body as the bullets ripped into him, killing him instantly.

"Zulu, this is Victor," Duncan spoke calmly. "X-Ray is down, I repeat, X-Ray is down."

"Victor, what is your status?" Leblanc queried.

"Overwatch dirty," Duncan said grimly, indicating the action was still taking place. He watched through his headset as a flatbed truck rolled up quickly next to Brodeur's bullet-riddled Citroen. The occupants of the BMW quickly went to work, one securing a tarp over the car, the other positioning the winch under the front. In less than 30 seconds, they were gone, as if nothing had ever happened. "Overwatch clear," he said grimly.

"Roger that," Leblanc said, then shouts overran everything. "Compromised," he managed to say before he grunted, and his mic went dead.

Duncan said nothing else, knowing the mission was over and his teammates were likely all dead. If they weren't, they would be soon. He switched to access the surveillance cameras from ATMs, storefronts, and other building security systems within two blocks to make sure it was clear. He quickly moved to the driver's seat, started the car, and drove away into the rapidly retreating night.

Land lay silently inside the horizontal entry of the lower shaft. The death of others was nothing new to her, but this infuriated her. If only they had been more careful, taken one more night to be sure their intel was correct. If they had been willing to listen to her, to have even considered her a viable member of the team, she may have been able to get them correct, uncompromised data. If they hadn't pushed her to the side, she may have been able to...

She shook her head slightly. No, that wasn't how things worked. "What ifs" had their usefulness, but times like this demanded a focus on what *is*. She was currently lying at the edge of an elevator shaft in an exhaust duct, her HUD display flashing red and telling her to hold position. She knew one of her team-mates—that's what they were, whether she or they liked it very much—was dead, and two others were either dead or captured. Duncan would have left the area as soon as Leblanc said "com-promised," and Chapman was...well, he was The Ghost. He wasn't saying anything at the moment.

She was all alone. And she needed to figure out what to do next.

Hawkins and Cortez arrived at Woodley's house within minutes. Ambulances, fire trucks, and police cars covered the grounds, their flashing lights making Hawkins' head hurt even worse. Several media vans were already pulling up, and Hawkins grunted in frustration. He was glad to have Cortez here—she would be able to take care of them, although she did nearly run one over trying to get to the house.

SAC Williams stood waiting by the front door. A body lay under a sheet nearby. Hawkins looked, but he didn't see Woodley anywhere. Simmons saw Hawkins climbing out of Cortez's car, and jogged towards him.

"Hey, are you okay?" Simmons asked.

"I'm fine," Hawkins replied, then realized he didn't look fine. His white dress shirt had turned black from smoke and red with blood—he wasn't sure whether it was his, one of his attacker's, or both. Cortez had made him put on an FBI windbreaker and ball cap during the ride over. "Where's Mark? Are Sarah and the kids okay?"

"Woodley's family is okay; they're sitting in the back of an

ambulance over there." Hawkins looked in the direction
Simmons had nodded and saw one of the ambulances had several
agents and officers standing particularly close to it.

"Simmons, where's Mark?"

"You're about to fall over. Let's get you into this ambulance
so they can check you out." Hawkins noticed two stretchers with
figures lying under sheets on them. He couldn't get his eyes
focused enough to see if any of the bodies were the right size to
be Woodley. The adrenaline was wearing off, and he was staring
to get light-headed. Simmons led him to one of the other ambulances, pulled open the door, and helped him inside. The paramedic closed the door behind him. In the ambulance Mark
Woodley lay on a stretcher. Woodley's chest was covered in
blood, and his shirt was torn from where the paramedics had cut
it open. Hawkins was stunned, his mind unable to accept what
he was seeing in front of him.

It wasn't possible. Woodley couldn't be gone.

"Mark," he said softly. "Man, I'm so sorry."

"This is what it takes for me to get a nap nowadays."
Woodley said without moving.

The relief Hawkins felt was almost physical, like a crushing
weight lifted suddenly. "Geez, Mark," he said. "How are you
feeling?"

Woodley opened his eyes and looked at his friend, then
winced. "Looks like I'm doing better than you. I need to get off
this stretcher so they can take care of you."

"I'm fine," Hawkins said, hoping if he said it enough his head
would accept it as fact and stop hurting.

"You look like a house blew up with you in it," Woodley said
as he sat up and shifted over.

"Funny you should say that," Hawkins said as he sat down
next to his friend on the stretcher. "Simmons said Sarah and the
kids are okay?"

"Yep. The kids slept through most of it, but Sarah almost

blew the cops away when they came to let her and the kids know it was safe. "

"You did give them the code phrase, right?"

"I told them to say, 'hook 'em, horns.' Guess they didn't say it loud enough."

"They probably said 'Roll Tide."

"In that case, Sarah would *definitely* have shot them."

"Any idea who these mutts were?"

"No, but they were kitted up just like the guys who came for you. You did okay over there, I guess?"

"Four for four, but my house is gone. All of my parents' cars, too."

"Man, I'm sorry, Hawk. I know how much those meant to you."

"Just stuff, Mark," Hawkins said, not sure he fully believed it yet. "We need to identify these guys and find out who sent them. Otherwise they'll likely just send more after us."

"Unless they think we're dead," Woodley said, and the ambulance suddenly lurched forward, its lights and sirens activating as it raced into the street. Hawkins' head started swimming at the sudden motion.

"The way the paramedic is tossing this bus around," Hawkins said woozily, "that may not be a cover story."

CHAPTER THIRTEEN

Samantha Land was listening to the sound of her own breathing. She had been inhaling the recycled air in her helmet for long enough now that it was beginning to get a slightly stale taste. The filter would safely recycle air for several more hours without a problem, but Sam was suddenly aware of how long she had been waiting in the duct. As the Case Officer watched the display in her helmet continue to flash an advisory to hold in place, she went through how the operation might have been compromised. Chapman and Duncan were the only ones to get away, but she knew Chapman would never compromise an op. Sam didn't know Duncan as well, but Chapman considered him a brother, so she gave him the benefit of the doubt. At that moment her comm beeped and a message appeared in the HUD.

"Athena, this is Ghost. Copy?"

"Copy," she replied, her spoken words converting to text. "Are you 10-4?"

"Roger that," came the reply, the green letters of the message a welcome respite from the flashing red that washed out her HUD. "Are you secure?"

"Working on it," she said. "Where was the compromise?"

A single word appeared in her view. "Earpieces."

"Our comms were on a secured channel. No one could hack that frequency without us knowing." The Agency handlers monitoring her own helmet comms would have picked up any intrusions on the frequencies used by anyone she communicated with.

"Not the frequency," Chapman texted. "The equipment." Of course, she thought. She hadn't been tracked because hers had been dropped in water and shorted out. Chapman didn't have them, so he was clear. "What about Duncan?"

"He has a subdermal implant like mine." Chapman referred to a small receiver surgically implanted just below his ear at the base of his skull. It had been years since that particular technology was made available to operators, and many didn't care for the idea of a permanent radio embedded in their heads, Sam included. "Morgan wanted nothing of it, so he always used whatever was available. I had always told him his cavalier attitude would cost him one day." The screen was clear for a moment, then another message scrolled across: "Today was that day."

Sam's entire HUD switched to green and flashed "CLEAR" three times before returning to standard night vision. The shaft below her showed a green path.

"I've got my clear-to-move signal," she said.

Chapman's message scrolled across. "Confirmed, all tangos are offsite. Recommend you clear the area and head for the regroup point." Sam made her way down the shaft as fast as she safely could. The fan stopped once again long enough for her to exit the shaft. She retraced her steps, keeping her head on a swivel as she made her way back to the Ducati. She started the bike, pulled a U-turn, and headed away. She watched her rearview mirror to make sure no one was following her. The display in her helmet blinked green, "CLEAR TO SAFE-HOUSE." She ran the bike hard down several streets, taking a couple of high-speed turns to make sure no one was following, and blended into the early morning traffic. She turned onto a street within sight of the Louvre and pulled the motorcycle behind a small bakery. A storage container the size of a small box truck opened as the motorcycle approached and then pulled inside. The door closed behind her, and several small LEDs came to life magnetic locks clamped into place. Sam climbed off the bike and retrieved a backpack that hung on the wall. In it was a change of clothes. She stripped down and put on the new outfit, consisting of jeans, running shoes, a grey hoodie, and a white leather jacket. Her finger touched a stud on the side of the helmet, used it as a pointer on her HUD to select "Color Change," then "White/Gloss." The surface of the helmet instantly changed from matte black to a shiny gloss white that matched her new jacket.

In the backpack she also found a new air filtration canister for the helmet. She raised the visor, and the smell of rubber and gasoline almost overwhelmed her in the compact enclosed space. She found the release stud on the back of her helmet, pressed it, and a small black cylinder popped out. She quickly replaced it with the new one from the backpack and closed her visor. The system reset, and she had fresh air once more. She put her previous outfit in the backpack and replaced it on the wall. She typed an access code on the keypad next to the backpack, and a door slid open revealing another section of the container. Another Ducati sat waiting, this one a fiery red. She climbed onto the bike as the door opened and rode away.

DNI Jack Price wasn't sure what he had been dreaming about, but he knew it was a good one. That's why he was more than a little irritated by the ringing phone at his bedside waking him. Over the course of his long career in the Intelligence Community he had grown used to calls in the middle of the night, and he always answered them by the second ring. This time would be no different. He glanced at the caller ID as he answered and saw "CC."

"Good morning," Price said, sounding as wide awake as he

now was.

"Not so 'good' here," Chris Chapman said. He briefed Price on the situation in Paris, providing every detail possible down to the minute. Chapman had worked and been friends with Price long enough to know the DNI viewed every element of operational minutiae as important. One never knew when some important bit of intel would be cloaked in a seemingly unimportant detail. Such attention to detail had also saved Chapman's life and that of his operatives many times over the years. Price listened, absorbing it all, not speaking until Chapman had finished.

"Too bad about Brodeur. How's Sam?"

"Just hit a quick stop, then heading back to base. I'm on overwatch near her location and there's no compromise."

"Duncan?"

"Clear," Chapman said. "I'm in contact with him. He's taking appropriate measures."

"Do we know the status of Leblanc and Morgan?"

"Other than the fact they were loaded in a van and carried away, no. I didn't have enough eyes to effectively follow and I lost them. They were not amateurs."

"Understood. Do we know the point of compromise?"

"I believe it to be the earpieces the contact at the nightclub supplied."

Price nodded to himself. "I assume he would be part of Duncan's 'appropriate measures.'"

"That would not be an incorrect assumption."

Niles Richter was lying in bed, alternating between drifting off to sleep and staring at the ceiling. Shadows rolled across his small apartment as the City of Lights lived up to its name. He hadn't slept well since he had come on site to work in his cover as a bartender at that creepy goth nightclub. He was to provide the plans for the Surmonter building for the insertion team, as well as the earpieces for the job, then get out of town. He had been a contractor for British Intelligence the last several years after leaving the German military's intelligence service. Contract work had been far more lucrative than service in the military ever had, and as long as one stayed with the Western European nations there generally wasn't too much bad blood.

Then something happened that never had before. Someone knew about the op he was supplying intel and radios for. They wanted the plans and equipment swapped out for their own, and they were willing to pay handsomely for him to do it. He knew that when word got out that he had sold out an operation he would never be trusted again in that world. But for the kind of untraceable money they offered him, he would happily buy a place on a beach in a country with no extradition and live out his days. He had no family, and no real friends, and he was certainly tired of cold and bleary winters. Sandy beaches, blue waters, pretty girls in minimal clothing, and all he could drink was worth any compromise to his professional standards. Money bought silence, and he would be able to afford to mute everyone he would come in contact with.

Even so, he couldn't kid himself into thinking this was a bloodless betrayal. Giving bad intel and compromised equipment meant people were going to die. Well, he thought to himself, people die anyway, whether it has to do with me or not. And so he had done what was asked of him, and they had been good to their word. More money than he thought he would ever see had been deposited to a numbered account, which he promptly changed over to an account of his own. He had seen enough double-crosses to know promises made were not always promises kept, and bank transfers could be undone. It was also why he slept with an H&K 9mm under his pillow. His apartment was rigged with the best anti-intrusion hardware available. Nothing was getting in. Nothing other than too much light to get a good night's sleep. He sighed and closed his eyes again. Yes, his conscience bothered him slightly, but later today he would be getting on a boat in a Mediterranean port that would take him to a locale less friendly with the West. Then he would charter transport to a safer destination. He closed his eyes again, and envisioned blue water, white sands, tanned ladies, and brown liquor. He opened his eyes as the shadows moved again. He definitely would not miss all of this light when one was trying to sleep. He closed his eyes again, and envisioned sleeping on that same beach under a blanket of stars, one of those tanned ladies keeping him company.

His eyes snapped open as an iron hand clapped over his mouth and nose, and he made out the silhouette of a man. He felt something hard and metallic pressed against his forehead, and he immediately knew it was a suppressor. As the light brightened in the room again, he could see that the man was dressed in black from head to toe, his eyes barely showing through a narrow slit in his head covering. The figure jammed the suppressor harder against Richter's forehead, causing him to wince in pain.

"If you reach for that weapon, I'll spray your brains out the back of your skull," the figure said in a thick Cockney accent. Richter nodded under the weight of the suppressor and the man's hand, which had completely cut off his air supply at this point, lifted slightly. As if acknowledging the thought, the figure spoke again. "If you try anything stupid at all, I will likewise forcibly remove your sorry gray matter. Understood?" Richter nodded, and the figure lifted his hand slightly more.

"How did you get in?" Richter managed, before the figure struck him hard on the forehead with the suppressor.

"Trade secret," the figure replied. The weapon remained painfully pressed into Richter's forehead, but the hand remained slightly above his mouth and nose.

"Are you going to kill me?"

"Probably," the shadow said. "How long it takes? Well, I would say that's up to you. But then I would probably be lying." He pressed the weapon even harder. "And nobody likes a liar."

CHAPTER FOURTEEN

Thomas Hawkins sat alongside SAC Walter Simmons and ASAC Mark Woodley in one of the Jacksonville Field Office's conference rooms. It did not feature the technologically advanced wonders he had access to in the Washington FO, but it was secure, soundproof, and enabled high-resolution video conferencing. On the large screen at the end of the table were several faces: FBI Director Van Horn, AD Shear, and Hawkins' squad mates from the CT squad in Washington.

"Since there were no survivors in the attacks on Hawkins and Woodley, interrogation was impossible, but we're running their remains through our databases to see if there are any hits. We've passed it on to our friends in the alphabet soup to see if they have any luck," Simmons said, using a slang term to refer to all of the Federal law enforcement and intelligence agencies.

"We'll figure out who they were," Jenn Moreland said. Barry Morris was leaning over her shoulder looking at the camera, while Dave Culver was at his own workstation. His face appeared in a separate box on the TV screen, and it was clear that he was typing away while they were meeting. Hawkins was certain that he was hacking into someone's database looking to find something useful.

"The question is, who did we tick off badly enough to send hit squads after the two of us?" Woodley asked, grimacing in discomfort as he shifted in his seat. They had been unable to remove the armor-piercing round at the hospital—fortunately it had *not* hit an artery as he initially believed—and his shoulder ached. It wasn't the only piece of metal in his body, and probably wouldn't be the last.

"These guys were pros, and they had some serious kit."

"The only case we worked on together that made news was GODKILLER, and William Matheson is dead. His whole group is. You kicked Seth Warrick off a ship in the middle of the Atlantic and Sam shot his girlfriend and their other partner dead in New Orleans. We seized all of Matheson's assets, so the money is dried up. There's no one left there."

"Well, maybe there's somebody else in France who hates us," Woodley replied. "We may not have done it all, but our ugly mugs were the faces on the news. As far as somebody is concerned, we sure caused a lot of trouble for them."

Culver snapped his eyes up from his keyboard and looked directly at the camera. "Someone in France hates you?"

"Wouldn't be surprised," Woodley said dismissively.

Morris and Moreland turned away from the camera to look at Culver sitting several desks away. "You think this is connected to what we got hooked up for?"

Shear cursed under his breath. "What kind of kit did the shooters have?"

"Military grade," Hawkins said. "Night vision gear, level III armor, suppressed full-auto MP-5s, steep penetrators, even explosives."

"Can we be that lucky?" Morris asked.

Woodley shook his head. "What are you guys talking about?"

"We got a tip yesterday morning from a DEA agent in South Carolina about a bust they made that went south. The guy they were serving a warrant on was dead when they made entry. He was moving a lot of drugs, and I mean a lot, which they found.

He was also moving a load of military hardware, fully automatic weapons, grenades, all military level stuff, which they did *not* find. They called us because they suspected possible terror connections, so we started digging."

"Their digging set off alarms at Langley on an investigation they're running," Shear interjected. "Their 7th floor called our 7th floor."

"We got our butts chewed pretty good," Morris said. "But we worked it out. Turns out there's a French company that looks like they're up to no good."

"What French company?" Hawkins asked.

"The name's Surmonter," Culver said. "Finance and logistics. Founded shortly after World War II. They own literally dozens of smaller companies around the globe, most of which are nothing more than fronts to hold money. And there is a *lot* of money."

"Who owns it? Any connection to Matheson?"

"We can't find any solid records as to who's at the top. Their main office is in Romania, so that's made tracing ownership almost impossible. As far as a connection to Matheson? None that we've found, but we can sure check that line if we're clear."

Shear nodded. "You're clear. There's a possible connection to known terroristic activities. That's our job to look into."

Director Van Horn nodded his agreement. "I'll let the AG know what's happening."

"Could I speak with you and Director Shear privately, sir?" Hawkins asked.

"Of course," Van Horn replied.

"Barry, I'll check back with you guys in a few." Morris nodded, and their faces disappeared from the screen.

"Well," Woodley said as he stood, "I'm assuming this is CIA spook stuff." He and SAC Simmons walked out of the conference room and closed the door behind them. They understood the rules of the game.

"What's the chance this has to do with the case Sam is working in Paris?"

Shear chuckled. "You would know more about that than us."

Van Horn agreed. "You know Langley is going to 'neither confirm nor deny' us if we ask."

Hawkins' phone chimed in his pocket. He looked at the screen and cocked an eyebrow. It was CIA Director Sullivan. He told the two men who was calling. "Looks like my chance to ask." He tapped the screen. "Madame Director."

"Agent Hawkins," she said tersely. "Are you alone?"

"I'm in a virtual meeting with Director Van Horn and AD Shear."

"That's fine, but it doesn't go beyond them. This is unofficial, but due to the nature of your squad's investigation, your involvement as a liaison, and your personal relationship with Samantha Land, I wanted you to hear it from me. Case Officer Land's operation was compromised. She is okay, but several members of her team were either captured or killed. In case this leaked out, which I don't believe it will, I wanted you to hear it from me first."

His heart sank in his chest. "What happened?"

"I can't speak to that over this line," the CIA Director said. He knew his phone was heavily encrypted, so there was something else in play. "If you want to come in, I'll be glad to meet with you in my office and brief you on what we know."

"I'll be there as quickly as possible. Thank you," and he ended the call. He told Van Horn and Shear what D/CIA had said.

"The closest Bureau jet is in Atlanta," Van Horn said. "I can have it there in an hour."

"Thank you, sir."

"Have Woodley join you," Shear added. "We need to get him out of Jacksonville anyway. It's easier for him to play dead for a few days up here than down there."

"Yes, sir." They ended the video meeting, and Hawkins

walked out of the conference room. He saw Woodley sitting in Simmons' office. The look on his face when he walked in told them something was definitely wrong.

"Hawk, you okay?" Woodley asked.

"Walt, I've been ordered back to DC," Hawkins said flatly. "DC has dispatched a jet to pick me up. AD Shear has requested that Mark come back with me on the plane so they can put him to work up there, out of sight."

Simmons nodded. "Sounds like a good plan. Saves me the logistics of trying to requisition transport for him." He looked at Woodley. "We've got Sarah and the kids packed up and heading out of town for safe keeping. We'll have several agents on them until we're sure this is resolved."

"Thanks, Walt." Woodley stood and followed Hawkins out of the office. As they went to leave, Woodley sidestepped into the conference room and motioned Hawkins inside. He closed the door and turned on the white noise generator.

"Okay," Woodley said with his hand on his hips. "Before I get on a jet with you, Mr. CIA Spook, I want to know what's up. And don't give me that compartmentalization crap, either. What's the deal here?"

Hawkins looked his friend in the eyes. "Sam's in trouble. The NOC op she was working in Paris went down the tubes. Most of her team is either dead or captives of unknown parties. I think it has to do with something my squad is working on, but she'll only talk in person."

"I'm in," Woodley said.

"I don't know enough to know what were in for."

"Doesn't matter." If Sam needs help, I know you're going to do something stupid. And if you're going to do something stupid, I'm in."

"Fair enough," Hawkins said. "Let's go to Washington."

. . .

Samantha Land walked out of the steam-filled bathroom into the bedroom of her apartment. She felt like she would never get the grime of the night's disastrous mission scrubbed away, but she had succeeded in at least feeling somewhat cleaner than when she returned home thirty minutes earlier. The blinds were closed, blocking most of the rising sun's light from entering. Out of habit she walked the perimeter of her temporary home, verifying that the doors and windows were secured and the security countermeasures were in place. Nothing was impenetrable, she knew—much of her adult life had been spent breaking into places no one was supposed to be able to breach—but this place was as secure as she could hope for. She walked back into the bedroom, locked the door, and lay down in the bed. She closed her eyes to review the events of the previous 12 hours, trying to replay every moment in order to pick up something she could use moving forward. Even though she was no fan of the men who had either been captured or killed, she wouldn't have wished such misfortune upon them. She knew better than to blame herself for what happened—they had made a grave tactical error when they pushed her out, compromising their own operational capabilities, and they had paid for it. She wanted to be able to prevent such failures in the future.

That was always the problem when working with a team: the whole was only as strong as the individual participants. If one member didn't carry their weight, the whole team suffered, and too often that meant the mission suffered as well. At the end of the day, the mission was all that mattered. Not her feelings, not her teammates, not even her own life. The mission came first, every time. She had adapted to that reality long ago and made her peace with it.

From her earliest days as an athlete in high school, Sam had been taught the value of resting when rest was available. It would be several hours before she would hear from the Langley analysts whether or not her deployment of the nanotech was successful, if the almost microscopic hacker bots could breach the servers and broadcast their findings to the CIA's waiting ears. She knew she would not likely hear from Chapman for a while, either. She was certain he and Duncan would be busy, but there was nothing for her to do at the moment. So she kept her eyes closed, pushed the thoughts of espionage from her mind, and thought of Thomas Hawkins. She took a deep breath, smiled, and promptly went to sleep.

CHAPTER FIFTEEN

The Gulfstream 550 had barely come to a stop when Thomas Hawkins charged down the stairs to the flight deck at Ronald Reagan International Airport, Mark Woodley trailing close behind. The FBI agents had made quick use of the shower facility on the aircraft to get cleaned up and change clothes before landing. The Airport Police awaited to take them to Hawkins' car, parked in a lot reserved for federal vehicles for better security, and they likely wouldn't have let the battered and disheveled agents in the Ford Explorer the way they had looked previously. The agents and the police officers remained silent on the brief ride to the lot. Hawkins and Woodley tossed their bags into the trunk, and the two men quickly made their way onto the parkway towards the Washington Field Office.

"So," Woodley finally said, "what's our plan here?"

"We're going to see what my squad has turned up. Then I'm going to see what Shear will authorize."

"Which, I can assure you, will not include us being cleared to go to France."

"We'll see," Hawkins replied. Woodley normally knew how to get Hawkins to lighten up when the younger man hit a mood, but this time he held his tongue. The big Texan was in a mood as well, so they rode in silence to the FO. It was early enough that they were ahead of rush hour, and Hawkins was putting the spurs to the black Charger. They pulled up to the security check-point, Hawkins showed his credentials, and the FBI Police officer waved him quickly through. When they arrived at the Counterterrorism Squad's office, Hawkins' people were ready and waiting in the conference room.

"Welcome back, Hawk. ASAC Woodley," Morris said as he extended his hand. "Pleasure to meet you. Glad you're both okay."

"Tell me what you've got," Hawkins said tersely.

Culver already had data digitally stacked on the opaque walls. "Surmonter is definitely going to a lot of trouble to hide their money. There are at least twenty fronts we've been able to find that have no products, no services, and yet tens of millions in revenue each year."

"Why has nobody ever noticed this before?" Woodley asked.

"No one has ever had a reason to ever look before. What they do is boring. No one cares about construction loans on mid-risk ventures that return reasonable profits. They pay their fees, page sure all of the i's are dotted and t's are crossed, so every-body who would be watching are happy."

"So they've got a lot of money," Woodley said. "That doesn't exactly guarantee they're the bad guys."

"It's not what they've got that's the problem, it's what they've been doing with it. They have been diversifying through their various fronts. As we began digging, we started seeing some familiar names," Culver said as he started tapping the glass pad on the conference table. Some of who definitely got our atten-tion." Invoices, bank transfers, and photos started appearing on the walls around them. "A couple dozen shipping vessels were financed a decade ago by Surmonter for Xuffash Transport Systems."

The room grew deathly silent. Everyone looked at Hawkins

expectantly. He stood looking at the invoice, and the image of the shipping company's owner.

"Ra's al Xuffash," he said finally.

Culver nodded. "The weapons used by the guys who attacked you? Missing hardware tracked to 'misplaced' cargo from one of Xuffash's transports a couple of years back."

"That's a pretty clear connection," Woodley said.

"It gets worse. Construction for BEAR's manufacturing facility? Financed by one of Surmonter's mysterious subsidiaries."

Woodley swore quietly. "Was William Matheson on their freaking board of directors?"

"It might be worse than that," Morris said grimly. "Show him." Culver manipulated the glass again, and more spreadsheets loomed large.

"They have two small fronts, very well hidden. So well done, in fact, that we wouldn't have connected them without a lot of cooperation from the alphabet soup. They look like mom and pop storefronts, a bakery in Nice and a bike shop in Calais; actual, verified physical locations. Both well-reviewed on the Internet. And they both virtually managed to bankroll a couple of significant French political campaigns." Culver tapped the glass pad in front of him, and a picture materialized on the walls around them.

French President Louis Paquet.

Woodley cursed again—louder this time—at the exact moment Assistant Director Robert Shear walked into the secured conference room.

"I've clearly come in at the right time," Shear quipped. "What have I missed?" Culver quickly ran back through their findings.

"We've been coordinating with Langley and Secret Service on this and, surprisingly, everyone has been playing well together," Culver said proudly. "Secret Service confirmed some of the transactions through Romanian channels. Bucharest happily gave up a couple of minor asks for the Section Chief over there. And you've got a guy named Niels over at CIA who dug up the Xuffash connection."

"Xuffash was a bit of a project for him last year," Hawkins offered.

Shear was not convinced. "It's certainly damning, but at this point it's nothing more than circumstantial as far as Paquet is concerned. We're going to need a lot more than what we've got so far."

"We may have that covered," Culver continued. "Langley found out that Paquet's family has connections to some kind of secretive group founded about the same time as Surmonter. It seems that several families got together and pooled their wealth to form this company and then have been working it from the shadows for decades."

"'What do we know about this secretive group'?" Hawkins asked.

"Unfortunately, that's the catch. There's a lot of rumor and innuendo, but no one has anything concrete."

"Then how do we know this is connection is between Xuffash, Matheson, Surmonter, and Paquet is anything but coincidence?" Shear asked. "From our perspective it seems clear, but we've got to offer up evidence, not conjecture. I would say that angle is far from covered. There's nothing actionable here, certainly not against the sitting president of a nation that is supposed to be one of our allies, strained though that relationship may be."

"Sir, we're still pursuing those leads," Culver said, the frustration evident in his voice.

"Then keep pursuing them," Shear said. "I'm not saying this line of thinking is without merit, but until we have a smoking gun it's nothing more than supposition. And I can't ask the AG to go to bat for something with the President until we've got something substantive." He looked at each of the gathered agents in turn. "I personally think you're on to something. Drill down and see what else is there. I have confidence that if there's something to find, you all will find it. Now if you all don't mind, I'd like to talk with Hawkins and Woodley." The other agents filed out of the room and closed the door behind them.

"Where there's smoke, there's fire," Woodley said.

"I'm not disagreeing," Shear replied, "but I'm saying it's going to take a whole lot more than what we've got here. Unless Langley knows more than they're letting on."

"That's almost certainly the case. Don't you think, Hawk?"

Hawkins was silent for a moment, taking in all of the images on the room's display walls. "Why the hit on us? Why now? Matheson and his people are dead. Why would Surmonter risk bringing attention to themselves?"

"Doesn't seem like a lot of risk to me," Woodley said. "They were flying under the radar pretty well for a long time."

"And now they aren't," Shear said.

"Exactly," Hawkins continued. "We know the guns used in the hit on me and Woodley came through Xuffash." A thought struck him. "Did we ever source the weapons the bad guys had on the transports bringing the battle virus in?"

"Those were gathered up by the military," Woodley said. "They seized all of that when they cleaned the ships."

Shear raised his eyebrows. "But we've got the guns from the shootout in New Orleans." He picked up the receiver from one of the phones on the conference table. "Bill, it's Bob Shear. Listen, I need you to pull the info on the guns we grabbed in New Orleans last year. Yeah, the bioweapon event...Yeah...I need to know everything there is to know about those weapons, from the day they came out of the factory until the day we picked them up in Jackson Square. Send it over to my email ASAP. Thanks." He replaced the receiver in its cradle. "Maybe that will tell us something useful."

"But it still doesn't answer the question: why send hit teams after me and Hawkins? That was a lot of trouble to take out two federal agents. For what purpose?"

"This was personal," Hawkins said.

"I know it sure feels that way, Hawk."

"No, I mean it. They came to our houses. They attacked you with your wife and kids at bedtime. They came after me and burnt down my house. They guy who dropped the det pack looked at me and said, 'Got ya', before he blew himself to smithereens. That was pretty personal." He didn't mention about what the man had said about Hawkins arriving in hell before "her."

"So, what are you thinking?" Shear asked.

"Whoever ordered this wasn't just trying to kill us for something we did, they weren't trying to get us out of the way. They were trying to *hurt* us. They wanted us to suffer. This was payback. Then you have the intrusion on Surmonter in Paris that goes down the tubes. Sam is on that mission. They missed her, but that may be why they took the other members of her team captive instead of killing them. They want to find her, too."

"We can't prove that," Shear said, the tone of his voice inferring that he agreed with what Hawkins was saying.

"But I know who can help prove it," Hawkins said. "I'll be back."

"Where are you going?"

"Across the river to my other office."

CHAPTER SIXTEEN

"And you're absolutely sure of that?"

"Verified identities, Hawk," Barry Morris answered. "Every one of the operators you guys stacked were mercenaries, all with backgrounds in various European militaries. None of them were known to come across the Atlantic before. Europe and Asia were their only known AOs."

"I suppose that should make us feel special."

"It should make you glad to be feeling anything at all. Those guys were no joke. The fact that you and Woodley smoked them says more about you than it does them."

"I appreciate the confidence boost," Hawkins replied. "I'm going to need it shortly." He ended the call, turned off his phone, and secured it in the center console of his car. The walk to the entrance of CIA Headquarters felt colder than usual, the sharp wind digging its cold tendrils through his layers of clothing. He made his way through the security checkpoint in the lobby and rode the elevator to the seventh floor. Hawkins paused for a moment, took a deep breath, and walked into the outer office of the CIA Director. Carlisle Welch was sitting behind his desk on the phone we he saw the agent walk in with purpose. He quickly ended the call and rose to his feet, waving his hands.

"You can't go in there without an appointment, Agent Hawkins," Welch said excitedly.

"Afraid I am," Hawkins said, and walked through the Director's partially closed door. Dorothy Sullivan sat behind her desk, a cup of coffee in one hand as she looked at a massive monitor on her desk.

"Well," Sullivan said with a hint of a smile on her face, "Good morning, Agent Hawkins."

"General, I apologize," Welch almost shouted. "I told him he couldn't..."

Sullivan waved her hand at her flustered assistant. "It's alright, Carlisle. Close the door and make sure we aren't disturbed." Welch huffed his displeasure.

Sullivan motioned for Hawkins to take a seat, and the FBI agent heard the office door close behind him as he sat. Now *he* was the one feeling tense.

"I can't say I'm surprised to see you this morning, Agent Hawkins. I'm glad to hear you weren't seriously injured."

"Thank you, ma'am. The attack on ASAC Woodley and myself are directly related to why I'm here."

Sullivan continued to sip her coffee. "So, what can I do for you, Agent Hawkins?"

"Madame Director, what is the location and status of Samatha Land?"

"You know the rules, Agent. That is need-to-know only, and you don't. I'm sorry."

"I believe that whoever ordered the hit on me and Woodley knew Sam was going to be at Surmonter."

"And what makes you say that?"

"Because the guy who blew himself up trying to kill me told me that I was going to get to hell before she did."

"You know, your instructors at the Farm couldn't say enough good things about you," Director Sullivan said. The redirect was abrupt, if not outright startling. Hawkins was glad to hear the compliment, of course, but it was not lost on him that he was being tested and scrutinized. He had met Sullivan a handful of times since completing his round of training to be co-opted into the CIA as an operational liaison. She had personally approved him and the liaison position, but it had been DNI Price who made it happen. Hawkins was considered one of Price's people; it remained to been seen if he would be one of Sullivan's. There was nothing as overt as a power struggle between the DNI and D/CIA—Price had staunchly supported Sullivan's appointment, and for her part she felt only the highest level of respect for the legendary Price. The reality, however, was that the IC had clearly drawn lines of trust, and it was easy for those lines to trip people up. Sullivan would want to know that not only could the CIA trust Hawkins, but *she* could as well. "I'm glad that DNI Price was able to convince you to come on board with us as liaison here at the Agency."

"Yes, ma'am," Hawkins replied. "I'm honored to be here. When I was first asked, I wasn't sure I was cut out for it."

"I understand," Sullivan said. The Director removed the rimless glasses she wore, interlaced her fingers on the desk in front of her, and leaned forward slightly in her chair. "Agent Hawkins, do you know why you're *really* here today?"

"Well, Madame Director, I believe it's because I strongly suspect that whoever is responsible for the attempted assassination of two federal agents last night also tried to kill Case Officer Land in France."

Sullivan nodded slightly. "So you're here for the sake of an investigation."

"I believe there's a connection, yes."

"You told an Assistant Director of the FBI on your way out the door of the Washington Field Office to come here that the Bureau and the Agency could both take your career and 'go pound sand' for the sake of an investigation?"

"Should I even ask how exactly you know that?"

"It was nothing fancy, I assure you," Sullivan said, taking

another drink from her Marine Corps mug. "He called to give me a heads up that you were coming in hot."

Hawkins flushed slightly at the memory. "I apologized for that remark, ma'am. Assistant Director Shear and I have a very good relationship, and I let my emotions take advantage of that."

Sullivan waved dismissively. "He told me all of that. He wasn't angry with you. He just wanted to make sure I was prepared to receive a bad attitude from you, and not to have you arrested by CIA Police when you marched your way into my office. I've dealt with Tom Shear a few times over the years. You do know that there are very few people that he would let get away with talking to him like that." It wasn't a question.

"Yes, ma'am, I'm aware of that."

"You told him that you'd take it to the D/CIA personally. So, here you are." Sullivan smiled slightly as she sat back in her chair. "You've got guts, I will say that for you. I wasn't sure you'd actually make the drive over here."

"I believe that there is a connection, yes." Hawkins took a breath. "But you also know I am personally concerned about Case Officer Land's situation. I would like to officially request as liaison with the FBI that I be allowed to go over and pursue the investigation into the attempt on the lives of myself and ASAC Woodley and its possible connection to the failed mission at Surmonter and, if necessary, extract her for investigative reasons."

"I understand that, Agent Hawkins, and I appreciate your forthrightness." She took another sip. "But I can't authorize that."

"Madame Director, I meant what I said. I can't believe that we are just going to leave Case Officer Land trapped in what is borderline enemy territory. After everything she has done for this Agency..."

"First of all, France is hardly enemy territory at this point.

Secondly, she's operating as a NOC, Agent Hawkins. She knew the risks."

"I'm not saying she didn't. I'm saying we need to extract her."

"Part of being a NOC is the risk that you may be compromised in unfriendly territory and find yourself on your own. With Non-Official Cover, the United States Government has total deniability..."

"I understand, ma'am. I'm just saying that Case Officer Land is far too valuable an asset to just abandon. She likely has vital information on both her own mission and the FBI's investigation. That alone should be justification for an extraction."

"Officially sanctioned FBI agents running around Paris, potentially shooting up the place, is not exactly the picture or cordial détente we need."

"Then we'll go in under other operational parameters. They sent two hit squads to kill federal agents. They're likely trying to find a decorated veteran and Clandestine Service Officer and gain intel from her, kill her, or both."

"That's simply not feasible right now," Director Sullivan said, closing her eyes briefly and shaking her head slightly. "The situation is far too delicate to be sending in *any* armed United States personnel to bring out one lone officer. We are having to allocate our resources very carefully right now, because we have no solid hold on what France and Spain are up to. Or who else is up to something with them."

"And she's the primary asset you have left in France on this mission," Hawkins said. He could feel his blood pressure rising. "Everyone else is either hiding out at the Embassy or dead."

Sullivan stiffened almost imperceptibly. "We're going to get some people in there, but it's an issue of timing."

"Precisely," Hawkins replied with a bit more energy than he intended. "She's in there alone, with no backup and limited resources. She needs help, and she needs it sooner rather than later."

Sullivan reclaimed her fingers and leaned forward. "Agent

Hawkins, I am coordinating the efforts of the CIA with 16 other agencies right now, trying to get all of the intel we can on what these crazies are about to do next. I cannot spare the resources to go and try to find a needle in a haystack when the whole barn is about to catch fire."

"Madame Director, with all due respect, that is all the more reason why we should get her out of there *before* it all comes down. We know that she's somewhere in Paris, likely using one of the safehouses that the Agency keeps there. We just have to figure out which one before the bad guys do. You know what they'll do to her if they catch her."

Sullivan sighed, then held up her coffee mug. "You see this?" She pointed to the Marine Corps seal affixed to one side. "I wasn't a a JAG. I was operational. MARSOC. I ran with the big boys, and we did nasty stuff." She turned the mug and pointed to the words "Semper Fi." "Do you see this? 'Always faithful.' We lived and died by these words."

"Then you understand why I have to go to Paris."

"Look, son, I understand how you feel. I know that you and Land are close. But you also have to understand that I can't help you."

Hawkins hit the tipping point, and knew he had nothing to lose. "This is a load of crap! You know where she is! You've gotten people out of tighter spots than this. Why can't the Agency extract her?"

"Because we have been ordered to stay out for now," Sullivan said with a finality that told Hawkins she was following orders from up the chain of command. "SecState has made very clear that there are to be no further incursions of any kind until we are greenlit by the White House. No one out of Langley, or any other federal agency, can enter French territory without authorization from POTUS, period."

Hawkins stared at her for a moment. Sullivan met his gaze. He realized he had stepped out of bounds—*way* out—but Director Sullivan was just sitting there with a quiet yet intense calmness. He wouldn't have been surprised if she had bodily removed him, but she only looked at him. Something unreadable flashed in her eyes, but she said nothing more.

After another moment Hawkins finally stood. "I understand." He opened the door and realized it hadn't been shut completely. "Thank you for your time, Madame Director." As he stepped through the doorway, he nearly bowled over the D/CIA's assistant. Welch caught himself and looked up at the taller FBI agent with a deer-in-the-headlights look on his face, as if he were caught listening in on his parents fighting in their bedroom. "Have a nice day, Mr. Welch. I know the way out."

"Agent Hawkins, there is still the matter of barging in..."

"Do what you've gotta do," Hawkins said as he walked out the door, and down the hallway of the 7th floor towards the elevators.

Sullivan waved her hand. "It's alright, Carlisle. He's on full access now. He'll be going straight out anyway." The D/CIA picked up her phone. "Close the door all the way this time, if you would. And Carlisle?"

"Yes, ma'am?"

"If there's something you need to know that goes on in this office, I'll make sure you get a copy of the recording. Clear?"

"Yes, ma'am," Welch said as he sheepishly closed the door.

Hawkins nodded at the CIA Police officers at the front desk and walked out the front doors. He switched his cell phone back on and had just replaced it in his back pocket when it began vibrating silently. He looked at the caller ID, and saw only a jumbled mix of numbers, letters and symbols. He thought that extremely unusual, as his phone was programmed to display any incoming number, unlisted or not. If the President called from Air Force One, the phone should show the number and calling source. He tapped the phone's screen.

"Hawkins."

"Mr. Hawkins, I am going to tell you who this is, but I don't want you to repeat my name aloud."

"I understand."

"Good. My name is Chris Chapman. I am a friend of Samantha Land." Hawkins listened intently to the voice, only slightly distorted by the layers of active digital encryption. The man had a British accent—well, almost. Chapman's speech had another lilt to it that he couldn't quite place. "I am well aware of the difficult and unpleasant situation you are finding yourself in regarding Samantha. I also know that you are even more upset about it than I am. That is why I am calling. D/CIA Sullivan's hands are tied. She's a good leader and wants nothing more than to help you. Unfortunately, she can't. DNI Price is in a similar situation. Due to governmental oversight, both of them are currently unable to provide any substantive assistance. I, on the other hand, believe I *can* help you in doing something about it."

"I'm listening."

"DNI Price would raise far too many flags if he were to aid you in any official capacity. He and I go back a number of years, so we have an *understanding*." Even on the encrypted line, Chapman was being careful not to pull Price into the situation more than necessary. "You need to get into France, and I have the resources to get you there. I assume that you're interested."

"Yes."

Good, Chapman thought. *The young man knows how to carry on a conversation in a circumspect fashion.* No one would be able to crack the audio on Chapman's side, and anyone with electronic ears would only get static from the speaker at Hawkins' ear. What they could grab, however, was any responses Hawkins made. So far, anyone listening would get absolutely zero from the conversation. The D/CIA had called Price as soon as Hawkins had walked out, and in code speak had told him that the FBI agent was primed to head for Paris. It was all a matter of basic tradecraft from there. "Alright then. I'll provide party favors when you arrive, so no need to bring yours. Get to Reagan Airport. When you arrive, call me and I'll tell you where to go."

"Right," Hawkins replied, then tapped the phone to end the call. He got into his Dodge Charger and pulled out of the VIP lot, past the guard post, and back up the main drive to the front gate of CIA Headquarters. He half expected the CIA Police to stop him at the main checkpoint, but they let him pass with a nod. He pulled out onto 123 and headed back towards the Park-way. The late morning traffic was light, a far cry from the almost perpetual logjams present during the week. As he drove, he turned the situation over and over again in his mind. He hadn't been all that surprised by Director Sullivan's response. She had too many people in Washington breathing down her neck at the moment to go against a direct order from on high. While Sulli-van's behavior didn't surprise him, the assistant's did. Carlisle Welch was awfully unsettled for a man in his position. Hawkins had managed to rattle him fairly easily just by his presence, something that the Director of the Central Intelligence Agency's personal assistant should be immune to. Granted he was under a great deal of stress, and the D/CIA was obviously laying it down hard because one of her best covert operations officers was missing behind enemy lines. But even so, the man responded to Hawkins like someone who was under interrogation and had something to hide. The fact that he was eavesdropping through a partially open door didn't endear him to Hawkins, either. It could be that he had simply watched too many conspiracy movies over the years, but Hawkins genuinely believed that there were things working behind the scenes at the CIA that weren't for Sam's benefit, or his. He would have to be careful.

What would inspire Price to have Chapman contact him? How did he know where Hawkins was? Well, that one was easy. Most people in the know in the Federal Law Enforcement and Intelligence Communities understood that Jack Price was more than just the DNI to a great many. He had been a friend and helper to a lot of people over the years, and people in that community never forgot. DNI Price could lift an eyebrow a certain way and someone would see and interpret it to carry out a covert task. The new D/CIA's healthy relationship with the DNI would guarantee open communication between the two. And Sullivan was far from the only friend that Price had in CIA. The DNI had people on the inside who were loyal to him above anyone else and made sure he knew what he needed to know. Price had successfully recruited Hawkins into the Agency after the initial BEAR mess last year, and maybe that put a mark on Hawkins that he was one of Price's people and was to be treated accordingly. Hawkins didn't know that for certain, and he didn't need to. He just needed to get to Sam. She was all that mattered to him right now, and this was his ticket in country. Chapman certainly sounded connected. Or it could be that the whole thing was just a setup of some kind. Either way, he supposed, he would soon find out.

CHAPTER SEVENTEEN

The beeping of a cell phone brought Samantha Land out of a restful sleep instantly. She reached over to the nightstand and glanced at the screen long enough to recognize the number before answering.

"You said to let you sleep a few hours," E.J. Niels said. "I've got news on your mission. But first I wanted you to hear from me before word got to you any other way. Someone tried to kill Hawkins and Woodley last night in Jacksonville. They're okay, but it was bad."

"How bad?" Sam asked, sitting straight up in bed.

"A four-man hit squad went to each of their houses. The only fatalities were bad guys, but they shot up Woodley's house pretty good. And Hawkins' house burnt to the ground. The word on the news is that two federal agents were killed. They're using that to try and get some lead time on whoever was behind it."

"Do they have any leads?"

"Boy, do they," Niels said proudly. "Thanks to us."

"What do you have? Are our little friends talking?"

"They're singing like the Brooklyn Tabernacle Choir. While you were sleeping we grabbed some serious gold," Niels said as his eyes scanned the multiple monitors at his desk. The excitement was evident in the CIA technical genius' voice. There were few things he loved more than retasking surveillance tech in real time. Digging through mountains of indecipherable digital flotsam to find information the bad guys didn't want found was one of those things. He caught her up on the intel on Surmonter, including the possible connection with Matheson, Xuffash, and Paquet.

"Okay, that's definitely bad," she said. She was relieved to hear Hawkins and Woodley weren't seriously injured, and the possible connections troubled her. She brushed her other questions aside for now. "But that's not my priority. Did you find anything about the backpack nukes?"

"That's where the bad news comes in. I found a file buried in several subdirectories that I think is what we're looking for. The problem is that it's local storage only. It's not connected to an external server. I can't get to it remotely." The phone buzzed as Sam was talking. She looked to see a text from Chris Chapman. It said, "Call me ASAP."

"Of course not," Sam said. She knew better than to ask Niels how the one file she needed the most was inaccessible. No matter how good technology got, there would always be the need for an operator to go hands on in the field. "So I'm going to have to go back inside."

"That is a terrible idea," Niels replied in an astonished tone. "You can't even think about that. They're going to be on high alert for any intrusion."

"We don't have a lot of options, do we?" The silence on the line answered her question. "Get word to Sensei that I'm going in, and I'm going to get that data."

"Roger that," Niels said. "There'll be a package for you on your doorstop in 45 minutes."

"Are you airdropping personnel?" she joked.

"Not yet. Eyeglasses. All the tech of your helmet without... well, without you walking around with a helmet on."

"Probably better for discretion."

"They're brand new. Like, yesterday new. I tried to get them to you before your insertion, but they weren't ready in time. All of the perks of the helmet without the bulk."

"Or the protection," she interjected.

"I didn't say to throw the helmet away. Trust me. Those glasses will be your friend."

"Got it. I'll keep you posted. Let me know what's going on with Hawkins."

"Roger that. Stay safe." As soon as the call ended, Sam dialed Chapman.

"Just got an update from Langley," she said. "They can't get to what we need."

"I know," Chapman said. "They sent a packet to my email. Risky business goin back in."

"I'm open to suggestions."

"You've got a pretty good path established from your first go 'round. Are you going the same way?"

"If I had another option, I would consider it," Sam said. "Since I don't, I'm making do with what I've got. We need to know if they actually have those devices and, if so, where they are."

"We have to take them out of play, no doubt. We're just down a couple of team members at the moment. On that note, we do have backup coming. But they won't be here until late tonight at the earliest."

"Can we wait that long?"

"Do we have a choice?" Chapman asked rhetorically. As frustrating as it was, Sam knew they did not. She couldn't risk entry in broad daylight. She mentally ran through what else was on the top floor with the server. And then it occurred to her.

"Maybe we do."

Hawkins picked up Woodley from the coffee shop down the road in McLean following his meeting with Sullivan and was now driving down the Parkway. He caught Woodley up with what had transpired at Langley, and the phone conversation afterward with Chapman.

"Chris Chapman?" Woodley repeated. "That guy's is a legend. They call him 'The Ghost.' Rumor has it he's the only foreign agent to ever make it into CIA Headquarters undetected." There had been an unofficial competition for decades involving Tier 1 teams from nations considered to be the United States' closest allies. These teams would attempt to make entry onto the grounds of CIA Headquarters and see who could make it the farthest without being detected and caught. No one had ever made it very far. The exercise provided two main purposes: to allow CIA to constantly evaluate and upgrade its security measures, and to let even their allies know that the only way into Langley was by invitation, and then under careful scrutiny. There were a couple of American teams that had gotten too close for comfort on a couple of occasions, but no foreign team made it through the no man's land to approach the buildings. The only people to ever penetrate security during the exercise were the CIA's own Clandestine Service Officers, and only a couple weren't caught until they had made it into secured areas. Only one foreign agent had ever made it through, and it had earned him the nickname "The Ghost." He was found by the Director of CIA at the time, sipping tea at the Director's desk. He and then CIA Director Jack Price had been close friends ever since.

"You know, if you do this your career with the Bureau is likely over," Woodley said matter-of-factly. "And CIA. And you'll probably go to federal prison, now that I think about it."

"I don't care," Hawkins replied. "Sam is more important to me than anything else. Besides, she's the only one in position to get the information about what's really going on. And there's no way she's going to be able to pull this off without some backup."

Woodley nodded. "I understand that," he said with a sigh of resignation. "Okay. I'm in."

A surprised look crossed Hawkins' face. "I can't ask you to get involved in this, Mark."

"You don't have to," Woodley replied. "I'm volunteering."

"You know that the world is going to come crashing down on you, too."

"Remember, they came after me at my home. With my wife and babies there." Woodley never got serious for too long, but Hawkins swore the car got hotter for a moment from his friend's controlled rage at what had happened. "Not gonna let that go unanswered." The moment passed, and jovial Woodley was back. "Besides, Price already reached out to me and asked me to accompany you."

Hawk looked over at his friend. "Are you kidding me?"

"We are working 'unofficially' with several key personnel in CIA and FBI to help pull this off. That way Price and Sullivan can say they're not running any ops when the Oversight Committee starts asking questions."

"So why did Price really call you?"

Woodley shrugged, then paused for a moment. "I did some work for Price and the Agency during my SEAL days."

"So..."

"Yeah, yeah," Woodley said as he threw his hands up. "I'm a CIA spook."

Hawkins shook his head. "Pot, meet kettle," he said with a chuckle. "One more thing we'll have in common since we're kissing our careers goodbye."

Woodley made a "pfft" sound. "You're rich," he said nonchalantly. "We can always start our own agency."

"If we aren't locked up in prison," Hawkins offered.

"Or dead," Woodley said with a chuckle. "There's always the possibility of dead."

"I recommend we avoid all of those options, if possible."

"I concur," Woodley said. "So, what's the plan?"

"We're supposed to get a ride to Reagan. Once there, I'll

reach out to my contact. He'll give us additional instructions then."

"Once we get on that plane, we're on our own."

"We're already on our own, Mark. At least now we'll be able to do something about it."

CHAPTER EIGHTEEN

The guard posted at the front entrance of Surmonter was used to seeing all kinds of people coming and going. People of every nationality conducted business with the finance company, some wearing grungy work clothes, and others wearing high-end fashion. He had served in the French military after finishing high school, and the 20 years of experience in various combat zones gave him a good pension and a strong resume for the job. It had also given him his fill for combat. He wasn't looking for action any longer. He worked 5 days a week, from 0800 until 1700. His was a boring job, but it was peaceful, it paid well, and it afforded him the chance to people watch. And occasionally there were some really nice-looking people.

This afternoon afforded him one such person. A woman walked through the main entrance into the spacious lobby and drew his attention instantly. She had straight electric blue hair cut just above her shoulders, bangs hanging just over eyes that were almost the same color. She wore a gray overcoat which she removed and hung on a rack by the entrance. Beneath it she wore a form-fitting black long sleeve exercise shirt with straps that criss-crossed her chest and plunged to a deep "V" shape. Black leggings with mesh panels and black sneakers completed the athletic ensemble. A strap that ran over her shoulder suspended a black FILA duffle bag. He could see her muscles flexing as she walked, the LED lights hanging from the ceiling shimmering off the material. His first guess based on her legs was that she was likely a dancer, perhaps a ballerina, but her arms and shoulders indicated that she may have been a gymnast as well. She walked with a sureness of purpose that told him she was used to getting what she wanted.

"Hello, ma'am, can I help you?"

"Good afternoon, friend," she spoke. Her French was tinged with a slight accent. Russian? "I'm here for a private training session with Monsieur Barton."

"Do you have an appointment with him?"

Her blue eyes seemed to burn into his brain, even through her glasses. "Of course, darling," she purred. "Why else would I be here?"

"You don't appear to be on his calendar for the day."

She pivoted slightly, making sure he could see all of her outfit. "My name usually doesn't appear on the calendar of my clients."

A slight sweat broke out on the man's upper lip. "I understand, madame. Just give me a moment to verify with him."

"Of course," she said as the guard picked up the phone and dialed Barton's office. He had no way of knowing that the woman could see in the heads-up display on her glasses the number being dialed, and the call being routed to a phone that would be answered by someone who was definitely not Barton.

The guard replaced the receiver. "My apology for the inconvenience, Madame. He said for you to come directly to his office.

"Thank you, darling," and she walked toward the elevator. He was extremely disappointed when she stepped into the elevator and out of his line of sight. He never really envied managers like Barton, overpaid executives with too much money in the bank and too much fat on their belly. Right now, however, he very much wished he could be in the man's place.

She made her way to the 6th floor, then walked to Barton's office. She opened the door into a surprisingly massive room. The office had walls that appeared to be white marble, contrasting against the dark gray marble floors. Everything was trimmed in bright chrome and backlit with white LEDs. Barton sat at a massive glass and steel desk, with floor to ceiling windows behind. A triple monitor took up much of the desk's real estate. He peeked around one side. There sat Vin Barton, 56, married, Master's Degree in accounting and finance. A man who never made waves, Barton had stayed beneath corporate politics and worked his was up to the chief financial officer position at the Paris Surmonter office a decade ago. Much like his office, he was simple and without frills, but had everything needed to make a business run smoothly. He had never been in trouble, not even a parking ticket. He had proved himself adept at handling finances on a staggering scale without making waves. He did his job, and nothing more. Nothing more was needed of him, so he was left alone. It was perfect.

"Excuse me," Barton said, clearly confused by the beautiful woman who had just entered his office.

"Hello, monsieur," the woman said as she set down her duffle bag. "I'm here for your personal training session."

A look of confusion crossed his face. "Training session?"

"Yes," the woman said. She turned around and bent over to retrieve something from the bag, distracting the man with the view. "You ordered a personal cardio and body weight training session."

The certainty with which she spoke, and the woman's attractiveness, further confused him. Had he scheduled someone to come in and start him on an exercise regimen? His wife had certainly been complaining to him about his weight, how he was going to die before retirement if he didn't lose some of the weight he had gained over the last few years of riding a desk. It suddenly dawned on him—knowing that he wouldn't do it on his own, his wife had likely ordered the exercise trainer for him.

That was why security hadn't called before sending her up. If they had said someone was here to help him exercise, he would have turned them away without asking any further questions. As the woman turned around and walked towards him, he scanned her from head to toe. This was certainly one way to get him into exercising. His wife would not likely approve of the curvaceous coach who had been sent to start his fitness regimen, but there was no reason for her to know such details. "Of course," he said finally. "I'm so busy I must have forgotten." He touched a button on his phone, and the security man from downstairs answered. "Yes, please see to it that I'm not disturbed for the next couple of hours. I have a personal training session," then switched the phone off.

"Very good," the trainer replied, setting several items on the floor. She squatted and rolled out a pair of foam yoga mats. It occurred to Barton as she laid out several resistance bands in a careful formation that his heart rate was increasing just watching the woman move. *Already getting some cardio*, he thought to himself. She picked up a small plastic box and moved toward him. "Before we begin, my agency requires that I do get your vitals for liability purposes." Her eyes narrowed slightly, and she smiled. "They don't want you getting…injured by our workout," she said breathily. Sweat was already beading up on his forehead. She looked at him for a moment, as if waiting for him to respond. "Are you going to change into your workout clothes?"

Panic flashed across the man's face just for a moment. "I, uh, forgot to bring them."

"That's okay," the trainer replied calmly. "That happens more than you would think. You can do what would be most comfortable, but I recommend you at least remove your shirt and your dress pants." She paused and smiled. "As long as you are wearing undergarments, of course."

"Of course," he repeated. She set the box down on the desktop as he undressed to a white undershirt and black boxers. He took his seat once more, and she placed an automated blood pressure cuff on his wrist and a pulse oximeter over his right forefinger. The trainer them removed a small plastic cylinder attached to a metal handle.

"I need to get a sample of your blood so we can establish your metabolic profile," she said, leaning in close so he could get a good look. "I want to make sure I have all the information I need to ensure you get the best workout possible." The man could see himself in the reflection of her glasses, and he immediately changed his expression to look more at ease. He was a successful man of wealth and influence. He shouldn't allow himself to get flustered by a beautiful athletic trainer. Of course she would want to be with him. He had so much to offer. His confidence boosted, he asserted himself somewhat. He reached a hand around and grabbed the woman's backside.

"Believe me," he said, "I want the best workout possible."

"Oh, you're definitely going to get that. Hold still," she said, and stuck the cylinder against the man's neck. He barely flinched. He was proud of himself. He smiled at the woman, and she smiled back. He felt his hand slip away from contact with her as he drifted off into darkness. The woman stood quickly and removed the blood pressure cuff and pulse oximeter. She propped open Barton's eyes and scanned them, then fireman-carried the unconscious man to his sofa. She undressed him completely then tossed his t-shirt and boxers down in different spots. He would wake up naked and confused in about two hours, but he would be certain that he had indeed had an excellent workout. She quickly repacked the duffle bag and set it by the office door, then went back to his desk and looked at the computer screens. Back at Langley, E. J. Niels was able to see exactly what she was seeing. Directions popped up on the HUD on her new glasses. They worked just as well as the HUD in her helmet.

A virtual pointer appeared in her field of view as Sam navigated through the computer desktop. Commands would occasionally pop up on her glasses, and she would type in what Niels told her. It took several minutes, but she finally found what she was looking for. It was a blocked folder, with no file name or other designator to locate it. If one wasn't looking for it, and knew the digital markers to find such files, it would be as though it didn't even exist. She opened the file using the commands Niels sent, which would make her current access untraceable to this computer. Someone would be able to see that the file had been accessed, but they wouldn't be able to track from where. Barton's computer was giving her both the access and the anonymity she needed. The downside was he seemed like a decent enough fellow from the file she read on her glasses as she had walked into his office. She didn't want him getting killed over what she was doing. Better that he would only think he had a good time that he couldn't remember than suffer for his unwilling participation in her mission.

The file opened and revealed little. Several pages had been scanned from what looked like a Russian military manual and an accompanying lab report. What the file lacked in size, however, it more than made up for in impact, much like the subject of the file itself: a tactical suitcase nuclear bomb. "Suitcase" wasn't exactly accurate. It would take a good-sized hiking backpack or duffle bag to carry the nearly 35kg device, but it was still man-portable. The other pages showed transport requirements to avoid detection, and a list of possible site deployments. In what appeared to be various hand-written notes, several city names were scrawled, as if the document was continually being updated and rescanned. Washington and New York were crossed out, along with several other major cities. Five U.S. cities remained, with various notes written around each. There was only one city outside of the United States that was listed, and it appeared there was no discussion about it whatsoever, that it was a settled target.

Paris.

Her HUD displayed a message from Niels that he had everything they need. Her display went red almost immediately after.

"COMPROMISED" flashed three times, then "Two Armed Targets Inbound, 45 seconds. Pistols. Clear to Engage." Someone was clearly alerted to the file being opened. The security guard downstairs must have been sharper than he let on if he connected the dots that quickly. *How* they knew didn't matter at this point; *that* they knew was the current problem. She closed the windows on the computers and reset it to how she found it. "30 Seconds." She considered attempting to leave through the ventilation system, but she didn't want to attract unnecessary attention to that path. The transmitters were still doing their job, and she definitely didn't want any of that discovered at this point. "15 Seconds." She unlocked the office door.

Two men burst into the office, security guard from the lobby and another man in a suit and tie. Both had their guns in the close ready position as they moved quickly into the room. They quickly spotted the naked man on the couch. The security guard barely felt the needle that jabbed into the left side of his neck. The last thing he heard as he slipped into unconsciousness was the sound of the other man grunting in pain as a foot drove into the back of his right knee.

Sam ducked, anticipating the suit's pivot toward the source of the attack. She knife-handed the man's wrist and drove the ball of her fist upward into his chin. His pistol clattered away and he grunted, but he was able to snap a left cross that caught Sam on the side of her head right above her ear, knocking her glasses off. He followed with a right that missed, but then drove his right knee into her midsection. He then made contact with another left across her jaw that sent her tumbling to the floor. She rolled quickly to her feet. *Okay*, she thought. *This guy wants to get serious*. She assumed a boxer's stance, then moved in closer. He feinted with a right hand then struck with a left. She dodged it easily, backing away slightly. She noticed he was favoring the right knee. *He made it worse when he hit me with it.* Between the knife-hand to the right wrist and the injured right knee, the suit was in more trouble than he realized. He couldn't brace to deliver a solid right hand, which was clearly his strong side, and his right leg would no longer fully support him. She faked a jab, then pivoted and side-kicked him in the gut. He rocked backward several steps, the wind knocked from him. He tried to press the attack once more, but Sam hit him with two hard jabs to the face, then landed a spin kick to the side of his jaw that broke it with a sickening pop. The man folded up and hit the floor. She picked up her glasses and checked the display. Green letters flashed, "Extract Via Stairwell ASAP." She grabbed her duffle bag, tightened the straps to turn it into a backpack, and sprinted into the hallway. She took the steps three at a time on the descent and emerged into the lobby. She jogged across the empty lobby, grabbed her coat, and went outside. She went two blocks before she reached a storm drain access door that glowed green in her HUD. She lifted the cover and lowered herself into the vast sewer network that ran below the Parisian streets

CHAPTER NINETEEN

Well, Donald Molson thought to himself, *it doesn't get much worse than this*. He looked at himself in the golden-tinted mirrors that lined the banquet hall. He was wearing a tuxedo, of course, as one should at events of this caliber. His wife had insisted he purchase this one, and it had been expensive, but he had to admit he looked pretty good in it. Maybe a little like the spy he was turning out to be. He was the Legal Attaché for the FBI, but most days he felt like he was working in the Intelligence Community. The stakes were so high in this world, much higher even than when he had been Assistant Director in the New York Field Office. Now he was less than two dozen feet from the Vice President of the United States and the President of France, with some of the wealthiest and most powerful people in the Western world around them.

He glanced at the VP's Secret Service detail, watching everyone tirelessly. He had come to begrudgingly admire his colleagues from Treasury over the years. There was generally no love lost between the Bureau and the Secret Service, but Molson had outgrown petty rivalries. If you did your job well, he respected you, regardless of what your badge said. And there was no one better at executive protection and financial crime than the Secret Service.

The French President had his own security detail, of course, and they looked to be far more agitated than their American counterparts. They appeared as though they were actively searching for someone, as if they were expecting a problem. That pushed one of Molson's buttons. What did they know that the Secret Service didn't? Was there a threat they didn't share? Or were the Secret Service personnel just that much better with their game faces? Whatever the case, Molson had the feeling that something was up. He turned to gaze around the room and saw a familiar face walking his way, whiskey glasses in each hand.

"You look like you could use one of these," Philippe Dupain said as he handed a glass to his friend.

"As always, your timing is impeccable." Molson took a sip and nodded. "And you didn't go cheap, either."

"Nothing less than the very best for my friend," he said. "And, it is an open bar."

"All the better," Molson said as he took another drink. "Are we having fun yet?"

"Your Vice President has had a very successful stay here with us. The fractured relationship between our two countries is well on its way to being restored."

"But?"

Dupain smiled. "I don't know what has become of the world when a man cannot even have smoke at a party." He reached into his pocket and removed a silver cigarette case. "Join me outside?"

Molson nodded and followed as Dupain walked up a staircase that led to the level above where the well-heeled partygoers impressed one another with their fashion choices and name-dropping. The Frenchman led the way through a service hallway that opened onto a small balcony overlooking ventilation units pumping away noisily. The cold night air jabbed at their skin, the wind blowing with enough force that even Dupain's torch lighter struggled to stay aflame long enough to light their cigarettes. The Frenchman took a drink, then a long puff, before he spoke.

"Something is amiss, Donald. Last night there was an attempted break-in at an office building here in Paris."

"That isn't particularly unusual," Molson said.

"No, but what is unusual is the response. Word on the street is that heavily armed mercenaries killed or captured the perpetrators and cleared the scene in less than five minutes."

The FBI agent nodded. "Now *that* is unusual." He took a puff from the cigarette. "What was the police response?"

"None whatsoever. The police were never notified."

"Let me get this straight. Guys with guns show up and kill and/or kidnap would-be thieves and nobody called the cops?"

"There's more," Dupain said. "There was another incident earlier today. Someone made entry into the CFO's office and a fight broke out. Two security men were taken out, and the perpetrator escaped." He winked wryly. "They said it was a beautiful woman."

"And where exactly did this happen?"

"A place you are going to want your people to take a very close look at," Dupain replied as he handed a piece of paper to Molson. "There are several people at this party who are not going to want it looked into, I can assure you."

"It sounds like somebody is already taking a look at it pretty closely. And *persistently*, if the same people were behind the second incursion." Molson pocketed the paper and raised an eyebrow at his friend. "This is awfully close for you, my friend. You okay in this?"

"One doesn't get to where I am without having certain protections available," the Frenchman replied. "Don't worry about me. I plan on coming out ahead of this one, I assure you."

"Even if this *does* involve some of your people?"

"They are not my people," Dupain said, taking another puff. "Not if they are involved in this."

"And what exactly do you think 'this' is?"

Dupain drained the rest of the whiskey from his glass. "World War 3, Donald."

Hawkins couldn't help but think about the last time he had been winging his way over the Atlantic toward France on a mission for the FBI. It was hard to believe it had been little more than a year earlier that he and Samantha Land were sharing a flight that would be the start of—what? A case that would change his career, a relationship that would change his life—it could be argued, he supposed, that both the case and relationship had changed his career *and* his life. He was now working as much for the CIA as the Bureau, and once again had been assigned a mission with Sam. He looked over at Mark Woodley, dozing quietly in one of the leather-upholstered seats in the Gulfstream 550. As glad as he was that his friend was with him on this one, he wished Sam were there much more.

His chest tightened slightly at the thought—what if something bad happened to her? Although very few federal agents actually lost their lives in the line of duty, it was nonetheless a possibility everyone involved understood and accepted. Sam's line of work was far more dangerous than the average government employee, however. The CIA's Clandestine Service Officers were highly trained experts, but they weren't superheroes— the memorial stars etched into the wall and marked in the book at the lobby of CIA Headquarters testified to their mortality.

Hawkins had faced enough loss that he understood the toll it took, but he also knew that hiding from the risks of living wasn't really living at all. He believed everyone had a purpose, a mission, that they were created for, and to shirk that duty was to welcome deep-seated misery. He was reminded of a t-shirt he had seen recently at a track day he attended. The shirt had a cartoon of person driving a race car wildly around a track, the caption above and below saying, "Something is going to kill you —it might as well be something you enjoy." He still felt guilt from time to time about how much he actually enjoyed his work. His current tasks were far different than what he had done as a young pastor before his recruitment into the FBI. Hawkins scarcely could have imagined only a few years earlier the things he would experience in his relatively short time as an FBI agent. His turn in white-collar crime had shifted quickly to a game-changing global bioterrorism plot that he helped to successfully thwart. Now he was going into what could be considered hostile territory to carry out a clandestine mission for the United States government and, hopefully, provide needed backup for the love of his life.

Hawkins stood from his own seat at the bank of communications equipment, sensor packages, and computer workstations at the front of the aircraft. As he walked down the narrow aisle he noticed Woodley had set a map of Paris down in the seat facing him. Hawkins saw scribbled notes and highlighted routes snaking their way across the Parisian streets on the large diagram. Woodley's time as a Navy SEAL had ingrained into him the importance of knowing your AO. The old adage of never going into a place you didn't have more than one way out of was a non-negotiable. Although Woodley never went into significant detail about his past exploits, Hawkins knew his friend had gotten in and out of more hairy situations than he ever would. It gave the younger man no small comfort knowing that Woodley was covering the bases.

Hawkins sat down into one of the surprisingly comfortable leather chairs at the rear of the aircraft and reclined it slightly. He thought about looking over the files of the people he was going to be meeting up with again, but he already knew the details on them by heart. Sleep would benefit him more than study at this point, so he closed his eyes and allowed the hum of the jet's powerful engines to lull him to sleep.

CHAPTER TWENTY

The sun had started to rise and shine its light over Paris, the streets quickly filling with more vehicles than city planners had ever intended. Hawkins sat at a small outdoor café with a cappuccino and chocolate-filled croissant. A black watch cap and pea coat helped shield him from the chill morning air. The light tint on his aviator-frame sunglasses helped cut down some of the early morning glare that radiated onto the patio where he sat, the slight warmth it added to the chill air well worth the inconvenience. He tapped away on his tablet when the blue LED flashed twice. A new window popped up, a green background with black letters—impossible to read from the sides or using electronic measures. Only the one holding the device and wearing the correct lenses could read such a message. It was from E.J. Niels, the technical wiz at Langley who had been such a help the last time he had been in France. The text box read: "Attendee is bravo to your location."

Two minutes out, Hawkins thought. "Photo?" he typed.

The reply popped up in the box: "Attendee knows who they're looking for."

So, I wait. Hawkins had sat on plenty of wiretaps and stake-outs, but he never got used to the waiting. Patience had never been one of his particular strong suits. One of the instructors at Quantico had told him that all great detectives hate mysteries; their desire to solve, and therefore eliminate, them is what makes them great. He wasn't sure he was a great detective, but he at least shared their hatred for the unknown. He wondered who had tried to kill Woodley and him. He wondered what the connection was between a drug dealer in South Carolina and a finance company in France.

He wondered where Sam was.

He ate the rest of his croissant and, exactly two minutes from Niels mark, a man walked up to the table.

"Excuse me, monsieur, there are no other tables. Would you mind if I took a seat here with you for a moment?"

"Of course," Hawkins said, and gestured towards the other chair. The man took the seat. He was wearing a gray wool over-coat and scarf that covered the lower part of his face. A gray wool driving cap sat low over his forehead. He made a motion with his hand toward the waiter, who nodded in understanding and hurried away.

"Cold as it was back in New York at this time," the man said.

"Much like it is in Washington," Hawkins replied. The other man set his phone on the table and pushed a button on the side.

"Welcome to Paris," Donald Molson said.

"Thanks. I only wish I were here under better circumstances."

"Don't we all," Molson acknowledged with a slight nod. He thanked the waiter as he returned with a cup of coffee. "This is turning out to really be a hot mess."

"You've got something then?"

"That's an understatement," Molson said. "I just hit your phone with the files. You're going to get a call in a few minutes from an unknown number. Answer it and do exactly what you're told. Don't say anything, just do it. I've got things I've got to take care of on my end. You need to find what you're looking for, then get out of the way. There's going to be assets coming into play to take care of the issue here. You and yours need to be gone before that happens. And you absolutely cannot get caught doing something stupid, or this whole thing blows up in our faces. Literally. Understood?"

"Perfectly. Thanks for the help."

"Don't mention it." Molson chuckled once. "Literally." He finished his coffee, picked up his phone, and left money on the table. "*Adieu*." He stuffed his hands into his pockets and walked away.

Sam had taken another shower as soon as she awoke. She had cleaned up after emerging from the sewers in a local hostel, then again when she returned to her apartment before she went to bed. She still felt like the stench of the sewers was attached to her somehow, even though she knew it was impossible with all the shampoo and soap she had used. She switched on the Saeco Xelsis coffee machine on the kitchen counter, then checked her phone for messages. Nothing. There was no word from Chapman or Duncan, and no emergency messages from Niels. At least she hadn't been compromised. Seeing that the water had reached a sufficient temperature in the machine, and she pressed the Americano option on the touchscreen. The whirring and grinding began as the warm, rich scent drove the last remnants of the sewer from her recent memory. She took a sip and sat down with the cup at the small table in the breakfast nook. There was nothing to do but wait until she received her next orders. The waiting was tough, but she was used to it. She had lost track of how many hours she waited in some out-of-the-way spot for her mission to get the green light. One of the most memorable had been in Moscow with Chapman a couple of years ago. He had really earned his "Ghost" nickname on that one. She was certain there were some Russians who still had nightmares over it.

Her phone buzzed. It was Chapman. She checked the message and cocked her head slightly.

"You have a visitor."

She tapped the virtual keyboard on her phone. "Who?"

"A bird and a bull."

Hawkins and Woodley? She was excited at the prospect of having them in her AO. "What are they doing here?"

"Really?" was the reply. She smiled. He knew exactly why the two FBI agents were there, and it only partly had to do with the mission. Although they had never met, Chapman liked Hawkins. He had actually crossed paths with Woodley back in his SEAL days, when Chapman was the "old man" at Hereford. Forty years of age was hardly old, but the Ghost's age was the only thing the younger SAS members could give him a hard time about. "They just had the files passed to them. I'll send you their address when you're ready."

"I'll head out momentarily," she responded. Chapman sent the address of the safe house Hawkins and Woodley were going to be using. It was on the other side of Paris; one she had used before. It was not as posh as her current place, but one that would be more appropriate for a couple of burly American men. She quickly dressed, making sure her pink wig was securely in place, and headed outside.

Hawkins waited five minutes before finishing his coffee and leaving cash on the table, tipping just the right amount so as not to be memorable. As he stood his phone chirped from his inner pocket, the caller ID only showing asterisks. When he answered he heard several clicks, indicating that digital encryption was processing the signal.

"Welcome to Paris, Mr. Hawkins," Chris Chapman said.

"Thanks for the deluxe accommodations," Hawkins said. The flight had indeed been luxurious, a private jet that featured leather couches and appointments any high-level executive or movie star would appreciate, computers and surveillance equipment notwithstanding. The car they had been provided was a 10-year old Mercedes, but in excellent shape and with low miles. The apartment, however, was decidedly rougher. It was in a part of Paris where tourists dared not step, the splendor of the city lights dimmed by crime and decay. The car made them look like mid-level criminals with big connections, which guaranteed that the street-level hoods who haunted the area gave them a wide berth.

"I was fairly certain you two would stick out at the Four Seasons."

"You aren't wrong," Hawkins replied. "We do appreciate your help. How's our mutual friend?" Although the phone was encrypted, one never knew who might be listening on the street. No need to call out names unnecessarily.

"All good. I'm about to send her your address. We'll meet at your place to compare notes and discuss strategy."

"Sounds good. What resources do we have?"

"Sam, a former SAS colleague name Benny Duncan, and yours truly. I'll bring plenty of hardware. I trust you found your walkaround piece sufficient?"

"Certainly," Hawkins answered, conscious of the tiny Sig Sauer P938 tucked into his waistband and the three spare mags on his opposite hip. He preferred handguns with more heft, but the small Sig was and big on concealability and accuracy—a definite perk in his current circumstance. "Again, much appreciated."

"Happy to help. I'm sending you a file to supplement the information from the Legal Attaché."

Hawkins knew better than to ask someone nicknamed the Ghost how he knew about the meeting and who he had met with. He was suddenly very aware of how exposed he was, and the growing certainty that Chapman had eyes on him at that very moment. He resisted the urge to look around. "I'll look it over momentarily."

"Excellent. Head back to your place. We'll meet you there shortly."

Hawkins ended the call. He walked two blocks from the café before he spotted the older Mercedes S600 parked at the curb with blacked out windows. As he approached, he heard the door unlock, and he climbed inside. Although the darkened glass made the interior much dimmer than the Parisian streets, it was far warmer.

"Glad you're staying nice and warm while I'm doing all the work," Hawkins said.

"I know you hate driving in city traffic," Woodley said. "At least I turned your heated seat on. So, what do we have?"

Hawkins opened the files sent by Molson first. He glanced at the small led on the dash that indicated the car's white noise jammers were operating properly. "This definitely goes in the worst-case scenario category. Did you ever hear about the rumor that Russia had developed a couple of suitcase nukes?"

"Low-yield, fast-clearing tactical weapons meant to do a lot of damage and cause even more panic," Woodley answered. "Nothing makes people want to roll over like the sight of a mushroom cloud on the horizon. I may or may not have been on a couple of missions trying to track them down back in my SEAL days without success. If they're real, they've been in the wind for a long time. The brass wrote them off as propaganda. The thought was some extremist would have popped them off by now if they were really out there."

"Then you'll be happy to know we have a lead on two mini-boomers in the wind, and apparently in play by Surmonter."

"Somehow I am not encouraged by that," Woodley said dryly. "What does a glorified mortgage company want with tactical nukes?"

"My squad back in DC has been working this pretty hard, along with some of the other agencies. They've actually connected the new French President to Surmonter."

"Paquet?" Woodley asked. "Are they sure?"

"Pretty sure. The dummy corporations go several layers deep, and its subtle enough that it probably wouldn't hold up in court, but its there."

"What's his play? How's he tied up in this?"

"Apparently the French president's family had ties to a group called La Fin des Temps, a socialist cult created shortly after the end of World War II. The groups' unifying goal was, apparently, to usher in the end of the world."

"Of course it was." Woodley shook his head. "Why can't people just be happy when they get rich and powerful?"

CHAPTER TWENTY-ONE

"Jack, is this some kind of joke?"

"Mr. President, I can assure you that if I wanted to tickle your funnybone I would use a different tactic."

President Hathaway rocked back in his chair in the Oval Office. "A secret cult has possession of the two suitcase nukes the Russians lost thirty years ago. *And* the President of France is in on it. *And* he's part of a weird French cult of post-Nazis that want to setup up their own one-world government with Paris as the seat of power." Price was silent. "Do you have any idea how insane that sounds?"

"Yes, Mr. President," Price said deliberately, "I do. But how may insane things do you have come across your desk on a daily basis that not only require your attention but also your direct action?"

"I concede your point."

"I take no pleasure in being right, sir."

"The hell you don't," POTUS said. "What do we have that's actionable?"

"We have boots on the ground in Paris that are moving in on the suspected location of one of the nukes. I would like to have one of our NEST teams work with MI-6 and SAS on it, as they have been extremely helpful in partnering with us on this operation. We also believe that the other nuke is indeed on U.S. soil.

Hathaway cursed. "Do we have any idea where?"

"We've ruled out the obvious choices—New York, Washington, Chicago, L.A. We have reason to believe it may be out west, specifically Las Vegas, but we've not received solid confirmation on that. We have teams that are ready to deploy at a moment's notice anywhere in the country."

"Why Vegas?"

"Lots of tourists, including internationals. Much lower security at street level than some of the other options. And there's a great big Eiffel Tower replica there."

POTUS nodded. "There's that. So why would they want to set off a nuclear device in the capital of their potential one-world government?"

"In order to generate sympathy. If they are trying to make up for the mistakes of the past, offering an olive branch to the U.S. and all of their allies they alienated with the whole BEAR Pharmaceuticals incident, and then they're attacked? Russia could easily be made to be the scapegoat, as though they're trying to take advantage of a perceived weakness on the part of both the U.S. and France."

"And the U.S. would lose face because we didn't stop it."

"Our capabilities are certainly much greater than France's, and the whole world saw it last year."

"And people would really think we would allow an attack on our own soil just to let France take a hit?"

"Mr. President, I'm sure you're well aware of the conspiracy theories regarding the office of the President and Pearl Harbor? Or, more recently, 9/11? Is there really any limit to what people will believe?"

"Yes," POTUS said, "it appears they won't believe the truth."

"Then, Mr. President, it's up to us to make sure the truth is what sets us all free."

. . .

"Of course it's hot, you dump truck. It's the desert. It's hotter than the hinges of hell out here."

FBI Special Agent Rick Obermeyer laughed at his boss, the scorching Nevada sun perched almost directly overhead. "I don't mean the air temperature. I'm talking about the chili on this hot dog. This baby is packing some heat!"

HRT Commander Bill Hall turned his head slowly to look at the man beside him. Obermeyer had been on the Hostage Rescue Team with Hall since he was placed in charge of the unit a handful of years ago, and they had been through quite a few hairy missions in that time. He was fairly certain they had not done anything riskier than eating at the roadside diner they were currently parked at. "How you could possibly be eating that thing when it's a billion degrees is beyond my scope of under-standing. You do know we're going to be outside doing drills the rest of the day in full gear?"

"Don't worry, Goat," Obermeyer replied, using the new call-sign Hall had been given. The Bureau had gone with static call-signs to make interagency operations easier, As was the norm, one's nickname was given out by their unit. "I'm sure they'll sit on my belly just fine."

"We named you 'Dually' for a reason, you know," Warren "Warcoach" Pitman offered up, wrinkling his nose. "'Stinky Diesel' took too long to say."

"He'll always be number two in my book," Carl Jenkins—"Legs"—interjected. The group laughed and made various motions of holding their nose or fanning the air away.

"Don't worry," Jerome Stanley said. "I made sure to pack plenty of Tums for Dually here." He patted the backpack with "Replay" stitched across a small patch.

"Well, you're riding in Sparks' Suburban, I can tell you that," Hall said, pointing to Jay Buck as he made his way from the SUV parked next to his own. The two black vehicles were covered in dust and had no visual cues that they were FBI vehicles, but they were just as obvious as if they had the Bureau's seal emblazoned down the sides.

"Hate to be the bearer of bad news, but lunch is over," Buck said as he approached. "We've got a priority call coming in at the training facility in 15."

"Alright girls," Hall said, "saddle up." He watched as Obermeyer crammed half of a chili dog into his mouth, chewed it three times, then swallowed. "For crying out loud, what is wrong with you?" He pointed at Pitman. "Hey! The trash compactor isn't riding with me."

"Sorry, Goat," Pitman said with a massive grin. "All the gear bags are scattered all over my 'Burb. No room," and he, Jenkins, and Buck sprinted for their truck.

Hall looked at the smiling Obermeyer, then at Stanley. "Well," he said as they headed for their truck, "at least you've got some Tums."

Special Agent Dan Sloane was used to hectic. It had defined his life for the better part of 15 years, from his entry into the United States Marine Corps and up through the ranks in MARSOC. When he joined the FBI he assumed, like many, it would be a much more laid-back schedule. There were certain to be long nights, and the inevitable transfer to a Division one didn't really want, but at least an agent would be home with his family more than a MARSOC operator would. Such was the case until Sloane joined the Bureau's elite Hazardous Device Response Unit. The HDRU was tasked with dealing with improvised explosive devices anywhere in the United States within two hours or less. They weren't called in for pipe bombs or things that local agencies could handle. If the HDRU was called out, it meant a very big explosion was about to happen and their unit was needed to prevent that from happening. Sloane's job in MARSOC had made him a natural candidate. When the Bureau asked him if he was interested, he jumped at the chance. He had done extremely well in training, and within three years had made commander of the unit. His knowledge of Special Operations logistics put him ahead of the game, and his knowledge of IEDs and conventional high explosives—including nuclear weapons—made him the clear choice. The logistics experience was more helpful than he had initially realized. For obvious reasons the HDRU had vast amounts of resources available to them, including numerous aircraft and teams on standby 24/7. It meant his wife didn't have her Special Agent husband around much more than when he was MARSOC, but at least he wasn't deploying to some desolate corner of the planet for months at a time. Hectic followed him, however, and familiar or not, it was no less stressful.

"The Vice President is about to go wheels up in Paris, but we've got resources on the ground there," Alan Fisk, the Director of the Secret Service's Technical Security Division said. "I'll have them on standby to assist in any way they can. They've got a lot of toys if you need them." As the name suggested, Technical Security Division was tasked with all of the technological logistics of the protective responsibilities of the Secret Service. Anywhere the POTUS, the Vice President, or anyone else under their protection went, they had assets available that bordered on science fiction. Fisk's experience as a Tier 1 operator in the Army provided for not only operational knowledge but connections as well. An excellent relationship with the Directorate of Science and Technology over at CIA also helped to ensure that they were on the bleeding edge of what everyone was working on, technologically speaking.

"I really appreciate it, Alan," Sloane said. "I'll ping you back as soon as I know what we need." He ended the call and switched to another. "Sorry, Martie, are you still there?"

"I am," Dr. Martie Guest replied. Guest was the Director of the Nuclear Emergency Support Team team based out of Los Alamos. "We've got Search and JTOT teams spinning up, but we need to know where to send them."

"We need sweeps of the Vegas metro area, and Paris as well."

"That's not helping me, Dan," Guest said worriedly. "Those suitcase nukes don't give off wide-ranging rads like a bigger unit would, or even a leaky small unit. Rumor has always been that the reason no one has been able to track them was because the Soviets had really packaged them well."

"I don't have anything more specific yet, but we've got boots on the ground working it. I've got my HDRU ready to go here in 30. State says some of our boys are already making their way into Paris, with SAS running blocker as needed."

"I'll have the Search teams try to divide and conquer, but this is going to be a needle in a haystack until we get some more specific intel," Guest said. "If this winds up being them, it will definitely be nice to finally get those little noisemakers off the table. They've been making DOE brass sweat for a lot of years."

"Everybody that knows about the suitcase nukes has been sweating, but if this is them, then we'll take them out of play."

"We'd better," Guest said, "or we'll all be looking for new jobs."

Sloane scoffed. "If these things go off, our jobs will be the least of our problems."

CHAPTER TWENTY-TWO

Sam had grabbed the key for the Ducati motorcycle stashed half a block away from her secondary apartment as she walked out. Dressed in cargo pants, an insulated sweatshirt, black leather jacket, and the blacked-out helmet, she made her way to the bike's provisional resting place. She had temporarily abandoned the first dwelling and left the Porsche parked there. She knew it was almost impossible that anyone would have associated her with her primary apartment, but it was always a good idea to have a backup plan, and she always had several. Like the other dwelling, this apartment was on the top floor of a building bunched in with a cluster of virtually identical brick structures well over a century old. The buildings were built so close together that they almost touched, mating up against newer buildings that had replaced old structures torn down to make way for the inevitable march of progress. Hers was equipped for a quick escape thanks to an antique fire ladder, although it likely wouldn't be flames that would drive her out. One never knew, though, and Samantha Land had earned a reputation for being as prepared as anyone in her position could be.

The apartment was leased out under another name and was in turn one of several secret United States government holdings carefully protected, thanks to the wiles and creativity of the wizards back at Langley. Each of the safehouses were under the name of French citizens with complete histories, and Land knew all of them by memory. If questioned, she could adopt the identity of the lessee without missing a beat, explaining that she was a young woman who had inherited some money and was busily traveling the world, thus explaining why she might not be seen for extended periods of time. Her neighbors in the building weren't really a problem, as they all likely had something to hide as well, and therefore wished no attention brought to them or anyone else in the immediate area.

As she mounted the Ducati motorcycle, she mentally rewound the surveillance footage of the areas around both residences. She learned long ago that a few well-placed remote cameras provided extremely useful intel on the areas around a safehouse. She had been watching the comings and goings of people in both neighborhoods each night while she had been in Paris, and had memorized the movements and mannerisms of the regulars in her immediate area. She noticed a conspicuous absence of police at both locations.

What had really drawn her attention was a dark four-door sedan carrying four men. The past two evenings—after the botched Surmonter Op—the vehicle would travel across several blocks, depositing its passengers in the neighborhood. The four men had walked the same route both nights, trying to look around without being noticed. They hadn't found her, of course, and there was no way to be certain they were even looking for her. Paris was a large city, and there were certainly many people doing things others would want to stop. But she also knew that she was playing a dangerous game, and it was always safest to assume someone was watching.

Working under that assumption, she wondered how they had been able to zero in on her location. She was extremely careful, and Paris was indeed a big place. Someone would have had to clue them in, but who? Chapman wouldn't sell her out, she was quite sure of that, nor would Duncan. If the men who had been captured had been made to talk, they wouldn't have known where to tell anyone to look. No one else outside the 7th floor at Langley would know her location—either of them—so the list of potentials was very short.

She had watched as the two men she could see from her viewpoint wandered, trying to look interested in things in order to mask their what they were *really* searching for. She couldn't be absolutely certain they were searching for her, of course, but the fact that they were in this neighborhood for the last two nights told her that something was likely afoot. *Amateurs*, she thought. *If they had any idea of what they were doing they'd change it up a bit*. She couldn't complain, however, because it made the situation much easier on her. The whole thing reminded her of playing her father's old Pac-Man arcade unit when she was a kid, memorizing the patterns of the ghosts and allowing the yellow video game character to gobble the dots unmolested. The manager of the skating rink used to get angry with her because she could play the machine for an hour on one quarter. The comparison had amused her greatly. She had given several of the guards' names, as best as she could remember, that the ghosts in Pac-Man were called. It made it easier to keep track of their quirks that way.

The two men she had watched work the area around her first apartment she called "Pinky" and "Blinky". "Pinky" was the shortest of the four and had an unusually pinkish tone to his skin. "Blinky" acted as if he either wore contacts or had allergies, because he was always fidgeting with his eyes. The other two men, currently out of sight, were "Inky" and "Boo". "Inky" apparently spent a great deal of time outdoors as he had a dark tan, along with black hair and a black mustache. "Boo" was jumpy, always swinging his head around as if someone were right behind him. "Inky" mocked him for his jumpiness, and "Boo" would proceed to say hurtful things about the other man's heritage. She couldn't be sure they were looking for her, but they were clearly looking for someone, and they clearly had ill intentions for whoever it was.

It was at that moment that Sam realized a dark colored sedan had made the same last two turns she had. She tapped a control on the side of her helmet and the rear-facing camera zoomed in on the driver and passenger.

Inky and Boo unknowingly stared right into her camera.

How did they find me? was her first thought, then she began processing options. Although clumsily obvious and certainly not clandestine service veterans, they were no less a threat. She had given them all cutesy names, but she knew that they were dangerous and would kill her on a moment's notice if they were able to locate her. She also had no question in her mind that she could, and would, kill each one by whatever means necessary if she had to. She instinctively reached for her pistol. It was still there, in the concealment holster tucked in the front of her waistband. She had three additional magazines for the weapon, each holding Teflon-coated rounds capable of penetrating body armor with ease. Counting the magazine in the weapon and the one round already in the firing chamber, that meant she could, under ideal conditions, stop 29 people from capturing her. Realistically, she would not be so lucky. The 9mm was a good round, and would certainly kill a person quite efficiently. It was, generally speaking, a one-shot wonder only if the round struck the head of the target. Otherwise, it could take several shots to sufficiently bleed a target as to make it drop. She preferred to simply outmaneuver her pursuers. It was best to avoid a firefight on the streets of Paris during the daytime if at all possible. She needed to escape, meet up with her team, complete their mission, and get out, not win the whole fight by herself. She thought of Leblanc and Morgan, wondered what these men had done to them, and wondered for a moment what they would do to her if she was captured.

. . .

"Shouldn't Sam have been here by now?" Hawkins asked impatiently.

"She's no doubt taking the scenic route," Benny Duncan said. "You know she's going to be watching out for a tail."

"Duncan's right," Chris Chapman said. "I sent her the dossier I'm about to share with you. She's probably reviewing it first before heading over. Which gives me time to go over it with you."

"We've chased some crazy stuff before, Chris," Woodley said, "but this sounds like something off one of those social media conspiracy videos that keep popping up in my message folder."

"What makes it worse is that this is all too real. Surmonter's origins are traced back to the same people who founded La Fin des Temps."

"'The end of time,'" Hawkins said. "Nice. Who are they and what do they want?"

"La Fin des Temps started out as a Protestant sub-culture in the French Underground Resistance during the Elaine days of Germany's takeover of France. As Hitler began to reveal more and more of his evil nature, the group began to focus heavily on the biblical book of Revelation and the end times. While they vigorously opposed Hitler and his Third Reich, they came to feel that his goals may not have been all that wrong."

"They were in the middle of a Nazi takeover, and they thought that maybe Hitler was right?" Woodley asked. "Sounds like the definition of 'insane' to me."

"It wasn't Hitler they agreed with," Chapman continued. "Their philosophy shifted, and they came to believe that the world would be best served by a one world government led by someone like the Anti-Christ figure from the Bible."

"They definitely were not Biblical literalists," Hawkins said.

"That much is certain," Chapman replied. "While their origins were Protestant, they were increasingly secular. While they did not believe they would literally bring about the end of the world, they believed the only way to accomplish true victory, true human unity, would be to follow that model: establish a leader whom people would look up to, bring everyone together after a period of conflict, then destroy anyone who threatened the new order. The way to ensure this would be to bring forward a charismatic leader who could bring people to the table and then force everyone in line."

"This sounds like how every totalitarian government starts," Woodley said. "What made them think they would be any different from Hitler, Mussolini, Stalin, or any other despot throughout history?"

"Ego," Chapman replied. "What else? After the war's end, several families formally started working toward this end. They recovered a significant portion of the wealth Hitler and his cronies stole and hoarded it together, forming Surmonter as a primary company in 1948. They also started nearly two dozen companies over the next two years, apparently for no other reason than to have shell corporations through which they could move money around. Beginning in the early 1950's, money started flowing from several of the wealthiest families involved into some sort of campaign slush fund. Each family raised up their own potential leader, and all of those involved would throw their full support behind the one who began to show the most promise."

"This is where our boy Paquet comes in," Woodley said. "I'm assuming his family had the winner."

"In more ways than one," Chapman said, trailing off momentarily before coming back into sharp focus. "But yes, Paquet apparently demonstrated the greatest aptitude, so the other families with potential candidates had to fall in line."

"Did they?" Hawkins asked.

There was a moment's hesitation on Chapman's part. "They did not."

"You know an awful lot about this group, Chris," Woodley said, "and this info doesn't sound like it's coming from a briefing at MI-6."

"That's a story for another time," Chapman said. "We have too much else to focus on at the moment."

"Fair enough," Hawkins said. "So why are we here? We know there's a lot of money involved. We know that there is a secret cabal working to put their leader in place to move toward a one-world government. France just seems like a strange place to launch that from."

"Perhaps this is why they're making a move to increase France's standing on the world stage. No better way to do that than look like they're the pitiable victim of international bullies."

"I'm assuming the U.S. plays that role."

"Possibly, but not necessarily. Remember, these are Russian weapons that are in play. If their plan is to use them, what if it's made to look as though Russia is making a move on the West?"

"Would anybody really buy that?" Woodley asked. Everyone in the room looked at him with raised eyebrows. "You're right," he conceded. "Forget I asked."

Chapman shrugged. "It is also quite possible that they have something else in mind entirely. With groups like this, motives are often difficult to ascertain for those on the outside looking in."

Hawkins leaned in. "I assume you're the one who put DNI Price on to this. So, what made you start digging?"

"A massive old church was purchased by one of the shell companies connected to La Fin des Temps a while back. It had been inactive for years, but there's been some activity there over the last few months. Satellite spectrum analysis of the area indicates nuclear material has been brought in and out, and there are indications that something may currently be present. We know the Russians had two small tactical nukes go missing shortly after the fall of the Soviet Union. Woodley and I were on several joint SAS/SEAL ops years ago trying to locate them."

"I thought there was speculation that they were just propaganda bogeymen used to flex the Soviet Union's muscles," Hawkins said.

"People in our COC certainly thought that," Woodley added.

"We *know* they're real," Chapman said with a finality that put any doubts to rest. "Somebody in Soviet command with access was offered a vast sum of money and the promise of silence, and two small nuclear devices vanished into the ether. My government, yours, and of course the Russians had been in a quiet race to find them ever since but had almost given up. The guy who sold them was eventually found—at least his remains were. He and his family died in a house fire in New Zealand nearly thirty years ago. The bombs, however, were not."

"Where did they go?"

"It was generally assumed that they were being hidden in a cave in Afghanistan or some other godforsaken part of the world. I actually suspected they might have been in Northern Ireland back in the early-90's. I had thought it to be a perfect weapon to be used in the conflict there at the time. Can you imagine one of those going off in London in 1993? Or Londonderry?" Chapman shook his head at the recollection. "I did my own searching then, but that didn't pan out."

Woodley nodded. "So, where do we go from here?"

"We wait for Samantha a little longer," Chapman said. "Traffic is notoriously aggressive this time of day."

CHAPTER TWENTY-THREE

Jean Leblanc awoke to what felt like hundreds of needles striking his bare skin. It took him a second to realize it was merely ice-cold water, then another couple of seconds for his mind to truly engage itself. He thought at first he must have a terrible head injury because all he could see was a bright spot, then realized that it actually *was* a light—a shop light of some kind, shining directly into his face. He tried to cover his face but realized that his arms were fastened above him in a "V" shape, and he was suspended from chains hanging from the ceiling. Most of the weight was on his arms as his feet barely touched the ground. He looked down and saw he still had on his web belt, trousers and his boots, but the pouches on his pants and belt were all open and empty. He had no shirt on, and the cool room was made more uncomfortable by the chilly water that soaked him. He saw a hint of movement, then a fist swung in and struck him on the jaw. His head snapped to the right, unprepared for the blow. Before he could recover, another blow struck him in the abdomen. He felt what was coming next but couldn't help himself—he vomited profusely. Another bucket of water splashed him.

"I don't want to get myself too messy," a voice said. It

seemed to come from far away and had a surprisingly pleasant British tone. "Do you think you can refrain from vomiting any more?"

"If you can quit punching me in the gut, I think we can come to an agreement, yes," the Frenchman replied.

"Very well, for the moment," the pleasant British voice said. Although it was pleasant, it had an oily quality to it. Jean thought for a moment that it was, perhaps, how the devil might sound. "Your friend over there has been particularly helpful." The silhouette looked to his left, and Leblanc could barely make out another figure.

"Morgan?" he asked, unable to hide the shock in his voice. Morgan had worked with him before on a number of ops, had even saved his life at least once. The betrayal was unfathomable. "You could...?"

"It's amazing how much more accommodating a person can be once you know what to offer them. Fortunately, he agreed to work with me once I learned what buttons to push." He paused for a moment. "I wonder, Mr. Leblanc—what button of yours do I need to push?"

Leblanc scoffed. "What do you want from me that the traitor wouldn't tell you?"

"I need you to...verify some information, as well as fill in some gaps. Mr. Morgan isn't fully aware of the names of all personnel involved. He identified you as the team lead, so it only stands to reason that, even in the compartmentalized world of the intelligence Community, that you would know all about your team. I would very much like for you to confirm that information with me."

"You seem to be a pretty smart person. I'm sure you could tell me more than I could tell you."

Jean heard the sound of metal against metal, and the shape of a man approached him, silhouetted by the bright light. The figure looked all the more devilish in silhouette, a slim form that moved like liquid poured across a smooth surface. He held up a shadowed hand, and Jean could recognize the outline of a surgical scalpel.

"You're too kind," the voice said. He stood, unmoving, for a moment. "I'm ready to move on to some new things." The form began moving in the darkness, just out of sight, like a shark sizing up its prey. "I need to be certain I'm properly tidying up loose ends, and there are still a few floating around out there. Oh, don't worry. I know who most of them are, and will be taking care of them in short order. But I am a man who prefers certainties. Now, tell me who you're working with."

"Certainly," Leblanc said calmly. "The Russian mafia."

The devil chuckled, then made a "tsk"-ing sound. "I can see I'm going to have to get myself messy after all."

Bill Hall and his HRT team sat in the darkened room waiting for the meeting to start. The HDRU team was with them, and they were small-talking while waiting for Sloane to come in and get things started. They had been doing some cross-training exercises together at the Nevada training facility for the last few days and had already made connections. Several of them had worked together before, which always went a long way toward building new relationships in the tight knit community of quiet professionals. They were all extremely competitive and loved to brag about their accomplishments, but a large portion of this week had been about working together. There was no doubt each team had their strengths, and would be better suited to certain tasks, but each team would benefit from learning some of the finer points of the others' specialty. When Sloane walked in, the room fell silent.

"Alright people, here's what we've got. Word's come down that we have a tactical nuclear device in our AO. This is not a drill, ladies. This is the real thing."

A couple of whispered curses wafted through the room, along with a whistle. Hall spoke up. "Do we have a solid lock on it?

What's the nature of the device? Do we know who's got it? What the layers of defense are?"

"NEST Search is working the Vegas metro area right now. Word is it's one of the missing suitcase nukes the Soviets developed in the late 80's. We believe it's been put in play by a group of relative unknowns affiliated with the current French president seeking to create instability among the U.S. and its allies. They have deep pockets and have already demonstrated their ability to have high-bend hardware and the personnel to use it. A NOC team sent in to investigate in Paris was compromised. These weren't rookies, either. They're all seasoned intelligence operatives."

"So, we've also got a leak somewhere," one of the HDRU agents said.

"Safe to assume that," Sloane responded. "JTOT is rolling, but they're going to need some help covering ground. We've got a big area to watch and an uncertain timeframe, so we're going to divide and conquer. Bill, I'd like to split our squads half-and-half. That way if one teams rolls up on it first, we've got device experts on it."

Hall nodded. "I'm good with that. Obermeyer, Jenkins, you guys are with me. Pitman, Stanley and Buck are with Sloane."

Sloane nodded his agreement. "My team will take North Las Vegas out to Red Rock; your team will cover the south around Spring Valley and Paradise. We're action ready in fifteen."

Samantha Land looked again in her display at the men in the vehicle a couple of cars behind her in traffic. She was not one to lack confidence in her abilities. She had years of training and experience, and had been in a number of very sticky situations. She had not, however, been caught. She also had not been in a situation of this magnitude without any way of contacting backup. It occurred to her that it didn't make for a good potential outcome.

That last thought didn't stay long. If you thought you were going to get caught, you probably were. It was a waste of time and energy to worry. All one could do was prepare to the best of one's abilities and hope that when all hell broke loose that it went your way. And she planned on making sure that was exactly what happened. She squeezed the clutch, dropped a gear, and twisted the throttle. The Ducati reared back like an angry stallion and ripped through an opening in traffic. She could see the car behind blocked in by traffic. They didn't look concerned, which concerned her.

A moment later she knew why. Two motorcycles roared out into traffic in pursuit. She assumed it was likely the other two men she had seen. They knew she was on a bike, and they were prepared. The first two just flushed her out. Maybe they were better than she thought. She thought about calling for assistance from Chapman, and therefore Hawkins, but decided against it. She was more than capable of taking care of these four herself. All she had to do was outrun them. She was confident they wouldn't want to draw attention by shooting in broad daylight any more than she would. Several hard strikes against her back proved her wrong. Her armored jacket and helmet kept several rounds from punching holes in her head and back. Sam took a hard left directly in front of traffic and ripped down a narrow side street. She locked the rear brake and spun the bike back in the direction from which she had come. When her two pursuers rounded the corner, she drew her pistol and fired two shots each directly into the visors of their helmets. Both men flew backwards off the bikes and hit the ground like leather covered sacks, their bikes sputtering away and flipping onto the sidewalk.

As she holstered the pistol and started to ride away several more shots struck her on the side of her helmet and right side, knocking her off the bike. The sedan was unable to get through traffic, so the men had left and were pursuing her on foot. They were closing fast. She drew her pistol and fired off three shots. She knew she wouldn't hit them, but she counted on them slowing down enough for her to get to her feet. She tried activating the phone built into her helmet but quickly realize the bullet impacts had spider-webbed the visor and damaged the electronics. There was no help to be had from Langley, and no way to call for backup. She was on her own. She was already sore from the shots she had taken, even with her armor, which told her they were likely using .45 caliber rounds with a lot of kinetic energy.

Sam fired another shot, swapped mags, and sprinted across the street into an alley that led between two hotels. As she ran a metal pipe swung from a doorway and struck right on the helmet's visor. The impact knocked Sam off her feet and onto her back, her pistol clattering away. She was thoroughly dazed by the impact, and almost lost consciousness before willing herself back. She looked through the shattered visor and saw a man she didn't recognize reaching down for her. He looked up and called out in French, indicating that he had her. She took the moment of distraction to drive her fist into his throat. The man stumbled back, desperately struggling to breathe. She rolled to her side and removed her shattered helmet as she stood, pressed a hidden stud inside, and stuffed it on the man's head. It immediacy burst into flames, destroying any evidence of its true capabilities, and sending the man to the ground flailing wildly. As she turned to find her pursuers a fist struck her hard in the abdomen, doubling her over, then what must have been the butt of a gun struck the back of her head. She stumbled against a dumpster, striking her knee on her way to the ground. She looked up in time to see a foot rushing toward her face before darkness claimed her.

Jean Leblanc was in a bad spot. The French spy's head hung, his chin touching his chest. It had taken a while, but he had finally started screaming in spite of himself. Blood and sweat covered the man's upper body, and his head rolled back, looking toward the ceiling. A sound like a sigh escaped from him as he shifted slightly against his bonds.

Leblanc's inquisitor stood beside him, almost peacefully. The source of his suffering had never raised his voice during the questioning, but let his fists, scalpel, and various other tools and instruments convey his displeasure with the French intelligence operative. Leblanc tried to focus his eyes, but he could feel them crossing against his will. Actually, *eye* was more accurate. He couldn't see anything out of his left eye any longer. It hurt badly, and seemed to be swollen shut, but he wasn't entirely sure his left eye even remained any longer.

What stung as badly as any of the physical wounds was the betrayal of Wally Morgan. During the torture and interrogation, he heard the silhouette tell Morgan to initiate the clean-up, followed by what must have been the sound of Morgan walking away. Leblanc struggled to make his pain-addled brain work through it. He could not believe a Quiet Professional would sell out. How had this man gotten to Morgan? Maybe he really was the devil.

Still, if he could only get a moment to catch his breath, to get a brief respite. He was a trained intelligence officer and had been instructed in ways to resist interrogation. If he could just hold out until the man gave up, even briefly, he could find a way out. There was *always* a way out.

The devil chuckled, then Leblanc noticed he couldn't hear the other man because someone was screaming. It took a moment before he realized it was his own throat making the sound. He knew there was excruciating pain, but he could no longer determine the cause of it, or even specifically what hurt. His entire world was nothing but jagged sharpness and blunt impacts. One last blow to the jaw seemed to clear his head for a moment, snapping him back to reality from the nightmare dreamworld he was floating in. He felt something in his mouth, like pieces of hard candy, and spit, then realized that several of his teeth were now on the floor. He almost thought that was funny.

"While this is certainly a great deal of fun," the devil said, "I'm starting to get fatigued. Let's try one more time, and we'll be all finished here." He leaned close to the Frenchman, who reeked of sweat and other body odors. "Who dispatched your team? What do you know about Surmonter? What are the names of the others we should be looking for?"

Leblanc's head seemed as if it were almost disconnected from his neck, rolling from side to side. "The Tooth Fairy sent us," he tried to say, the words almost indecipherable through his broken teeth and shattered jaw. He sounded in his own head as if someone else were speaking. Leblanc found the disconnect both shocking and comforting. "And you must find Santa Claus. He's the one calling the shots."

The devil in silhouette made no sound at all. Throughout his interrogation, Leblanc had heard the man chuckle, grunt, breathe, swear. But the sound that unsettled him the most was the lack of it.

"Then I suppose we are finished," the voice finally said, and the silhouetted figure stepped behind the light. There was a metal on metal sound again, and the figure soon reappeared. Leblanc could not get his eye focused well, but he could tell that the man was now holding a pistol. His tormentor raised the suppressed weapon until the barrel was aimed directly at the bridge of Leblanc's shattered nose. "Anything else you'd like to add?"

Leblanc spit on him, or at least tried. He thought a tooth hit, but he was sure some blood did. "Viva la France."

The devil smiled. "Not for long," he said, and squeezed the trigger.

CHAPTER TWENTY-FOUR

"I look forward to the day I never have to walk into a strip club again," Mike Rhodes said as he adjusted the South Carolina Gamecocks cap on his head.

That elicited a grunted chuckle from his partner. "I never thought I'd hear those words come from your lips," Logan Nash said. The two DEA agents were walking into the club where Luna Roberts, their confidential informer, was working. It was just before the lunchtime rush, when guys would take advantage of the all-you-can-eat buffet while they watched the show on stage. Luna had texted Nash that she thought the driver who worked the night Cheevers had been murdered had walked in the door, and within 10 minutes the agents were walking inside.

"Come on, man," Rhodes said. "You know exactly what I mean." Nash indeed knew, all too well—both men attended the same church every Sunday. It was a larger church, so there was a certain degree of anonymity afforded them, and even drug dealers went to church. These men pretended to be among the worst humanity had to offer, their undercover work an all too necessary part of their job duties. But the reality was they were simply playing roles, often forced to go completely against the direction of their own moral and spiritual compasses. Nash had wrestled with that issue many times, and finally settled on the fact that it was all for the greater good. It didn't make what they had to do any easier most of the time, but it did help them to sleep at night.

"Yeah, yeah," Nash replied. "Come on, let's see if this is our boy." He was suddenly aware that there was no one working security at the front door, and there was no one at the admission window either. The music was blasting, the subwoofers rattling the walls, but there were no human sounds. As they entered the main part of the club they saw why. The security guard was lying face up on the floor, his head twisted at an awkward angle. Half a dozen men lay sprawled across tables, on the floor, one bent over backwards across the edge of the stage. The girls were nowhere in sight. Both men drew their weapons. Nash motioned towards the backstage area, and they moved quickly towards the curtained entrance. As the agents drew closer, they could hear the sounds of someone banging on a door and shouting. Nash peeked through the curtain and saw their target: every bit of 6 and half feet, 350 pounds of angry assassin was pounding on the door to the dressing room, demanding to be let in or he'd kill them all. Nash watched the man drop his shoulder and ram the door. It was clear it wouldn't take many more hits before it gave way, and then he would be in the middle of several agitated females.

"Federal agents!" Nash shouted. "Don't move," and called the man a colorful metaphor.

The man turned and looked at the two agents. He smiled, drew a pistol faster than Nash had ever seen, and fired.

Donald Molson was leaving his office for the day a full two hours earlier than usual. He rarely made it home before 7:00 most weekdays, but he was going to be well ahead of schedule today. He had made reservations at his wife's favorite restaurant for her birthday, no small task as it was generally booked 6 months in advance. He had forgotten to make the reservation early enough, but was able to pull some strings and get a table overlooking the Eiffel Tower. He owed a favor in return now, but that was how so much of the world he lived in worked.

As Molson walked out of the secured elevator into the parking garage and saw his driver had pulled up farther than usual, the taillights glowing on the BMW 7-Series sedan as it idled quietly. As he wondered about the change in pickup location, his phone dinged. He saw immediately that it was Philippe Dupain, and it was one word: "DANGER." Molson immediately placed the phone back in his pocket, acting nonplussed by the message so as not to tip off anyone watching. If Dupain sent a message like that, then it was serious, and it was imminent. Molson took two more steps, then spun behind a concrete column for cover as two suppressed bullets clinked into the window of the vehicle he had just been standing next to. He reached into his waistband and drew his own weapon. He had no idea how many attackers there were, what their position was. But he knew he was all alone, with 30 rounds, and very little cover. He had been in some tough scrapes, but this one was going to be hairy.

It suddenly occurred to him how angry his wife would be if she found out she had missed dinner at her favorite restaurant because he had been shot.

"Bad guys and churches," Benny Duncan said contemptuously. "What's the world coming to?"

"Some would say it's always been that way," Chris Chapman offered.

Mark Woodley chuckled without any real mirth. "Hawk, you're about to go two for two on terror plots involving churches. I think you're jinxed."

"I don't believe in luck, but if I did it would be running true to form," Hawkins replied. Woodley and Duncan were looking over a set of technical drawings of the old church, marking points of entry and possible locations for the device, while he and Chapman were looking at the loading screen on the computer before them. Within moments the faces of DNI Price and Assistant Director Shear blinked into view.

"Okay, here's the latest," Shear started. "We've got NEST teams mobilizing in the Las Vegas area trying to get a bead on device number 1. One of our teams was in the area for cross-training and is responding with them for overwatch. Director Price reallocated some assets to help with the search, but so far we're coming up empty."

Price spoke as if on cue. "A NEST team is heading to the church along with a joint team of SEALs and SAS. They're about to go wheels up from Hereford, so they're a little less than 90 minutes out. What's your status?"

"We're ready to head to the site, but we've been waiting on Sam," Hawkins said. "So far she's a no-show. Getting a little concerned."

"You know she's more than capable of taking care of herself," Price said confidently. "If she's not there, she has a good reason."

"We're leaving in five," Chapman interjected. "If Sam's not here, she'll know where to meet us."

"E.J. over at Langley is going to be running comms on our end," Shear said. "I'll have the team leads patch you into their comms when they're getting close. Keep us posted as to what you find onsite." Their faces disappeared from the screen.

Hawkins looked at the door, expecting Sam to walk through at any moment. When she didn't, that empty feeling in his chest returned. Price was right—she was more than capable of taking care of herself. Maybe she was leading someone off the trail, or maybe she decided to stay on overwatch until they arrived at the church.

Or maybe something bad had happened to her.

"You know she's the toughest one of all of us," Benny Duncan said as he worked the action on one of several MP5Ks not the kitchen counter. "If we don't get on it, she's gonna take it out of our hides."

Hawkins saw Chris Chapman looking at him, his head barely nodding in silent agreement. They were right, of course. They had a job to do, and the job always comes first. He chambered a round in his P226 pistol and tucked it into his belt holster.

"Let's get to work," he said.

CHAPTER TWENTY-FIVE

Sam awoke to the realization that she was freezing. It took her mind a moment to clear, to figure out where she was and what was happening. She prepared to stand, then realized she already was. Her wrists were bound over her head and attached to a cable that was hanging from the ceiling. Her feet touched the floor, but only barely. The room was dark, with only a work light aimed in her direction. The glare from the light made it impossible to see anything else around her, including how many people were in the room with her. She was sore everywhere, and tried to take a quick inventory of her injuries. She had the coppery taste of blood in her mouth and could feel it around one corner of her lips. Her jacket was gone, and her t-shirt was torn, but everything else seemed to be okay. It definitely wasn't as bad as it could have been. She gingerly moved and flexed each joint as much as possible to determine if any bones were broken, and so far she seemed solid.

As her eyes adjusted somewhat, Sam began to make out her surroundings a bit. She was in a long rectangular room with a tall ceiling, and she seemed to be located toward one end. There were tall windows evenly spaced out in the distance in front of her, covered but still allowing a small bit of light through. It suddenly dawned on her. She wasn't being held in an empty warehouse.

She was being held in a church.

"Glad you could join us," a voice said from the darkness just beyond the light. "I've been expecting you, even before I knew for sure that you were in Paris."

"Sorry I didn't make reservations," Land said, weaker sounding than she would have liked. Through her quickly clearing mental fog it seemed as though the voice was familiar.

"No bother at all. We always have room for a pretty lady," the voice said, and a man moved into the lit area. Sam's head cleared immediately when she saw who her captor was.

"Warrick."

It was like looking at a ghost. Seth Warrick, who had been an instrument of death to hundreds in the BEAR ordeal, was standing before her, alive. Mark Woodley had been confident that Warrick was dead, likely with a broken neck, but certainly drowned after he kicked him into the ocean while destroying the last of BEAR Pharmaceuticals battle virus.

And yet, here he was. He walked smoothly, almost gliding across the floor of the dusty cathedral. She noted Warrick looked even thinner than when she had last seen him, outside of Paris at BEAR headquarters. It seemed as if his skin had been shrink-wrapped over an armature of bone and muscle. In the stark, silhouetted light his deep-set eyes made him look like the Grim Reaper in a fashionable black suit.

The smile that seemed out of place crept once more across his skull-like visage. "Hello, Officer Land. So nice to see you again." He balled his right hand into a fist, pulled it back, and punched Sam in the jaw. She tried to roll with the hit, spinning her head back and to the right, but he still got a good shot in. She felt the blood begin trickling out from her lip and down her chin once more. "I am so glad you're here."

"Why Seth, I didn't even have the privilege of kicking your sorry bones into the Atlantic. Such hospitality..." Land was interrupted by Warrick punching her again, this time in the abdomen. He grabbed her hair roughly with his right hand and drew in close.

"Oh, I owe you a great deal, Officer Land," Warrick said, his voice a harsh whisper. His breath smelled of mint and brandy. "You killed the only thing in this world I cared for, my beloved Manon, in New Orleans. I never dreamed I would have such an opportunity as this, and I plan to exploit it to the fullest."

"The attempted rape of a teenage girl notwithstanding," Sam replied, "I'm sure Manon didn't have a problem with your extracurricular activities, especially since you were going to kill the girl's whole family anyway." The mention of the hit on Ra's al Xuffash and his attempted molestation of the girl infuriated him, but the fact that Land and Hawkins had almost caught him then made it even worse. She could see that Warrick was furious, and was fighting to maintain his composure. *Good*, she thought to herself. Emotions tended to push people to make bad decisions, and she could capitalize on that. *Let me see if I can keep pushing those buttons.*

Warrick was silent for a moment, quietly stuffing his rage back into whatever dark compartment in his soul usually held it. "You all made a grand effort to be sure, Officer Land, but ultimately a wasted one," he said, rubbing his knuckles. "Your government's effort to stop me is nothing more than the labor of fools unable to find their way home. They don't realize that they've already lost."

"If we've already lost, you could just let me go. I promise I won't break your neck."

"I have no reason to doubt you, of course," Warrick said sarcastically, and walked into the shadows. "No, I believe in the importance of protecting oneself, to be certain. I don't take any chances with my prisoners. I wouldn't want them stabbing me in the back when I wasn't looking." With that, something large was tossed in front of the light. It took a second for Land to realize what, or rather who, it was: Jean Leblanc, or at least she thought it was. He had been so savagely beaten and mutilated that he was almost unrecognizable. A single bullet hole just above the bridge of his nose told her how the end had come. The rest of his body told her the end didn't come quickly enough. She wanted to scream, not out of fear, but out of rage. She would not give Warrick the satisfaction, however, and maintained her composure perfectly.

"Your hospitality leaves something to be desired," she said.

Warrick stepped back into her line of sight and grinned, a mirthless expression. "Oh, you have no idea." He swept an arm around expressively. "I take it you've gotten a sense of where you are, my dear. Ironic how places of worship keep playing such pivotal roles in our lives, yes? It was in one, not unlike this, that I discovered my true purpose, my true calling in life. Like me, your FBI lover walked away for a more...martial lifestyle."

"You think far too much of yourself if you think you're in Hawkins' league," Sam said with a smirk.

Warrick cocked his head slightly. "Really? Well, he did shoot an unarmed man on the steps of a church in cold blood. Several times, actually."

"Only because he and your little sweetheart were planning on releasing a biological weapon that would kill thousands of innocent people."

"No one is innocent," he spat. "Particularly those who claim allegiance to God. Houses of worship are all nothing more than stockades for sheep and the wolves who prey upon them." He paused, tensing slightly. "The love of my life perished only a few blocks from one, and *your* love will find your broken body here." He closed his eyes for a moment, seeing another scene in his head. His eyes snapped open quickly enough that Sam was actually startled by it. "And break you I shall." Warrick looked her up and down, like a hungry lion about to pounce on its prey. "You are quite lovely to behold, Miss Land. So strong, yet so soft as well. You know I have quite the appreciation for the female form." He stepped in close. "I am going to take my time and treasure every moment with you." He traced along Sam's jawline from behind her ear and down her neck with the forefinger of his right hand. He wrapped his fingers around her neck and began to gently but firmly squeeze. "Oh, I won't use all of the same methods as I did with your friend here, but we both know I have my own way of doing things." Warrick's grin grew into a deaths-head smile. "I assure you that I intend to make sure your suffering far exceeds that of Manon's."

Sam put everything she had into maintaining her expression. She didn't want to lose consciousness again around this monster, and she didn't want him to have the thrill of seeing her struggle. Instead her eyes bored into his. Even as she felt them beginning to roll back and the edges of her vision started to darken, she would not give him the satisfaction of seeing her falter. She wasn't afraid. Her faith was the antidote to fear. And she would not let him win.

As she felt her consciousness start to slip Warrick tilted his head slightly. The smile scurried from his face like a snake scurrying away at a predator's approach. He released his hold on Sam's neck, clearly disappointed. His eyes narrowed slightly, as if he were trying to examine her more closely, to see what was going on in her head. He shook his head quickly, as if trying to shoo away a troublesome insect, and Land realized she had won this exchange.

Before Warrick could say anything, his phone beeped in his coat pocket. He removed it, looked at it, then looked back at Sam. A hint of concern clouded his expression momentarily, then faded just as quickly. "I would love to get started with you, but I have other things to attend to first. We will have our time together soon enough," Warrick said as he turned away. "I just wanted you know that it was me whom you had to look forward to playing with."

"Thanks," Sam said tersely, and Warrick walked back into the darkness. A heavy door slammed shut at the end of the chapel. She took a few breaths through her nose to help clear her head. She felt around her teeth with her tongue, making sure they were all in place. Satisfied that she wouldn't be needing dentures anytime soon, she began turning the situation over in her head.

As hard as it was to believe, Warrick was still alive—bad news, because *he* was bad news. She knew what he was capable of, and had no desire to still be hanging like a side of beef when he came back. The only reason he had left her alone now, she was certain, was to give her some time to think about it, to look at Leblanc's tortured body and to be filled with dread at the prospect of being at Warrick's mercy. That wasn't going to happen, of course. She was a highly-trained and experienced soldier and CIA Case Officer, and it would take more than a couple of punches and some mind games to intimidate her.

Sam looked away from the shop light and up at the steel cable that held her bound hands above her head. Giving her eyes a moment to adjust, she then visually followed the cable up into the darkness. The ceiling was about 20 feet high at its apex, with exposed ductwork crisscrossing the beams supporting the chapel ceiling. If she could get up there, it might be possible to use the ductwork to move about the church facility and find where Warrick had gone. And what he was up to.

She stretched her body enough to get the toes of her boots planted on the floor, taking some of the tension off her arms. She wiggled her hands and found that the cloth material binding her wrists was actually looser than she would have thought. The metal cable she was hanging from had been looped through the material, then tossed over one of the crossbeams near the ceiling and secured to a metal loop on the floor.

Sam wasn't sure how long she would be left alone, so it was clear that if she was going to act it would have to be now. She took a deep breath, then put all her weight back on her arms again. She felt the blow Warrick had given her abdomen as she began pulling at the material, trying to work it against the cable. She pressed up on her tiptoes again, then pulled her full weight down, rubbing the material against the metal. After a few minutes her legs began shaking from the effort. Her head hurt, from the hits as well as the exertion. She felt the material give a little and spared a glance up to see that it was beginning to fray in one spot. She shifted her hands to better position the weak point directly against the cable, stood on her toes, and pushed off in the best jump she could muster. She caught her full weight with her arms and the bonds tore. She grunted from the pain in her abdomen and left side as she found herself falling the rest of the way to the ground. She sat there for a moment and looked at the tatters of the burlap-type material that had bound her hands. She rubbed her wrists gingerly, noting that although they were red the skin had not been broken. Her watch was gone, so she had no idea of the time, of how long she had been here. That wasn't the most important thing in her life right now, however— escaping this place was.

The CIA officer wrapped the palms of her hands in the torn material as she stood. After taking a moment to assess her leg strength—no serious injuries other than a banged-up knee— Land walked toward the utility light pointed where she had been hanging. It was a simple spotlight attached to a tripod. She turned the lamp, shining it all around the area. She aimed the light upwards to confirm her earlier glimpse and saw that the ductwork looked large enough to accommodate her, and the supports looked substantial enough to support her weight. *Spent a lot of time crawling through ducts lately*, she mused. *But this just might work.*

She turned the light to shine at eye level of anyone who opened the door—the glare would distract them and give her a couple of extra seconds to respond—then walked back to the cable. Her hands wrapped in the burlap, she grabbed onto the cable she had been dangling from and began climbing. She was about ten feet off the ground when she almost had to use her legs to climb, then found her second wind and pulled herself up onto the crossbeam that the cable was draped over. She dropped the cable back over the beam to where it had been hanging, then shimmied across the beam until she reached a vent in the duct-work. She pulled the vent cover off, clambered inside, then lifted the vent back into place.

CHAPTER TWENTY-SIX

Nash and Rhodes dove for cover as the big man fired off what must have been a full magazine in their direction. When the slide locked back, it took the shooter a second to react. Nash and Rhodes both returned fire as the man spun behind a corner wall. Rhodes spared a look at his partner.

"You know we need this guy alive, Logan."

Nash sighed. "Federal agents!" he shouted. "Come out with your hands up or we *will* shoot you!" There was silence for a moment, then the man tossed the gun out ahead of him, slide still locked open. He slowly stepped around the corner with both hands held high, making him look even larger. Nash and Rhodes were less than 6 feet tall, and although they were both stocky and muscular the man walking down the hallway towards them seemed like a giant. He was every bit of 6' 8", fair skinned with a buzz cut. Nash thought that the guy looked like every Russian strong man he had ever seen in a movie.

"You stop right where you are, Sasquatch!" Rhodes called out. "Turn around and back up toward the sound of my voice!" The man complied, and Rhodes holstered his pistol and readied his cuffs while Nash kept his pistol aimed at the center of the man's back. The girls were still making a lot of noise in the dressing room. Logan looked to the door and was about to call out to them when the big man spun, grabbed Rhodes, and tossed him into his partner, sending both agents tumbling to the floor. Nash's head hit the floor hard enough that he saw stars for a few seconds. Rhodes jumped to his feet and drew his pistol, but the assassin grabbed the gun from his hand and tossed it across the club. Rhodes was so shocked his eyes followed the gun instead of the man's fist, which landed solidly across his jaw and sent him sprawling. Nash took advantage of the moment and sprung towards the taller man, using the momentum to carry them out of the hallway and into the club proper. The larger man tried to get a grip on Nash, but the agent kept him off balance until the both tumbled over an upturned table. The assassin was fast for a man of his size, and was on his feet as quickly as the DEA agent. Nash ducked beneath a right hook, then caught the big man with a stiff left jab just below where his right ear met his jaw. The giant stumbled, and Nash followed with a fast combo to his body ending with an uppercut. The man's head rocked back, then he sprung forward and grabbed Nash. It seems like he used the DEA agent to steady himself for a moment before lifting him off the ground and tossing him like a father throws his child in a swimming pool. Nash crashed onto the top of the bar and rolled behind the counter onto the floor. He could hear his attacker moving toward the bar, pushing furniture out of the way. Nash looked on the floor beside him and noticed a whiskey bottle that managed to fall from the top shelf yet had not shattered on the floor. He grabbed the bottle like a football and popped up from behind the bar like a quarterback under pressure looking for a receiver. He found his target, and threw the heavy bottle as hard as he could at the charging giant. Still groggy from Nash's punches, the heavy decanter landed right on the man's nose with a sickening crunch, and the man folded like an old cardboard cutout. As he went down, Rhodes came running out of the hall-way. "Logan, are you alright?"

"I'm fine," he answered, wiping his palm across his forehead and realizing it was blood and not sweat. "No thanks to you. Once again, I do all the heavy lifting." He knelt down beside the fallen assassin and cuffed him. "You okay?"

"For a big guy, he sure doesn't know how to throw a punch. Hits like he plays for Clemson. Must have been a wrestler."

"Glass jaw, for sure. Toss me your cuffs, too. I'm going to hook up his ankles for good measure." Rhodes tossed the bracelets to his partner, who quickly fastened them. "Go check on the girls."

"Right. You good over there?"

Nash sat down on the floor, drew the Glock 30 from his ankle holster and pointed it at the man. "Yeah. I'm done dancing for tonight."

Donald Molson hadn't drawn his weapon outside of a training facility in years. He had always requalified easily—he was a natural shot—but the LEGAT still made the most of every opportunity to send some lead down range with other agents. Shooting had always been something of a relaxing pastime for him. The situation in which he currently found himself, however, did not elicit the same feelings. He was in a parking garage with at least one well-equipped shooter, using a suppressed weapon. If Molson hadn't listened to his inner voice he would have been standing exactly where the first two shots hit, and his dead body would now be bleeding out on the garage deck. But he had, and he wasn't, and now he had a chance. From his cover behind the concrete column, Molson used the windows of the two parked vehicles closest to him to get a survey of the area. He took note once more of his BMW idling, and was sure that his driver had been killed. The only vehicles in sight other than his own ride was the Fiat Ducato van next to him that took the bullets intended for him, a Volkswagen sedan, and a Mercedes station wagon parked against the far wall. The only place the shooter could be was behind the Mercedes station wagon.

As if in response, suppressed shots coughed from behind the wagon on the driver's side. Molson, pivoted lightly, then recoiled as shots also erupted from the rear of the Mercedes on the passenger side as well. *Two shooters,* he thought. *That makes this a little more difficult.* He was trapped behind the column, with two shooters drawing a bead on him. If he moved to the van, he would be in a worse position—they could shoot his ankles and feet beneath the raised work vehicle. He knew they would have to act quickly before someone discovered what was happening and sent support for him, so he assumed one shooter would likely keep him pinned down while the other tried to flank him.

Before he could decide on his next course of action, several unsuppressed shots rang out in the garage from the ramp in front of the idling BMW. It was silent for a few moments before a familiar voice called out.

"Donald!" Philippe Dupain shouted. "Are you still alive, my friend?"

Molson risked a peek and saw blood spatter on the wall behind where the shooters has taken up position. "Philippe, I've never been so glad to hear your voice." He saw Dupain checking the driver of the BMW, then motioning for him to hurry.

"Even when I'm offering to buy drinks?" The Frenchman said with a grin.

"As hard it may be to believe, yes." Molson glanced at his driver and saw him slumped against the steering wheel. "I assume there's more shooters topside. Do you have an extraction plan?"

"I took care of the other two gunmen who stopped by my office for a visit," Dupain said as they started up the garage ramp. "And yes, I have a work van that should keep us reasonably unnoticed for the time being. A bit ignominious, to be sure, but at least we will blend in."

"Two middle-aged men in suits carrying guns riding around in a work van," Molson said. "The very picture of 'blending in.'"

"The van is armored, has comms equipment, and lots of guns," Dupain offered.

Molson raised his eyebrows. "My kinda van," he said as they sprinted up the ramp.

CHAPTER TWENTY-SEVEN

It occurred to Sam that she had no idea where she was. She knew she was in a church, almost certainly the one Surmonter was using as the staging area for their planned nuke attack. She knew Seth Warrick was alive somehow and was running this operation. She knew that Leblanc was dead, and that meant Wally Duncan was most likely dead as well. She was crawling through the ductwork in almost pitch darkness, the only light being the slight glow emanating from the occasional vent. She closed her eyes and listened for sounds, voices, anything that might tell her which way to go. She heard the faint sounds of people talking, so she slowly made her way toward them.

A cold chill shot through her unbidden. There weren't many things that could unsettle the experienced soldier and clandestine service officer, but the sight of Seth Warrick had made her blood run cold. She shuddered at the thought of being tied up in his presence, and made a vow that would not happen again. She wasn't sure what made her skin crawl so badly at even the thought of Warrick. She thought it was almost like seeing a ghost, but it occurred to her that he seemed to be something far worse.

She crawled in the direction of the voices until the duct grew brighter. Lights shone through the vents in front of her, confirming the room was occupied by the ones doing the talking. She took a deep breath as she recognized the eerie calm of Warrick's voice. She listened carefully to hear what he was saying.

"So was the team able to get Molson?" Warrick asked. A moment of silence. "Then that means the hit team is dead. It's likely his friend in your administration came to his aid." Who was he talking about? "I have nothing to do with that. I have been tasked with ensuring the delivery of the weapon and its detonation at the appropriate time and place. I don't have time to babysit politicians." Sam could almost hear the shouting on the other end of the call. "Then take it up with your superiors. I have my own responsibilities to fulfill, Mr. Paquet, as do you. The clock is ticking. I suggest we get back to work."

Paquet? Warrick was speaking on the phone with the French President. Sam knew that her first priority was to make sure she lived long enough to pass on that bit of information.

Warrick continued talking. "Regardless of your feelings on the matter, it is time for you to leave Paris. The big moment is coming quickly, and we want to make sure you are safely away when that happens. Although the weapon is only a small tactical device, I'm confident the yield is sufficient to destroy a significant section of the city, as well as rendering it unlivable for some time due to radiation. Not to mention the unknown extent of an electromagnetic pulse." Warrick listened while Paquet spoke. "Yes, the team is in place in Las Vegas. We have made certain that there will be sufficient evidence to point in the appropriate direction to move the plan forward. Now, if you would, be so kind, please get on your plane. Thank you, Mr. President," Warrick said sarcastically, then ended the call. "Pompous fool. A little money and power and he thinks he actually knows something about how the world works."

A man laughed without any trace of humor. "Is he as bad as Matheson was?" He said in a thick English accent. Sam was completely taken aback—was that Wally Duncan? She edged closer to the vent to get a look. She spotted Warrick and two other men standing next to a desk in the center of the room. The man who had just spoken was seated in a chair in front of the desk, smoking a cigar and drinking a glass of what appeared to be whiskey. Sure enough, there sat her former "teammate," alive and well. He had been working with Warrick and his fellow conspirators the whole time. She reeled for a moment at the thought that one of the conspirators was the President of France. How in the world would they be able to stop this? She realized that the priority were the nukes, but Price needed to know about Paquet's treachery.

"I'm not sure anyone could be as annoying as that worm was," Warrick replied. He was so pathetic. I regret I didn't have the opportunity to kill him myself. Yet another thing I hold Agent Hawkins responsible for." Warrick paused and cocked his head slightly, as if a thought had occurred to him. "And yet another thing Officer Land will suffer for."

Duncan chuckled again. "I'd be glad to help with that if you'd like," he offered.

"No no," Warrick replied. "I'm afraid Officer Land is a treasure I shall most definitely keep to myself."

It was at that moment that Sam's abdomen suddenly spasmed, a result from the blows she endured only a short time before. The sudden pain caused her to shift slightly in the duct, which let out a metallic creak. Warrick and the three others in the room looked up at the duct. The two men next to Warrick aimed their submachine guns at the source of the sound.

"What was that?" Duncan asked.

Warrick smiled as he looked at the grate. Sam felt as though he were staring into her very soul. "Tell the squad to not set the timer just yet," he said, a smile crossing his face like a serpent crossing a bleached sidewalk. "It looks like playtime is going to be sooner rather than later."

"Where are we going, Philippe?" Donald Molson asked. He was in the passenger seat of the van driven by Philippe Dupain, who had saved his life only moments before. He glanced over his shoulder and noted the back of the vehicle was fully stocked with what looked like heavy riot gear—armor, pistols, rifles, and ammunition filled the mesh cabinets on the interior walls.

"To the airport," Dupain said as he wove the work van through traffic. "Your Vice-President is in danger."

Molson looked at his watch. "Air Force Two should be going wheels up in 20 minutes. He'll be with your President until then."

"That's the problem, Donald," Dupain said. "President Paquet is involved in all of this."

Molson squinted his eyes at his friend. "What are you talking about? How is he involved?"

"His family has been involved in Surmonter and La Fin des Temps since its inception. There have been many forces at work to ensure that someone form their group rose to power, and Paquet is their golden child. He is planning on allowing two nuclear devices to be detonated, one here in Paris, and another in the United States. He believes, along with his handlers at Les Fin, that this will shift the balance of power in a direction beneficial to their goals."

"Which are?"

"I am not sure," Dupain said as he cranked the wheel and pitched the van into a tire-screeching right turn. "But I believe your Vice-President may know too much, and he may likewise be in danger." He spared a quick glance at Molson. "Make your calls quickly, Donald. He is not the only one at risk."

. . .

Kirk Talbert, the Vice President of the United States, savored the brandy in his mouth before he allowed himself to swallow. He enjoyed the time he had been able to spend with Paquet, the relaxation it had afforded him. Feigning loyalty to President Hathaway had come to be almost more than he could bear, and he was thankful he wouldn't have to keep the charade up much longer. When the nukes were detonated, he would be blamed for it. It didn't matter who was actually responsible—the fact that nuclear devices detonated on American soil and in the French capital would be enough to set the stage for his ouster. The move to oust him amidst another terrorist strike would be swift, thanks to allies in the House of Representatives, and the outcry would be loud enough that the Senate would have no choice but to impeach him. That would mean the humble but willing Vice President would become the most powerful man in the world, and thus be perfectly positioned to move La Fin des Temps' plan forward. Paquet had a not insignificant role to play as well, naturally, but Talbert would be in the lead. The French President had expressed his willingness to do what was necessary, and had no problem with taking the secondary position as the plan proceeded. He had certainly been a gracious host, and if this was a sign of things to come, then things would go smoothly indeed.

"Your plane is going to be leaving soon, my friend," Paquet said as he exhaled a mouthful of smoke from his cigar. "It would be a shame if you didn't have time to finish your drink."

Talbert nodded. "You're right, of course," he said, and drank down the rest of the liquor. "That is truly an exquisite brandy, Louis."

"A custom formulation from a courtier," the French President said. "People are always looking for ways to curry favor. But you know all about that as well."

"Indeed I do." Talbert glanced at the cigar in his own hand, still unlit. "These cigars are a special blend from a wealthy sponsor. It's nice to have people with good taste—and good contacts. What time are the fireworks supposed to happen?"

"We have about 90 minutes, but we are far enough from the zone that we should have no issues. You will be long gone by then, so there is no worry for you."

Talbert looked at the door. "This will probably be my last flight on Air Force Two. Once Hathaway is impeached, it will only be a matter of time before I move up the chain. And then things will be different."

"Quite different indeed," Paquet said, taking along drag from the cigar into his mouth and exhaling.

"I have to admit, Louis, I am really impressed with how well you're taking the idea of playing second fiddle moving forward."

"Really?"

"Yes. I mean, you could have very easily have leveraged this for a bigger role for yourself, yet you have been so open to letting me take the leading role moving forward. I would have thought La Fin would have wanted a Frenchman to be the point man."

Paquet took another puff. "Yes," he said. "Well, I have been patient this long. There is no reason to rush things now, is there?"

"I suppose it depends on how much time one has," Talbert said.

A confused look crossed Paquet's face. Then his eyes suddenly grew large, his skin grew pale, and he leaned slightly forward as if he were having trouble breathing. An unseen vice squeezed him tight, and he clawed at his chest in a desperate attempt to ease the pain.

Talbert leaned slightly forward. "Is the cigar not settling well with you, Louis? I suppose the special blend isn't for everyone." Talbert took another sip. "Well, actually, that blend was specially formulated for you. La Fin does have a plan moving forward, but alas, your involvement ends with your unfortunate death from a massive heart attack. I assure you will do everything in my power to get you the help you need, but I'm afraid it will all be in vain." Paquet stumbled and fell onto the floor, mouthing words that could not fully form. "France is simply not in a position to take the lead on the global stage, but United States certainly is. Take comfort in knowing two things, my friend: first, you have greatly contributed to the fruition of La Fin's plans. And secondly, I will say such kind things about you at your funeral."

CHAPTER TWENTY-EIGHT

Samantha Land was, for once, in a situation she didn't have many options for. She was trapped in an air duct above four armed men, three of whom wanted to kill her outright and a fourth who wanted to take his time. The Case Officer knew her only real choice was to drop through the vent, fall ten feet onto one of the men, then try to fight her way out. Under ordinary circumstances Sam would have given herself pretty good odds, but considering the beating she had already taken and having no weapons she wasn't sure. If she could land on both of the goons with submachine guns, it would be possible to grab one and shoot the others dead before they could react. Although it would be preferable to keep Warrick alive for questioning, Sam couldn't afford to be choosy. She needed to stay alive long enough to let someone know about Paquet. Sam knew she had to strike fast, while they weren't sure what she would do. She would act quickly, violently, and if need be, go down fighting. Allowing them to take her alive was not an acceptable option. She took a deep breath and prepared to pounce.

Before she could push herself through the grate, she was startled by the sound of a door being kicked open and the sound of gunshots ringing out. She cringed reflexively, then realized the bullets weren't coming through the duct. She looked through the grate in time to see Warrick dive through a doorway and the two gunmen falling to the ground. Hawkins, Woodley, Duncan and Chapman moved into the room, weapons trained on Morgan, still seated in his chair. Duncan told the man to remain still in no uncertain terms.

"Hold your fire!" Sam called out. "Friendly in the duct above you."

"Sam?" Hawkins replied. The relief he felt was palpable, like a wave of warm water pouring over him. "Are you okay?"

"I could use a hand getting down." She opened the grate and hung down through the opening. Hawkins grabbed her legs and eased her to the floor. He hugged her tightly, and she returned the embrace.

"Are you hurt?" Hawkins asked.

"I've been worse, that's for sure. We've got a problem."

"Just one?" Woodley asked, peeking through the open doorway leading back into the church.

"The guy who just bolted through that door was none other than Seth Warrick."

Hawkins had to let that sink in for a second. "What? How is that possible?"

"There's no way," Woodley answered. "I know I broke that guy's neck when we went off the side of that ship. He had to have drowned."

"There is no doubt it's him," Sam said. "Absolute certainty."

"From bad to worse," Hawkins said. "If that twisted guy is involved..."

"There's just no way," Woodley repeated.

"Oh, it's him alright," Morgan finally said, peeking around the MP5K Chapman had jammed in his face. "Twisted bugger has all kinds of plans for you lot."

"Such as?" Chapman asked calmly.

"Take me with you," Morgan said, "and I'll tell you what you need to know."

"Seems like we've got plenty of reasons to trust you," Hawkins said.

"Don't you presume to judge me, FBI," Morgan spat. "You don't know anything about me."

"Apparently we don't either, Wally," Duncan said angrily before smacking Morgan across the back of his head with the side of his weapon. "Tell us!"

"Alright!" Morgan grunted angrily. "Paquet is working with Warrick and a group called La Fin des Temps. Surmonter is the primary front they've been using for decades to provide cover for their politics ambitions. They managed to get the two suitcase nukes and are planning to use them to destabilize the peace talks between the United States and France. One is right here, and the other is in Vegas."

"We've got teams moving in to take care of both," Hawkins said. "The teams should be here any minute, and the other teams are narrowing down the search in Vegas."

"Where are they, you lousy scumbag?" Duncan asked, moving to strike Morgan again before Chapman raised a hand to stop him.

"The one here is in the basement below the chapel," Morgan replied. "Warrick's probably on his was to activate it. If he does, there's no stopping it."

"What do you mean?" Hawkins asked.

"It means we're all dead," Morgan said matter-of-factly. "It's a locked timer. Once the countdown starts, any attempt to shut it off will detonate it."

"Then we gotta go," Woodley said.

Hawkins paused. "What about the one is Vegas?"

"I don't know."

"We need to know where that other bomb is."

Morgan began to sweat. "You need to stop Warrick before he activates the timer or we're all dead! We won't be able to get far enough away!"

"Tell us where the bomb is located in Vegas!" Duncan shouted

"I don't know where the one is in Vegas!" Morgan spat.

Chapman shook his head. "Well, I suppose that's all the help you're going to give us. Isn't it, Wally?"

Morgan made a "pfft" sound. "Gimme a break, Chris. Do you have any idea what Warrick and his buddies paid me? You know how little our own government pays us to do what we do. I deserve better than I've got."

"No, you don't," Chapman said, his voice maintaining a controlled volume. "You sold out your country, your team—your *character*—for money. You're nothing but a worthless sack of meat."

In that moment Morgan's hand moved almost faster than the eye could follow to his hip and produced a pistol. Chapman moved with equal speed, almost as if he knew exactly what Morgan was going to do. He easily caught the man's gun hand and turned the pistol back towards Morgan's own face, now wearing an expression of equal parts shock and panic. He was certain Chapman was about to force him to pull the trigger.

"A bullet is too good for the likes of you," Chapman said. As if out of thin air a savage looking karambit knife appeared in Chapman's left hand, and in one smooth motion he slashed Morgan's throat open. The man gurgled once, then leaned back in the chair staring wide-eyed at the ceiling.

Shouts could be heard coming down the hallway. "Warrick must have sent reinforcements," Duncan said. "We need to move."

Sam grabbed a weapon and spare magazines from the dead men on the floor. "Do we have any idea of the status on the incoming teams?"

"E.J., you got a status report for me?" Hawkins said. "I'm assuming you were able to get all of that."

"Yeah, Hawk, they're two minutes from wheels down at your location," Niels said over the earpiece. "You guys need to keep your heads on a swivel. President Paquet just had a massive heart attack at Elysée Palace only minutes before our VP was supposed to head for home. Price thinks there's something wonky going on with..."

The sound of gunfire interrupted Hawk's conversation. Woodley was sending fire down the hallway. "We've got company!" he shouted.

"We can't get bogged down here," Sam said.

Chapman spoke, his voice still perfectly calm. "You, Hawkins, and Woodley get after Warrick and stop him from arming that weapon." He pointed to a window on the air side of the room. "That leads to an alley that funnels to the basement level. Benny and I will distract this group."

"There's too many of them," Hawkins said.

"Not for long," Duncan said as he pulled an explosive charge from his satchel. He pushed a small button and the charge began beeping. Hawkins thought he heard the British warrior giggle as he let it beep twice before hurling it down the stone corridor. There were several shouts before the deafening roar of an explosion drowned them out.

"That's our cue," Woodley said, and the three clambered through the window into the alley.

"Mr. President, we need to get you secured," the Secret Service agent said as he burst into the Oval Office, three other agents trailing behind. The lead agent on the detail, Terrell Durrant, was all business, with an intensity that radiated off him like heat waves. President Hathaway had grown accustomed to occasional interruptions by his Presidential Protective Detail, or PPD. If there was any perceived viable threat to POTUS then the agents entrusted with guarding him would swoop in and take him to "The Bunker," an ultra-secure command and control center underneath the White House. While the suit-wearing agents were more than capable of dealing with threats, the

Counter Assault Team in the black military-style gear had the task of actively engaging hostiles. Capable was an understatement—Hathaway had watched CAT training sessions and marveled at their proficiency. They were operators of the highest level, equal or superior to any other Tier 1 team in the world. Durrant, the lead agent on his detail, had been a part of the elite CAT team before putting on a suit and tie once more. Hathaway briefly wondered what they were doing as he was being hustled down the staircase towards The Bunker. The President knew better than to try and talk to Durrant or the other agents until he had been secured in a safe location. Their sole focus was to ensure that POTUS was safe. Then, and only then, would they relax enough to answer any questions he might have.

With the President huddled down between them, the agents moved quickly down the passageway. One of the agents ran ahead and eventually reached a large metal door. He tapped a code into the keypad and passed his credentials over a flat black disc next to it. Several LEDs turned green, and the clicking of magnetic and mechanical locks signaled the door's release. The agent grabbed the handle and pulled the massive door open just as the President and his detail reached the opening. The agents remained huddled around POTUS until the door had securely locked behind them.

The President stood up to his full height and straightened his coat and tie slightly. "I'm assuming this has something to do with the backpack bombs?" Hathaway asked.

"I'm not sure about that, Mr. President," Durrant answered. "Intel got wind of activity in close proximity of the White House. I don't have any further details at this point."

"Mr. President," a voice called out. CIA Director Dorothy Sullivan was coming around the conference table with a file folder in her hand, National Security Advisor Karen Quinn hot on her heels. "Here's the latest. DNI Price is coming up on the screen momentarily." Sullivan handed the file to Hathaway, who began looking over the papers. As much as everyone had gone digital, he still liked to read reports the old-fashioned way.

POTUS looked up from the file, surprise wrinkling his brow. "Paquet had a heart attack? Where's Kirk?"

"Going wheels up on Air Force Two as we speak," Price answered. "Talbert was with him and called for help, saying Paquet had suddenly hit the ground. Massive heart attack is the official word. Talbert's detail got him out of there post haste."

"That's an unexpected turn. That removes Paquet from the board as a primary. Is it possible Talbert's clean in all this?"

"A lot of things are possible, Mr. President, but that doesn't make them true."

"Fair enough. So, what does that have to do with running me down here?"

The DNI looked over at Agent Durrant, who took the cue. "Mr. President, we received actionable intel that there is an active threat in the metro area," Durrant replied.

"What kind of threat? Is it one of the nukes?"

"No, sir," Price answered. "We've confirmed Paris and Las Vegas for those. Teams are moving in to disarm them as we speak."

"So, what is it?"

Quinn spoke up. "Secret Service got a ping on one of their top 10 players. Noted Spanish MOE spec ops sniper, from the 3rd Special Operations Group. Name of Mateo Fernandez. He went AWOL a handful of years back and has since become known as one of the top gunmen for hire out there."

"I remember seeing his name on a couple of PDBs," Hathaway said. Several prominent VIPs had been enjoying their day when a bullet landed in the middle of their forehead, and Fernandez had been the likely suspect in at least half. Word was that if he wanted a target dead, that's exactly how they wound up.

"And that's why we're not taking any chances, sir," Quinn said.

"But what's the play here? I thought the whole idea was to make me look bad, not kill me."

"Maybe they're looking for a backup plan," Quinn said. "If our teams are able to shut off the nukes, they need another way to take you off the board."

"Or maybe you aren't Fernandez' target," Sullivan offered. "But we can't take that chance. Until we know where Fernandez' whereabouts, and what his play is, you have to stay here."

"Well if he's not after me," Hathaway asked, "then who's his target?"

"Heart attack, my eye," Assistant Director Robert Shear said. "Surely nobody's buying that at the White House."

"They don't know what to think," Attorney General Jillian Stott said as she slipped on her overcoat. "Just got a text from the Chief of Staff. They're shuffling the President off to his underground bunker as we speak," Stott, Van Horn, and Shear were walking past the security turnstiles in the lobby of the Washington Field Office. "Secret Service is so skittish about POTUS right now they'll move him if the wind blows too hard."

"Do you want to do the conference call from here? You can just go back upstairs and use the secure conference room."

"No, we'll head back to Justice," AG Stott said. "My car's here at the curb already, and frankly, we need to be over there so we can coordinate our assets more easily with the other agencies." Shear held the door for the Attorney General and FBI Director as they walked into the cold DC air. Stott's black Suburban eased up to the curb as if on cue. It wasn't surprising— all three had been through this routine enough times their internal clocks could time the trip from Shear's office to the curb in front of the Field Office with consistent precision. A member of Stott's security detail stepped out from the front passenger seat and opened the rear door. "I'm pretty sure this workday just got a lot longer."

Shear was about to reply in agreement when Stott stumbled back into Van Horn as she started to climb into the back seat of the Suburban. He went to catch the FBI Director and had his hands on Van Horn's chest when he realized the Director was going all the way to the ground. The agent on the security detail moved forward to steady the Attorney General. Shear was surprised when the agent fell into the AG and they both tumbled to the ground. Shear turned to check on them when he realized his hands were wet. It took him a split second to realize it was blood. He ducked behind the rear passenger door as a suppressed rifle round slammed into it. The armor plating held, he noted with relief. He drew his pistol from his belt holster and shouted at the driver, still unaware of what had just happened.

"Shooter at our 12! Three down! Call it in!" The driver reached for the radio as the windshield spiderwebbed in front him. He drew back in surprise, then realized the rifle round hadn't fully penetrated the glass. He ducked down beneath the dash and radioed dispatch. Shear didn't dare risk peeking around the edge of the door—the sniper clearly had them dialed in, and the cornered Assistant Director had only a general idea where the shots were coming from. He looked and saw the Attorney General, the FBI Director, and the other agent lying on the side-walk out of the reach of his cover, blood spreading quickly across their clothing. It infuriated him to think that all he could do was wait for more shots to come.

CHAPTER TWENTY-NINE

"If there has ever been a search for the proverbial needle in the haystack, this is it," HRT operator Carl Jenkins said.

"This isn't our thing, Goat," Rick Obermeyer moaned from his spot in the back seat of the Suburban. "How are we supposed to play hide-and-seek with a nuke when we don't even know what we're looking for?"

"We're in the area, we've been asked to assist, and that's what we're gonna do," HRT Commander Bill Hall huffed. "The nerds from DOE are supposed to actually find the thing. We just have to be able to pop any tangos with bad intentions."

"Meanwhile, we just ride around taking in the sights with HDRU nerds following us," Obermeyer shrugged. "I suppose it could be worse."

"Like if, say, a nuclear device goes off close to us?" Jenkins asked.

"The nerds will do their jobs, and then we'll do ours," Hall said. He had never worked with anyone from the NEST teams before—fortunately, up until this point he'd never had a reason to. But Sloane, the hulking commander of the FBI's HDRU team, had and held them in high esteem. Hall liked Sloane and knew how he ran his HDRU team, so if the big ex-Marine said someone was good enough, then that was sufficient for him.

The road curved as they passed beneath the Mike O'Callaghan-Pat Tillman Memorial Bridge and the view opened up through the SUV's massive windshield. Before them loomed Hoover Dam. Hall had been there a couple of times with his family when he was younger, but that had been many years ago. He had forgotten just how massive the structure was, the pale concrete edifice looming more than 700 feet over the valley below.

Obermeyer leaned forward from the back seat. "Man, that thing is something, isn't it?"

Jenkins nodded. "I've always wanted to come out here and see it. This just isn't the circumstances I had in mind."

"I know, right?" Hall said. "But Obermeyer, I'm warning you. If you ask me where the Dam bait shop is..."

The men laughed and grimaced at the pun. "I don't want to hear anything about my jokes after you used that lame old line," Obermeyer said.

"You gotta stop," Jenkins said. "Jokes like that will make this dam leak."

The radio chirped to life as if on cue. "Moses to Goat," Sloane's voice echoed over the speaker.

"Go ahead."

"We've got confirmation on the target in your AO," Sloane said. "NEST team is en route and will be wheels down in 10."

"Roger that. What's the coordinates?"

"You're already there," Sloane replied. "The package is at the Dam."

The men all looked at each other. "Are you sure? Not exactly a low-key target."

"That's the point," Sloane replied. "And yes, we're 100 percent positive." Hall didn't bother to ask how they were sure, knowing he would just get the old need-to-know speech he had heard dozens of times. It really was for the best, he supposed.

He didn't care what kind of techno-voodoo the wizards came up with—he just needed to be told where the targets were. He and his team would do what needed to be done.

"Copy," Hall said. "Where should we be looking?"

"Top of the dam," Moses said. "Target has been painted by security onsite, but they are foot-mobile."

"Security has been told to stand down, correct?"

"Absolutely. They know of the threat, but not the specific nature of it. They've been told additional federal agents are coming in to engage. We're sending photos of the target and the confirmed tangos to your devices now. There are certainly shooters on overwatch. They're going to spot you as soon as you approach, so be prepared."

"Of course," Hall said. "Does anyone have eyes on them?"

"Negative, but we've got Homeland Security agents on site setting up a perimeter, and we're deploying additional assets as we speak. Should have more eyes in five."

Obermeyer tapped Hall's shoulder. "We can't wait, boss."

Hall nodded in agreement. "Do we have any idea what the time window is once they activate?"

"Negative, and we have reason to believe they are willing to die to ensure the mission succeeds."

Hall sighed. "Then we can't wait. We need to pop them and get our hands on the package sooner rather than later."

There was a pause before the radio came to life again. "I've got confirmation that the NEST team is seven minutes out."

"Then we've got to get to work so they aren't sitting ducks when they come in."

"You're weapons free, Goat," Sloane said. "We'll be there as fast as we can."

"Copy," Hall said, and switched to his team's tactical channel. "Warcoach, do you copy?"

"Roger that, Goat," the sound of the engine roaring over the radio almost as loud as Pitman's voice. "We're less than fifteen from you."

"Copy," Hall replied. "Come in hot. This is not an arrest situation. Our responsibility is to stop the tangos and make sure the NEST team secures that package. That means we need to get the bad guys attention and keep it."

"Affirmative, Goat," Warcoach replied, "coming in hot."

"We'll try to save some for you." Hall eased the Suburban into a lot at the entrance to the top of the dam. They looked at the two-lane road that crossed the massive structure. "I rode across this thing in a station wagon with my family in the mid-80's," he said.

"I wasn't alive then," Jenkins said.

"Thanks for that," Hall said. "If you're not careful out there, you won't be alive much longer, either."

"So, what's our play, boss?" Obermeyer asked.

"We need to draw the heat so the helo can get that NEST team on the ground. If that chopper gets shot up, then we've got a problem. Unless you happen to understand Russian and know how to defuse a tactical nuclear device."

Obermeyer chambered a round into his custom assault rifle. "Draw the heat it is," he said with a smile.

Hall and Jenkins likewise prepped their weapons, then the three men stepped out of the SUV at the same time the four HDRU team members piled out of theirs. If the tourists gathered at the dam on the pleasantly cool day were startled by the heavily armed agents piling out of the dusty black Suburbans they didn't show it. There were other federal agents in fatigues providing security at the dam, and people had grown increasingly comfortable with the sight of military-grade law enforcement at potential terrorist targets. The men gathered up by the front of Hall's SUV. The HDRU unit's squad leader, Nathaniel Evans, walked up to Hall. Evans looked like he had just walked out of a superhero movie, tall and muscular with short blond hair. His callsign, "Bulldog," didn't seem to fit. Hall would have to ask about that one.

"What's the play?" Evans asked.

"We've got a target rich environment, but they're currently blending in," Hall said. "Check your targets carefully. The bad guys will *not* be careful, but we have to be. Our goal is to save lives, but today we're going to stack some tangos. We can't risk them activating the package. Check your targets, call them out, and drop them. We know they've likely got shooters on over-watch, but we don't have eyes on them yet. Keep your heads on a swivel and we'll all go home. Questions?" The men were all silent. Although they had only trained together for a few hours, each one was a highly trained FBI agent who knew his job well. "Alright then. Let's go to work."

As if in response, shots began ringing out. Bullets peppered the area around the agents, and they dove for cover. They spread out behind several vehicles and began lining up their own shots. No sooner than the agents began to return fire they found themselves forced to get back behind their respective barriers, heavy rounds slamming in far too close to their heads. The snipers were making their presence known.

"Anybody have eyes on the snipers?" Hall called out.

"Other side of the bridge," one of the HDRU agents responded. "On the ridge."

"Gonna have to move our way up, boss," Obermeyer said.

Glass and shrapnel sprayed around Hall's position. "Safe to say we can't stay here. Bulldog, you guys lay down some covering fire. We're going to grab a better position."

CHAPTER THIRTY

The narrow alleyway ran between the massive stone structures of the church complex, opening suddenly into a small covered courtyard. Hawkins raised his hand, and Sam and Woodley stopped. The area was snug, no more than 15 feet square, and featured a short iron bench surrounded by roses. It was a beautiful area for reflection and meditation.

It was also a fatal funnel.

"We've got to get across there," Woodley said.

"Definite ambush point," Hawkins said.

"Doesn't change the fact," Woodley replied.

"Then we make it happen," Sam said. She nodded toward the arched doorway across the courtyard from them. "When they open that door, you drop them," and she stepped into the courtyard. She went three feet before the door opened and a man opened fire. Sam was already combat rolling out of his line of sight when Woodley put three rounds into the shooter's chest. A second shooter appeared and Hawkins fired two rounds, one striking the man in the throat and the other just below the nose. Both men fell in a heap. After ensuring the doorway was clear, they moved through the doorway and into the next building. Immediately in front of them was a set of stairs heading into a basement level, and a hallway that wrapped around the stairs and led into another area.

"Pretty sure it won't be downstairs," Woodley said. "They'll want it to go off at street level."

"It would do plenty of damage if it went off below ground," Sam offered.

"They're going to want a mushroom cloud," Hawkins said. "They aren't going for subtle, conventional damage. They want this to be high-profile."

"Then the hallway it is," Sam said. Woodley took point, peeking down the darkened corridor. When no shots rang out, he motioned the others forward. An open doorway in front of them beckoned. As they approached, the three operators could see it opened into what looked like a garage or storage shed. The ceiling was at least 15 feet high, and construction equipment was parked along the walls. At the far end was a double door that led to the parking lot next door. Three men stood in the doorway, one with a small satchel at his feet.

"Well, now" Warrick said, his voice echoing through the garage. "Isn't this a wonderful surprise? It's nearly Thanksgiving for you Americans, isn't it? I, for one, can't imagine being thankful for more than this, than having the three of you standing before me." Everyone was pointing weapons, except for Warrick, whose hands were clasped in front of him.

"Step away from the bag, Warrick," Hawkins said. "And put the weapons down now."

"I will most certainly step away from the bag, but my friends here will not be putting their weapons down."

"Suits me," Woodley says. "Gives me a chance to correct the mistake I made last year by not killing you."

"And a significant mistake that was, Agent Woodley, in spite of your best efforts. If only you had been a bit more thorough, Agent Hawkins might still have his home and his precious, dead parents' collection of cars." Warrick cocked his head slightly. "By the way, how is *your* family? I trust they weren't too traumatized by the guests I sent to your home."

"I'm going to have a little talk with you about that," Woodley replied calmly.

"I'm sure," Warrick said. "Officer Land, I apologize that you and I didn't get our quality time together."

Sam's response came in the form of gunshots, fired off faster than Hawkins imagined possible. The men on either side of Warrick dropped dead, but he didn't flinch.

"I'm a little embarrassed to say this," Warrick said in a voice that dripped venomous ice, "but I think I'm in love."

"She's taken," Hawkins said.

"So she is," Warrick replied. The sound of a helicopter grew louder.

"That sounds like the end of the line for you," Woodley said.

"Actually," Warrick said like a teacher correcting a child, "I'm afraid you've got that backwards. *Your* helicopter is still four minutes away. That is the sound of *my* helicopter arriving. And I'm walking out this door, or this nuke goes off right now."

Without hesitation, Sam fired again, two shots. Warrick twitched, but didn't fall. "That's it," he said. "I'm absolutely *certain* I'm in love," then turned and ran out the door. The three sprinted across the garage, Hawkins stopping to check the satchel on the ground. Sam and Woodley ran through the doorway in time to see Warrick climbing into the helicopter. They opened fire on the aircraft, and two men inside reciprocated with their own weapons. One of the shooters went stiff as bullets tore into him, and his body fell out of the open hatch. The turbine engine changed in pitch and the helicopter quickly rose from the ground. Sam continued to fire until her weapon ran dry, and although the helicopter bucked and smoked slightly, it quickly moved off into the darkening sky. She stood for a moment, watching as it carried Warrick out of their reach.

"We'll get you," she said under her breath. The sound of something hitting the ground next to her caused her to pivot, and she saw Woodley kneeling. She thought at first that he was either upset that Warrick had escaped, or was just exhausted. Then she saw the blood.

Inside the hangar Hawkins looked carefully at the satchel, a simple duffel bag that looked like those found in any athletic store in the late 1980's. It was roughly the size of the bags baseball players used to carry their gear, made of black nylon with white piping that ran around the ends and traced the line of the zipper. He noticed the bag was opened, and carefully peeked inside. He couldn't make out the letters—they were Cyrillic—but he understood the numbers all too well. The countdown was running, and showed 8:30 left. He was about to call out to the others when Sam ran back inside.

"Woodley is down," she said.

Hall, Obermeyer, and Jenkins were hunkered down behind the leading column on the Nevada approach across the dam. The fire coming from the terrorists' position was lessening thanks to the effective shooting of the HRT and HDRU members, but there was still no easy access to the nuclear device. Enemy snipers had them zeroed in pretty well, and to press forward meant certain death for members of the team.

"The clock is ticking, Agent Hall," the NEST commander said over the comms unit. "We need to get on the ground soon."

"If you want to land, go right ahead," Hall snapped. "We're pinned down with snipers sending fire on our position. Stand by." He switched channels. "Bulldog, you guys got anything for these clowns?"

"Those guys up top are making us keep our heads down," Evans replied. "they've got the angles on us. We're about to try something drastic."

"Negative, Bulldog," Hall shouted over the gunfire, "you hold your position. Stand by one."

"Copy," Evans replied.

"If that device goes off, everyone is dead, boss," Obermeyer said. "And we need to hold the HDRU guys back to work on the boomer. Let me move up and try to draw their fire."

"They couldn't miss you if they were blind," Jenkins replied. "I can move a lot quicker."

"Here's what we're going to do," Hall replied. "I'm going to move up and draw their fire. You guys are going to drop them when they pop up to get me."

"Boss..."

"That's an order, Dually," Hall said, leaving no room for negotiation. "We've got to make this happen, and I need you guys to make sure that we get it done. No matter what." The other men nodded their understanding. Hall turned to plan his route, then sprinted for the cover of a parked van. Bullets began peppering the ground near him as he ran. He could hear his team opening up on the targets, but rounds were still coming awfully close to him. He combat-rolled behind the van and paused a moment to catch his breath.

"Dually to Goat. Hold your position, they're still lining up shots on you."

Hall paused another moment, took a deep breath, then sprinted for the next vehicle. Rounds sliced through the air past him in both directions. He was almost to the pickup he had selected for his next cover when he felt an impact in the center of his chest that spun him around. He was able to use his momentum to carry him behind the truck, and he immediately took inventory of his injury. He felt for his chest, expecting to see blood, and was pleasantly surprised to see none on his gloved hand. The projectile had angled across the front of his vest, and while he would likely be bruised the bullet didn't penetrate.

"Boss, you alright?" Obermeyer asked.

"Good as gold," Hall said. "But I'm running out of luck. We're gonna need a little divine intervention here pretty soon."

The sound of a Barrett .50 caliber sniper rifle thundered across the area, and the agent assumed the worst. If they had that kind of weaponry, then the pickup he was crouching behind would provide as much protection as a sheet of paper. A second shot thundered across the narrow canyon, and Hall realized it was coming from behind his position.

""Ask and ye shall receive," Pitman called over the radio. "Two snipers down." Rifle fire resumed from behind Hall once more. His squad was now able to move into better position to take out the shooters. The big rifle boomed again, then once more. "Two more tangos down on the dam. Your squad is clear to move up, Goat. My unit will hold and secure"

"Copy that, Warcoach," Hall replied. "Much obliged. Squad, form up on my position. NEST, you are clear to land."

"Dually copies."

"NEST 1 copies, but we're having some difficulty."

"NEST 1, what kind of difficulty?" No response. "NEST 1, do you read?" Silence. "NEST 1, I repeat, do you copy?" Nothing. As tempting as it was, he knew better than to ask himself what else could go wrong.

Hall continued visually sweeping across the deck of the dam. He could see bodies lying prone across the roadway. The concrete barriers the snipers had been hiding behind had new holes drilled through them by the armor-piercing rounds from Warcoach's weapon. The other two tangos the Barrett had claimed were obvious by the damage done. The rest of Hall's team moved up behind him, then split in two. He motioned forward, and the two squads skirted the barrier walls on either side of the dam's roadway. Although it seemed the bad guys were all down, they still couldn't afford to be careless. Hall signaled with his fingers and his men began checking the bodies, careful to make sure none had dead-man's devices that would go off when they were moved. He took the lead and made his way to the large duffle bag, two members of HDRU, Evans and another agent, right beside him. He pointed to the bag, and the two agents carefully opened it.

Francis swore. "It's been activated," he said.

Hall looked at the agent. "Francis, right?" The other man nodded. "How much time do we have?"

"It's showing 7 minutes 43 seconds, sir," Agent Francis replied.

"NEST 1, this is Goat. The package is active, showing just over 7." Silence was the only response.

"What do you think? "Evans asked. "Do we wait for NEST?"

"We don't have time to wait for them to join the party. What are our options?"

Francis spoke up. "I studied Russian weapons technology and development. The guys on the bridge didn't switch this on. This device was remotely activated."

"Nice. So how do we shut it off?"

"That's the hard part, sir. Once it's been activated remotely the only way to shut it off is with a corresponding signal. If we try tampering with the sequence initializer, it will detonate."

"So, do we have the signal?"

Francis shrugged. "Only if one of our eyes and ears in the sky caught it."

Hall thought for a moment. "Can we at least move it?"

Evans looked at the other HDRU member squatting next to him, who nodded. "Yeah, it can be moved."

"Then get it in my Suburban. Right now." The two agents carefully lifted the explosive and started carrying it towards Hall's SUV. Obermeyer and Jenkins walked up as the agents hurried past.

"Uh, where are they going with that?" Jenkins asked.

"We've gotta get it away from this dam," Hall said, walking intently toward his vehicle without looking at either of his men.

"So where are we taking it?"

"We aren't taking it anywhere. I need you guys to stay here and secure the area Take care of any wounded civilians."

"Hold on, boss," Obermeyer said. "We can't let you drive off alone with a nuke in the truck."

"Really, Obermeyer?" Hall shouted. "What are you going to

do? Let it blow up here, take out the dam, and kill who knows how many people between here and Vegas? Are you gonna ride with me off into the nuclear sunset? No, you're going to stay here and do your job while I do mine. Francis said the device was armed with a remote detonator, and it can only be deactivated using the same frequency. Get on the horn and see if any of our wizards happened to grab a stray frequency that might be able to carry a kill signal."

"I'm going with you," Evans said.

"Not happening," Hall said.

"I'm not asking," Evans said as he jumped in the back. "If someone needs to put hands on this, you need someone that knows what they're doing."

"That should be me, Bulldog," Francis said.

"I need you on the horn with someone who can either get us the frequency code or can find a back door," Evans said. "They're always a back door," he said with a smirk, then closed the barn doors of the SUV.

"If we have the frequency, can they figure out the kill code?" Jenkins asked the HDRU agents who had gathered around the SUV.

Francis shrugged. "There were only a few possible codes the Russians had that would work on that style device. If somebody caught the frequency, then we've got a good shot at getting the right one."

"I'll take those odds," Hall said as he climbed into the driver's seat.

"Boss, we can't let you do this," Obermeyer said.

Hall paused for a moment and looked at his agents, men he had entrusted his life to for several years now. "Here's what you're going to do. You're going to get on the line and find some-body who grabbed that signal. Then you're going to get it to Francis here so he can send the kill signal to Evans so this thing doesn't go off over there in the desert and vaporize us. Then I'm going to drive back up here and tune you up for insubordination." He smiled at his teammates, then hit the gas pedal, aiming the Suburban towards the desert ahead. His mental clock told him they probably had five minutes. That was more than enough time to get the bomb safely away from the dam. The low yield meant it wouldn't have far reaching effects out here in the desert, and low radiation was part of the design intent. At least that's what the nerds had told him, so that's what he was going with.

"You alright back there, Evans?"

"I'm not glowing yet, so I've got that going for me."

"We take our wins where we can get 'em," Hall replied. "So, how did a guy who looks like you get saddled with the callsign 'Bulldog?'"

"I played football for the University of Georgia."

Hall groaned. "Are you kidding me? You're *that* Nathaniel Evans?"

"Not a fan?"

"Of the Florida Gators," Hall answered.

Evans laughed. "No hard feelings?"

"The way you guys beat us two weeks ago, I would say there are *definitely* hard feelings."

"I'll buy you a beer to make amends when this is over," Evans chuckled.

"I'm gonna hold you to that," Hall said. He realized that a lot was riding on the very people he loved picking on. He hoped that they could do their thing in time. *If not*, he mused, *at least we won't feel a thing*.

CHAPTER THIRTY-ONE

"I told you, I'm fine," Woodley said.

"You've two bullets in you, Mark," Hawkins said, concern weighing down his voice. He was tearing the shirt off one of the men Sam had killed in the doorway and ripping it into makeshift bandages.

"Just adding to my collection," Woodley replied with a grimace. What's a couple more?"

He took one of the folded pieces of cloth from Hawkins and held it against the wound in his lower left abdomen, while Sam pressed down on the bullet hole leaking blood from his upper thigh. Chapman and Duncan ran through the garage and out to where Woodley was sitting on the pavement.

"Bomb's been activated," Hawkins said.

"Saw that," Chapman replied calmly. "SAS is on the way in with a NEST team." The sound of a helicopter suddenly grew louder. "And that would be them."

"We need to get Woodley medical attention," Sam said. "He's losing a lot of blood, and we don't have the kit to stop it."

"We need the car," Hawkins said.

Duncan nodded. "On it," and he sprinted around the corner. The helicopter appeared over the rooftops, a sleek dark blue airframe with a white stripe across the bottom. Several black-fatigued operators, their faces obscured by balaclavas and crash helmets, poured out of the aircraft with weapons at the ready. Chapman stood and made several signals with his hand. One of the dark uniformed men approached him, while the others fanned out to clear the area.

"You The Ghost?"

"A pleasure, Commander," Chapman responded. "The package is just inside, and it is active. Remote activation of the detonation sequence."

Two of the other operators immediately moved forward. "On it," one said.

"Pleasure to meet you, sir," the commander said. "Just wish it was under different circumstances."

"It is what it is, Commander," Chapman replied. He noticed the medic was already taking a look at Woodley.

"They're right, sir," the medic said. "He's going to need surgical intervention to stop the bleed." Tires squealed and an engine roared as Duncan hurled the big Mercedes sedan into the parking lot. He rounded the helicopter and put the back door right next to Woodley. Hawkins and Sam helped the medic get Woodley in the car. Sam climbed in the back seat. Hawkins looked at Chapman.

"We've got this well in hand, son," Chapman said. "Get Woodley squared away." Hawkins hesitated for a moment. Duncan honked the horn twice, and the FBI agent jumped in the passenger seat. Duncan hit the gas and the sedan roared out of the parking lot. Chapman walked over to the package where the commander watched over the two NEST techs.

"What have we got?"

"Not sure we can do a lot about this on our end, sir," one of the techs said. "It looks to be on a tamper-proof timer and is set to go off in 5 minutes."

"Nothing is tamper-proof," the commander said.

"This is the Russians we're talking about," Chapman interjected. "They've been working with unusual frequency modulation signals since the end of World War II. This is a prime example. The only way to shut of the timer is with the matching signal from the same frequency. Any other attempt will cause it to detonate immediately."

Another operator ran up breathlessly. "Sir, the American teams have the same issue, but they believe one of their agencies may have intercepted the initiation signal. They're working to decode it now."

Duncan ran the big Mercedes hard, roaring away from the area as quickly as possible.

"Woodley's not in great shape back here," Sam said, the tension evident in her voice. "We need to get to a doctor quickly."

"I'm fine," Woodley said, but the weakness of his voice said otherwise. Sam continued to apply pressure to the wound in his thigh, while Woodley did his best to hold the makeshift bandage tightly against his abdominal wound. "I'm fully lucid, the bleeding has stopped, and everything is right with the world."

"We've *slowed* the bleeding," Sam corrected, "but we need to get him medical attention, and fast."

"I'm going to need more medical attention if Duncan drives us into a wall," Woodley said.

"Even bullets can't stop you crackin' wise, eh?" Duncan said with a chuckle. "He's fine." He cranked the wheel to the left and accelerated hard past several slow-moving cars. More traffic loomed ahead, and he had to get back on the brakes.

"Geez, Hawk," Woodley chuckled, "this guy drives even worse than you."

"Nice," Hawkins replied dryly. This was all going south quickly. The bomb was due to go off any minute, and he hadn't been able to do a thing to help other than get out of the way. Seth Warrick, a terrorist already responsible for the death of hundreds, had escaped, which meant more deaths would likely follow. Many more, if the bombs went off. He looked over his shoulder and saw Woodley grimacing in pain, Sam leaning over him while she kept pressure on the leg wound. Blood soaked the lower part of his shirt and the upper part of his pants, and Sam had it all over her. He saw two of the people he cared about most in the world, covered in blood, hurting and anxious, and he couldn't do a thing to help them.

And then Sam smiled at him. That glorious smile that made her whole face glow. Then there was a brilliant flash of light, and a moment later the back end of the Mercedes felt as though it had been struck by the hammer of an angry giant.

Hall glanced at the speedometer. The Burb was cooking along at 125 miles per hour. He was about 3 miles from the dam now. While the HRT commander was told that was a safe distance to avoid significant structural damage to the dam, he nonetheless kept the pedal down. There was no need to take a chance. He reached over and flipped off the siren but left the flashing strobes on. There was no one around him. If they were unable to stop the timer, he and Evans would be the only ones to die in the blast. He looked in the rear view, but other than his fellow FBI agent in the cargo area with a ticking nuclear bomb there was nothing to see. He looked ahead once more, fixing his eyes on what lay before. Whatever that might be.

"Are you using that machine?" the older woman asked.

"No, ma'am," Troy Chrisman answered. "A friend of mine was playing on it, but he went to get some drinks. "Feel free to give it a try, but be warned—he wasn't having much luck with it."

"Well, maybe he warmed it up for me," she said with a smile, and sat down next to him. She looked to be around 70—Troy was terrible at guessing people's age, but she reminded him of his grandmother, and that was how old she was. "My name is Marian."

"I'm Troy."

"Pleased to meet you, Troy. What brings you to Las Vegas?"

"Bachelor party for one of my buddies. Came out for an excursion before the wedding next weekend."

"Well that sounds like fun. I hope you boys are having a good time."

He smiled. She even sounded like his grandmother. "We are. So far, so good."

"Have you met any girls?"

Troy chuckled in spite of himself. "Did my grandmother send you here to spy on me?"

Marian laughed loudly. "If she did, I wouldn't tell on you," she said. "Where would the fun be in that?"

"Miss Marian, I like you already," Troy said jovially.

"Well that was easy," she laughed again. "Are you having any luck?"

"Not really. I've just about caught back up to being even."

"If that's the case, you're ahead. Most of the time people leave it all in the casino. That's why these places look as nice as they do."

Troy nodded in agreement. "What brings you here?"

"A bunch of my friends thought it would be good for me to get away for a few days," she replied. "My husband died three months ago, and they said I needed to get out."

Troy grimaced. "Oh, I'm so sorry."

"Think nothing of it. We had 45 great years together. I know where he is, and one of these days I'll see him again."

"You sound sure of that."

"I am," she said as she tapped the buttons that made the wheels spin on the slot machine. "You know, I really miss the old machines. The ones where you had to drop in coins and pull the arm down."

"I never got to play one of those," Troy replied.

"You missed out," Marian said. "But your best days are still ahead."

"How can you be so sure?"

"How can you be so unsure?"

That took him by surprise. "I don't know," he said with a shrug. "Past performance, I guess."

"Past performance is not a guarantee of future performance. Have some faith, Troy."

"Easier said than done."

"Maybe, but what's the alternative? Sitting around moping while the world passes you by?" She paused for a moment. "We can't change the circumstances that brought us to where we are, but we can choose where we're headed. I believe that every one of us was created for a purpose, Troy. We're all here for a reason."

"That's what my grandmother always said," he responded. He was silent for several long moments. "She died two weeks ago."

Marian nodded. "I'm sorry for your loss," she said. "Do you think she was right?"

"I used to. I'm not so sure anymore."

"Our circumstances don't determine our faith," Marian said. "At least, they shouldn't. Faith is, by its very definition, trusting in something you can't see."

"I suppose," Troy said.

"Well then, what do you think your grandmother would want you to do?"

Troy smiled, then leaned over to Marian's machine and swiped his card. "I think she'd want me to place a bet on your behalf." He pressed the buttons for the maximum bet and hit the "spin" button. The dials rotated at high speed until each one slammed to a stop on the oversized red "7"s.

"Would you look at that!" she shouts. "We've hit the jackpot!" Then brilliant light and deafening sound drowned out everything else.

TO BE CONTINUED

GLOSSARY OF TERMS AND ACRONYMS

AG—Attorney General
    AO—area of operation
    ASAC—Assistant Special Agent in Charge
    CAT—Counter Assault Team, Secret Service
    CIA—Central Intelligence Agency
    COMINT—Communications Intelligence; information derived from electronic signals
    that contain voice and/or text
    Constellation—several satellites working in union
    Crypto City—NSA Headquarters
    DCIA—Director of the Central Intelligence Agency
    DEA—Drug Enforcement Agency
    DNI—Director of National Intelligence
    DNSA—Director of the National Security Agency
    DIN—Defense Intelligence Network; top secret news gathering agency of the U.S.
    intelligence community
    DOE—Department of Energy
    DSS—Diplomatic Security Service
    ELINT—Electronic Intelligence; information derived from electronic signals that do not

contain voice or text

FBI—Federal Bureau of investigation

FCI—Foreign Counterintelligence

FISA—Foreign Intelligence Surveillance Act

FLIR—Forward Looking Infrared

FO—Field Office

GSW—Gunshot wound

HDRU—Hazardous Devices Response Unit, FBI

HRT—Hostage Rescue Team, FBI

HUMINT—Human Intelligence; information derived from actual human personnel in the

field, either overt or covert

INTELINK—Secure Intranet used by U.S. intelligence community

IOSA—Integrated Overhead Signals Intelligence Architecture

JCOS—Joint Chiefs of Staff

Langley—CIA Headquarters

LEO—Law Enforcement Officer

MI-6—British Intelligence Agency

MOSSAD—Israeli Intelligence Agency

NCTC—National Counterterrorism Center

NEST—Nuclear Energy Support Team, responds to nuclear threats

NNSA—National Nuclear Security Administration of the DOE; operates NEST

NSA—National Security Agency

NSAC—National Signals Analysis Center

OILSTOCK – High-resolution interactive geographic based software system that can store,

track, and display near real-time and historical SIGINT related data over a map background

Operator—Individual member of special ops team; i.e. SEALs or HRT

POTUS—President of the United States

PPD—Presidential Protective Detail, Secret Service

ROE—Rules of Engagement

SAC—Special Agent in Charge

SCS—Special Collection Service; cover joint NSA/CIA organization that specializes in
  worldwide covert operations

SEAL—Sea, Air, and Land; Navy Special Forces group

SecDef—Secretary of Defense

SecNav—Secretary of the Navy

SIGINT—Signals Intelligence; information gained by electronic surveillance (ELINT) or
  communications intercepts (COMINT)

Spook—slang term for a spy, particularly a CIA operative

STE—Secure Terminal Equipment

Tango—target

TTIC—Terrorism Threat Integration Center

Wetworks—term used for covert assassinations

www.ingramcontent.com/pod-product-compliance
Lightning Source LLC
Chambersburg PA
CBHW071556110726
47908CB00007B/2123